# THE BLUEBIRD

*Wings of the West Book 5*

## KRISTY MCCAFFREY

The Bluebird

Cover by Earthly Charms – earthlycharms.com

Edited by Truelove Press – truelovepress.weebly.com

Author Photo by Hannah McCaffrey – hannahmccaffrey.weebly.com

E-book ISBN-13: 978-0-9980907-0-2

Print ISBN-13: 978-0-9980907-1-9

kmccaffrey.com

kristy@kmccaffrey.com

*Books by Kristy McCaffrey*

## Wings of the West Series
The Wren
The Dove
The Sparrow
The Blackbird
The Bluebird
The Songbird (Novella)
Echo of the Plains (Short Story)
The Starling
The Canary
The Nighthawk
The Swan

## Stand-Alone Novel
Into The Land Of Shadows

## Short Story Collections
The Crow Brothers Collection
The West: A Romance Collection

## Long Novellas
Alice: Bride of Rhode Island
Rosemary
Blue Sage
The Peppermint Tree
A Mirthful Wish

## Contemporary Adventure Romances
Deep Blue

Cold Horizon
Ancient Winds
Sapphire Waves

"I...commend McCaffrey for the historical accuracy of her stories...a phenomenal read that I'd recommend to anyone who enjoys historical romance, with a hint of the other." ~ Jonel Boyko, Reviewer

"Ancient Hopi and Havasupai legends have a new voice in McCaffrey. Her inspired writing made her main character's mystical journey into another realm entirely believable and kept the pages turning long into the night." ~ City Sun Times

### *The Blackbird*

"With dastardly villains, plenty of action, a strong heroine, surprising twists and turns, and a sexy cowboy, all underlined by a sensual love story, this historical western romance has something for everyone." ~ Janna Shay, InD'tale Magazine

"A steamy, intelligent historical fiction set in the Arizona desert where the harsh environment matches the characters who populate it. Can two wounded souls find each other and flourish? Find out in Kristy McCaffrey's hard to put down, fourth book in the *Wings of the West* series, *The Blackbird*." ~ Chanticleer Book Reviews

### *The Bluebird*

"The reader will find themselves often sitting on the edge of their seats...a quick and exciting read!" ~ Belinda Wilson, InD'tale Magazine

"...a fast paced read with a depth to the characters and the story that kept my interest from the first page to the last..." ~ Jo, Romance Junkies

"...packed with adventure and action that left me breathless...quite unable to put it down!" ~ Maia, The Silver Dagger Scriptorium

*For Kevin ~*
*with all my love and gratitude*

"Lovers don't finally meet somewhere. They're in each other all along."
—*Rumi*,
13th century Persian poet, theologian, and Sufi mystic

# CHAPTER 1

*Creede, Colorado*
*April 1892*

J ake McKenna hitched a boot on a wooden bench in front of the mercantile as the determined fine figure of Miss Molly Rose Simms crossed the dirt street and entered Bertha's Saloon. Although he'd never met her, Jake had been watching his partner's sister ever since she arrived in Creede yesterday. He leaned forward and draped his forearms over his knee.

*Now what's she up to?*

Jake adjusted the brim of his hat to block the evening sun and strode across the Main Street of Upper Creede, dodging a buckboard and several horses. While entering Bertha's when the sun hadn't even set would hardly ruffle a feather in this town regarding his own reputation, Miss Simms' wouldn't fare as well.

She ought not be seen in such establishments at all.

Jake rarely patronized such places as Bertha's, but Robert—Miss

Simms' brother—did, at least early in his acquaintance with the man. He suspected Miss Simms was in search of Robert.

So was Jake.

He entered the establishment in one swift move, a bell on the glass door jingling as he closed it.

A woman appeared, wearing a silk robe and cheeks rosy with makeup. "We're not open just yet."

Jake removed his hat. "I know. I'm looking for the woman who just entered."

"She your wife?"

"No."

The woman arched an eyebrow and sized him up. "Wait here." Her ample bosom and wide hips jiggled beneath the thin fabric as she departed.

Jake scanned the parlor filled with fancy, plush couches and polished tables. Bertha's was more upscale than he'd realized. Perhaps Robert had good taste after all.

Jake fingered the brim of his hat until his frustration reached a breaking point. What was taking so long? He pushed aside the curtain guarding the hallway. There was no sign of his hostess, so he crept from door to door, listening for a clue to where Miss Simms might be.

He stilled when voices echoed in the hallway and slipped through the nearest door into a room containing an ornate iron bed blanketed with red coverings, a freestanding oval mirror, and provocative photos of females in various stages of undress. It was clearly meant for carnal pleasures.

Before Jake could hide, a woman burst in, spun around, and closed the door. She turned and slammed straight into him.

*Well, luck was on his side. His quarry found* him.

"Oh," she gasped. "My apologies."

Jake held Miss Simms by the shoulders to steady her.

"I have the wrong room," she added.

"Wait." He tried to keep his hold on her, but she slipped from his hands and headed for the door.

It opened again before Miss Simms could clasp the knob. At the threshold stood Charles Henderson, president of the First National Bank.

Miss Simms backed up and bumped into Jake. When she glared up at him, he was struck by the blueness of her eyes, reminding him of a peacock he'd once seen in Shanghai.

Jake lifted his gaze to Henderson and smiled, enjoying the man's obvious discomfort at having been caught—almost—with his britches down. The pompous buffoon had denied Jake and Robert financing last year when they were trying to develop the Lucky Dog Lode, despite samples assaying at 250 ounces in silver. They'd eventually sold the claim for $15,000; he debated whether to rub Henderson's nose in it again.

"How's the missus, Charles?" Jake asked.

The jiggly hostess appeared. Speaking to Henderson, she said, "I'm sorry, sir. I sent you to the wrong room."

Henderson, portly and sporting a bushy beard and mustache, narrowed his gaze on Jake. "The girl is fine. I like 'em petite."

Miss Simms squared her shoulders. "This is ridiculous. I'm here to see Mabel. I'm not for hire."

"That's a shame," Henderson replied. "But a bit of advice—I'd definitely stay away from *him*." Henderson indicated Jake.

A flash of anger filled Jake as Henderson ran his eyes down Miss Simms attributes. He had half a mind to tell Mrs. Henderson what her husband was up to. "Whoremongering suits you, Charles."

"I beg your pardon," the jiggly hostess interjected. "That kind of talk will not be tolerated."

Miss Simms had gone stiff before him. Maybe he'd gone too far with the ladies present. "My apologies, ma'am."

The hostess turned to Henderson. "I'm terribly sorry for the mix-up. I'll find you another girl immediately." As she guided the bank president away, she pinned Jake with an irritated gaze. "You were supposed to wait in the parlor."

"I'm impatient." Jake grinned. "And this girl will do just fine."

"I'm not for hire," Miss Simms repeated with exasperation.

As the perturbed hostess left to take care of her honored guest, Miss Simms spun around to face him. "I must request that you leave."

"We need to talk." He leaned around her and shut the door for privacy.

"About what? I don't even know who you are."

"Jake McKenna."

The flash of recognition on her face pleased him.

"You're Robert's partner?"

Not lately, but he'd play along. "Yeah."

"I was planning to see you next."

"Then it's fortunate that we've met. Although doing it in a brothel will certainly have the local biddies all fired up."

Up close, the resemblance between Miss Simms and her brother was more noticeable, both having the same dark hair and similar eyes, and the flash in hers reminded him of Robert's when the man was excited about a claim. In fact, she was a female version of her brother but a damn sight prettier.

"Do you know where Robert is?" she asked.

"I'm afraid I don't. He didn't know you were coming to town?"

She frowned. "He did, but when I arrived yesterday, he wasn't at the train station to meet me, and he hasn't been at his boardinghouse."

"I know."

"Well, if you know so much, then why don't you know where he is?" she demanded.

Her outburst caught him off guard. Before he could respond, the door opened again. It was a good thing he and Miss Simms weren't engaged in the usual activity for the premises—he doubted he could be that fast.

The hostess appeared. "Mabel will see you now," she said to Miss Simms, then she glared at Jake. "But not you. If you're not gonna pay for a girl, then you have to leave."

"Thank you," Miss Simms said. She spun back to him. "Mister McKenna, it was a pleasure to meet you"—She shook his hand— ". . . I suppose." And then she was gone.

*What the hell just happened?*

Molly Rose Simms wasn't anything like he'd expected.

---

THE FULL-FIGURED WOMAN who'd been helping her at Bertha's— was she Bertha?—led Molly to a bedroom at the back of the establishment. A young woman with curly, coffee-colored tresses met her at the door. Her light-blue eyes conveyed open curiosity, but an edge of cynicism surrounded her.

"This is Mabel. Don't visit too long. We'll be entertaining soon."

Molly was going to ask why men were already eagerly here if they weren't open yet, but she kept the question to herself. No doubt that man, Charles, was someone important and received preferential treatment. A slight queasiness still lingered over the presumption *she* would bed down with him.

And what about Jake McKenna? He hadn't tried anything, but, for a moment, he looked at her like he wanted to strip her bare and devour her right where she stood. Had he left or asked for another girl?

"Hello." Molly extended her hand. "I'm Molly Rose. I'm Robert Simms' sister."

"It's nice to meet you, Molly Rose," Mabel said slowly, her gaze guarded.

She slipped her palm into Molly's, the touch cool, a stark

contrast to the warmth of Mister McKenna's large grip engulfing hers just minutes ago. Molly ignored the flush of energy that still lingered from the tall man and their brief interaction—in a brothel, of all places. She was only here because of her brother.

Mabel stepped back and offered Molly a seat on a stool while the woman sat on the bed, frilly clothing strewn across the bedcovers. It seemed far less than what a woman should wear. Molly's gaze landed on a photo on the wall and she froze. A woman stood, hands on hips, wearing nothing but a pair of bloomers, her modest breasts thrust provocatively outward, as naked as could be.

Molly jerked her attention back to Mabel, embarrassed that her mouth was hanging open. Snapping it shut, she hid her mortification by clasping her hands together and resting them atop her gray skirt.

The urge to inquire if Mabel enjoyed what she did swelled inside, but Molly kept silent. That would be rude. Surely the woman did it because she had no other choice.

Mabel tugged the lapels of her dressing gown closed, then dropped her hand and sighed. "What can I do for you?"

"I arrived into town yesterday for a visit with Robert, but he never met me and I'm concerned. I don't really know where else to look." Molly cleared her throat. "A man at the hotel where I'm staying mentioned that Robert sometimes came here. He gave me your name." She added in a rush, "I hope that was all right. I was hoping that you might know something."

Mabel lowered her gaze.

"Do you know my brother?" Molly pressed.

The woman nodded. "Yep, I know Robbie."

Mabel glanced up and watched her, causing Molly to squirm under the scrutiny.

"What you say will be kept private, I can assure you," Molly blurted.

Mabel gathered the edges of her robe and tightened the sash at her waist. "Your brother hasn't been here recently, but other men I see..."

Molly waited, afraid to speak for fear of deterring the woman. She'd thought to go to the local law enforcement, but when she questioned the hotel clerk about the deputy marshal, his response had left her with more doubts than confidence. There was a wildness in this town that was hard to miss. It made little sense to come to a brothel for information—were women such as Mabel trustworthy?—but Molly was at her wit's end. Her mama had cautioned her against the impulsive actions she sometimes took, but her heart had told her to visit the prostitute.

Mabel's expression became so sober and sincere, Molly's insides twisted into a frozen knot.

"I'm sorry, Miss Simms, but Robert is dead."

# CHAPTER 2

J ake almost didn't recognize Miss Simms when she stepped onto
the wooden planks that served as the porch for Bertha's Saloon.
Gone was the vibrant, resolute woman he'd just encountered,
and in her place was a ghostly apparition.

In several strides, he was at her side and grasped her elbow.

"Are you ill?" he asked, guiding her to Cora's Restaurant. They
needed to talk, and Miss Simms was clearly in need of a cup of
strong black coffee.

She shook her head then slumped against him. He grabbed her
around the waist to keep her from falling to the ground.

"I take it things didn't go well with Mabel." He guided her up a
set of wooden steps and into the restaurant, then settled her at a
quiet table. He hung his hat on a hook and sat across from her.
"What's wrong, Miss Simms?"

She shook her head and fought back a sob. "Robert is dead," she
whispered, pinning him with a bleak, horrified look in her eyes.

Stunned, Jake asked, "Who told you that? Mabel?"

She nodded, a tear running down her face.

Jake reached inside his jacket, retrieved a kerchief, and handed
it to her. "How does she know?" He wasn't acquainted with Mabel

personally, but Robert had fancied a girl at Bertha's for a time. It must've been her.

"She said a man named James Winston told her that Robert had disappeared for good."

Jake swore under his breath.

"Do you know this man?" she asked.

"Yeah." He leaned forward. "Look. I don't think Robert is dead."

Hope lit up her features. "Why?"

"A lot of reasons but I wouldn't put much stock in what this Mabel knows. You should've just come to me." But he feared there was a reason she hadn't. It was why he hadn't approached her straightaway.

He smiled warmly when Cora, the elderly proprietress, appeared at their table, wiping her hands on the apron hugging her thin waist. She winked at him. "You've never had a young lady with you, Jake. What can I get you both?"

"Evenin', Cora. Coffee and pie."

"I've got apple, peach or cherry."

"I'll have apple." He looked expectantly at Miss Simms.

"Oh, no thank you. I'm not hungry."

"I think you should eat something," he insisted. "How about peach?"

"I'll bring a slice of both," Cora said. "It's sure nice to see you courtin', Jake."

"You know I'm sworn to you, Cora. Miss Simms and I are just visiting."

"Simms?" Cora exclaimed. "Are you related to Robbie?"

Miss Simms nodded, tears welling in her eyes once again. Damn that Mabel for so callously delivering news that might not be true.

"You haven't seen him lately, have you?" Jake asked the older woman.

"Well, let me think." She settled bony hands on her hips. "I believe he was in here last week, but just this morning I heard Ivan mention that he'd run into him in the hills."

"When?"

"I think he might've seen him yesterday."

Another customer signaled Cora, so she nodded and walked away.

"There you go," Jake said. "Robert's not dead." *At least, not yet.*

Miss Simms swiped at the wetness on her cheeks with his kerchief, and her features hardened. "Would you mind telling me what Robert is involved in that's so dangerous?"

Dealing with pretty sisters was something that Jake had never aspired to. He didn't want to explain to the young woman what Robert was up to these days. It was Robert's business, and he should tell her himself.

"I don't think he's in danger." In all likelihood, Jake spoke the truth. At least, that's what he told himself. "Robert and I have done a lot of prospecting in this area. I'm guessing he just lost track of time while in the hills. It happens. I think if you sit tight, he'll be along any day now."

Cora returned with a tray of cups and saucers and a pot of steaming coffee. She set a plate of pie before each of them along with a fork. "I know Jake takes his black, but would you like cream and sugar, Miss Simms?"

She nodded. Cora deposited both on the table. "Let me know if you need anything else."

"Thank you," replied Miss Simms.

Jake dug into his pie. He hadn't eaten since the noonday meal. Keeping an eye on Molly Rose Simms had consumed most of his time. He hadn't been entirely sure that she hadn't known the location of Robert, which was why he'd kept his distance initially. That, and the money. Since Robert had taken up with Bridget Lannigan, Jake wasn't certain of Robert's loyalties, and that uncertainty spread to his sister.

Miss Simms poured a dollop of cream into her coffee along with a half teaspoon of sugar, then stirred the brew slowly. "Exactly how long have you known Robert?"

"I came to the area last year, and Robert and I hit it off."

"And you search for silver veins in the mountains with him?"

"Yep, that's about right." He scooped his cup up by the rim and took a large swallow of coffee.

Miss Simms dawdled over her meal, and Jake eyed her piece of pie. She must have noticed because she pushed it across the table to him. He nodded his thanks and scooped a large bite into his mouth. "You really should eat something," he said around the food. "Cora has a decent stew."

"Do you always talk with your mouth full?" She bunched her eyebrows together. "You're not at all concerned that something has happened to Robert?"

A smile tugged at his mouth from her chastisement. "No sense counting eggs before they're hatched. I'll do more checking and see if I can find him. Why don't you go back to your hotel and rest? I'll let you know if I learn anything."

She watched him as if he'd been the one to lay the eggs. After a sip of coffee, she crossed her arms across her ivory blouse and leaned back in her chair.

Cora reappeared and retrieved the empty pie plates. "Would you both like anything else?"

"Miss Simms?" Jake asked.

"No, I've had quite enough."

MOLLY RESTED on the bumpy mattress in her hotel room, the thick quilt laying heavy on her. The sensation of smothering eventually prompted her to sit in the rocking chair in the corner. As the night lengthened, she oscillated forward and back, her mind filled with

Mabel's words, ricocheting like an errant bullet. Tears filled her eyes repeatedly.

With desperation, she clung to Mister McKenna's pronouncement. *Robert's not dead.*

It had to be true; the alternative was too horrific to consider.

She stood and paced, the hem of her nightgown tickling the top of her feet.

But then why didn't Mister McKenna know about Robert's whereabouts? They were partners, after all. While her brother had mentioned Jake McKenna a few times in letters home and had seemed happy with the partnership, the truth was she didn't know the man, and she had to wonder if he'd had anything to do with Robert being missing.

She'd been to Robert's room in a boardinghouse three times already to check if he'd returned, but more and more, the idea pressed on her that she should search the premises. And she preferred to do it without anyone knowing, least of all the boardinghouse proprietor, a gruff man who'd been annoyed every time she had inquired if her brother had yet returned from *wherever* he was.

Mabel's words whispered back at her, and Molly suppressed a shudder. She prayed that Mister McKenna was right—that Robert was simply distracted in the hills and had forgotten her arrival. He couldn't be dead. He just couldn't. How could she possibly convey such news to her folks? Her mama would be utterly heartbroken.

A sob hitched in Molly's throat. Her mama wouldn't be the only one.

She'd always been close to Robert since they were very young. Only two years her senior, he'd been her constant companion, at least as long as she could trail after him without him becoming cross. As they'd gotten older, he'd tolerated her because she'd proven herself to be as tough as the other boys in town, learning to shoot and rope and ride a horse like any good cowpuncher. It had made her pa proud, while her mama had simply shaken her head at Molly's bullheadedness. Thankfully, her mama still had Evelyn, the youngest and a good deal sweeter and prettier than Molly.

Molly made up her mind and quickly donned her darkest attire —a black skirt and a dark brown blouse—then tied an equally dark bonnet to her chin, the wide brim hiding the pale skin of her face. She slipped from her room and quietly let herself out the front entrance of Zang's Hotel, careful to close the door with as little sound as possible.

A glance up and down the street showed it to be empty although lights blazed from several establishments, all of them saloons, from the look of it.

*Did this town never sleep?*

She crossed the street then cut a path between two buildings so that she could make her way behind the buildings along the edge of Willow Creek. The water flowed briskly from the newly-melting snow of winter. Steep cliff walls loomed just beyond, lending an oppressive atmosphere to the already bustling mining camp. Robert's boardinghouse wasn't far. He'd reserved her a room at the hotel because it was nearby to him.

She covered her nose as the stench of urine blasted her, and then covered it again when the odor of rotting food replaced it. Moving swiftly to escape, she gasped for air. She counted the buildings to make certain she located the correct one since, from the rear, they all appeared similar. Earlier in the day, it had occurred to her that such an excursion might be necessary, and she'd scouted the possibility before her visit to Mabel . . . and the subsequent pie respite with the rugged Jake McKenna.

Shaking off that thought—what did it matter that she found him brawny in an oddly compelling way—she peeked around the building to make certain it was the correct boardinghouse, then crept back to the side window. When she'd come by in the afternoon, she'd unlatched a hallway window from the inside. Only now she realized that the opening was higher from the outside than she'd anticipated. She scanned around for something to stand on. A search in back—near the offending stench she'd just passed through—revealed a wooden crate.

She carried it to the window and pressed it into the ground, trying to get it as flat as she could, then carefully stepped up on it. Molly strained to lift the frame until it finally released in a sudden upward motion. At the same moment, the crate collapsed beneath her, and she clung to the window's edge, feet dangling.

She attempted to find purchase with her heels against the side of the building without making a ruckus, while the muscles in her arms began to strain. She didn't have much time before she'd be forced to drop back to the ground.

With a low grunt, she heaved herself upward and managed to haul herself high enough that she could swing a knee onto the wooden frame. She hoisted her torso into the boardinghouse and fell against the floor head first. Lying on her back and momentarily stunned, she took several steadying breaths before standing on shaky legs. She listened for anyone she might have alerted. When it seemed the coast was clear, she pushed the window down and closed it.

The boardinghouse entryway was dark although she spotted a few pieces of furniture. She tiptoed up the stairs to the second floor, cringing at the squeaking wood.

Three doors down was Robert's room. It would be locked, but she'd stolen the proprietor's extra key copy when she'd been by during the afternoon.

Her mama wouldn't be happy with all her subterfuge. Neither would Robert, for that matter, despite that it was for his benefit.

She pulled the iron key from her skirt pocket and unlocked the door as quietly as she could. Once inside, she closed the door and leaned against it, heaving a sigh of relief. Sneaking around was exhausting on the nerves.

In order to search properly, she would need light. She fiddled with the heavy curtain nailed in place above the window and tucked the edges tight to create a seal. She located a lucifer on the nightstand and struck a flame then lit the oil lamp, immediately turning the wick as low as possible. Carefully, she set the lamp onto the floor.

Where to start? The previous three times she'd been here, she hadn't actually been inside his room. And this was Robert's room, all right. Her brother was still a packrat. Filthy clothes lay in a pile in the corner. A narrow wooden table held a multitude of ore samples and various mining picks. The bedcovers were in disarray, and Molly found a partial loaf of dried-out bread on the floor beneath his bed. If their reunion had gone as planned, she would've been in here cleaning up for him instead of searching for a clue to his disappearance.

Lifting the lid of a trunk revealed more clothing, several books, and letters from her and Evie, as well as their mama. She held up *A Tale of Two Cities* by Charles Dickens. What a boring tale. The only thing Molly had liked about it was the descriptions of London and Paris, places she hoped one day to visit. But Robert had always gravitated to such morally angst-filled stories. Their Aunt Tess had started them young with *Sir Gawain and the Green Knight*. Molly preferred more adventure. *Twenty Thousand Leagues Under The Sea* suited her better, or *Alice in Wonderland*. She especially loved the tales of Ali Baba, Sinbad the Sailor, and Aladdin and his Magic Lamp from the *Arabian Nights*. She tossed the novel back into the trunk.

She scanned the ore table, but really, it was just a collection of rocks. She picked up the dirty laundry to see if anything was beneath it. Nothing. She wrinkled her nose at the odor and dropped the mess back to the floor.

She glanced at the crusty bread and dropped to hands and knees to retrieve it. It was as hard as the ore samples. Robert was lucky he didn't have ants yet.

As she sat back on her heels, her hand caught at the dusty rug beneath her. She tugged the edge back and noticed the flooring beneath didn't line up exactly. Positioning the oil lamp closer, she scooted back and pulled the rug away. Running her hands over the wood, the unevenness seemed odd, but trying to pry up one of the edges with her fingertips proved futile. She retrieved the smallest mining pick she could find on Robert's messy table and wedged the end into the space between the floor planks. After several tries, one finally popped out.

She pulled it up and away from its nesting spot and looked inside, but she couldn't see anything. She tugged at another plank, and it came free after a bit of wiggling back and forth. She picked up the oil lamp and peered into the crevice.

A small metal box was tucked farther back. She set down the lamp and reached her arm in and grasped the prize, dragging it from its hiding place.

It made her think of a story her Aunt Molly had told of her of a similar box she'd hidden near her ranch in Texas the night her folks —Molly Rose's grandparents—had been murdered. It was a dark tale, one that her aunt had shared only one time with her when Molly Rose was eleven and had come to Aunt Molly and Uncle Matt's ranch, the Rocking Wren, to visit for a summer.

Aunt Molly had hidden important and secret items inside her box, including a slingshot she had named The Wren. That summer, Molly Rose had made her own shooter, in an effort to emulate the aunt for which she was named.

Molly wondered what she'd find inside her brother's secret treasure chest as she lifted the lid. Gold pieces? Money? A handmade weapon similar to their aunt's?

A pile of papers greeted her, filling her with a twinge of disappointment.

She began to skim the documents. They were all mining claims, and they all seemed to be in Robert and Mister McKenna's names. The last one, however, caught her by surprise.

Jake McKenna and Molly Rose Simms were the proud owners of the Chigger Lode.

---

JAKE WATCHED from the shadow of a building as Miss Simms shimmied her way out of the window of Robert's boardinghouse. He'd been impressed when she'd hauled herself inside after the crate had given out. While she was proportioned just the way he liked a woman, he now had an appreciation of her strength.

He might've helped her except that in addition to him following her, another man also lurked nearby. And then there was, of course, the question of why she was slinking about in the first place. Was she searching for clues about her brother, or were the two of them cooking something up? Perhaps it had something to do with the five thousand dollars Jake was missing.

Jake hadn't planned on spying on her. When he'd dropped her at her hotel after their less-than-productive meeting at Cora's, he told her he'd be in touch as soon as he knew something. From there, he'd headed to the Orleans Club for a night of faro and his favorite rye whiskey. The saloon and gambling hall regularly cheated customers, but Jake felt it was worth it to see if he could glean any information about Robert. He'd come up empty.

When he left the establishment, he'd taken a path that led right to Miss Simms' hotel. He couldn't say exactly why—if he'd needed female company, there were plenty of girls at the Orleans Club that would've filled the bill—but here he was, nevertheless.

And then he'd seen the dark profile of a person hustling across the street. He'd known it was her immediately. He never forgot a fine figure, and this one ranked near the top.

Miss Simms dropped from the window. Her feet crashed into the broken crate, and she let out a muffled squeal. Without thinking Jake stepped forward to help, then paused. If he exposed himself, he might not be able to stop the other man if he should decide to attack. Jake hadn't been able to identify the third party in this covert dance.

Miss Simms untangled her feet from the crate and stood, brushing her hands down her pitch-black skirt. Then she glanced upward, and Jake understood her dilemma. She was unable to close the window. She stood for a moment and contemplated her situation. Jake watched the other man, the barest hint of his presence in the shadows.

The sound of a noise inside the house made her jump. She fled behind the buildings once more, abandoning the open window. The other man followed her, and Jake got a better look at him. A bandanna covered the man's face and his hat was pulled low, but Jake knew it was Chip Westfield. Chip and James Winston were thugs for Shep Lannigan.

Things just went from bad to worse.

Jake stayed undercover and moved along Creede Avenue, scanning between buildings for signs of Miss Simms. He paused at a livery and waited, his back braced against the building. She moved right past him, and Jake held his breath. If she turned her head just a bit more, she would see him, but the bonnet she wore shielded him from view. She crossed the street and took the hotel steps quickly, then entered the building.

Jake remained in his hiding place, waiting for the man who stalked her. A light came on in an upstairs room facing the street—Miss Simms' room, no doubt. After a fair amount of time had passed, Jake circled the livery back the way he'd come, in search of Westfield. Jake pulled his Colt from his hip holster and continued to move between the buildings by circling around the front first.

In the end, he found nothing.

The man had disappeared.

Jake's gut clenched like a skittish horse. He holstered his gun, entered Miss Simms' hotel and crept upstairs. By now, the light had been extinguished. When he listened at the threshold of the room he thought was hers, he heard loud snoring.

He sincerely hoped that wasn't Miss Simms.

He moved to the next room and tapped lightly on the door.

After a long pause, a slight crack appeared.

"What do you want?" she whispered.

"Someone's following you."

Her eyes narrowed. "I believe you're right, and I'm guessing it's not the first time you've done it."

"Not me. Well, not exactly." Jake glanced side to side and checked the hallway. "Can I come in?"

"How will my reputation survive it?" she groused, but she stood back and let him enter, shutting the door behind him. "Do you have news about Robert?"

She'd changed from her dark sneaking-around attire and now wore a wrap over what he presumed was her sleeping gown.

"No," he replied. "But I'm guessing you do."

"Why do you say that?"

"Look, I know you don't entirely trust me, but I know you went to Robert's room tonight." He held up his hand when anger flashed in her eyes and she opened her mouth to speak. "Yes, I was watching you, but I'm the least of your worries right now. Someone else was following you."

"Who?"

"A man who works for Shep Lannigan, and Robert's mixed up with the lot of 'em."

"Then maybe I should speak with them."

Jake shook his head. "No, you shouldn't. At least not until we can find your brother and learn what he's gotten himself into."

"What are you talking about?"

"Listen, we should get out of town."

Incredulous, she laughed. "Now?"

"Yes, now. I have a place we can go."

"You're deranged. We've only just met. For all I know, you could be the one against Robert, if that's what's truly going on."

Jake paused, watching the tigress before him. Why hadn't Robert ever told him his beautiful sister was full of spit and vinegar? "I can assure you, I won't hurt you. Robert is like a brother to me, and while we've had our ups and downs, I consider it my duty to look out for his sister. And right now, if you stay in town, I've a feeling you'll—at the very least—be harassed, but more likely, you'll get roughed up."

"By who? This Shep person?"

"He might think you know where your brother is." Jake lifted his hat and ran a hand through his hair. "Let's change your location and throw them off your scent."

He didn't really expect her to agree wholeheartedly with him, so he was taken aback when she nodded her compliance.

"Be ready in one hour and meet me behind the hotel," he said. "Pack light."

He left before she could change her mind.

# CHAPTER 3

I n the hours before dawn, Molly rode an even-tempered bay named Cinnamon out of Creede and into the surrounding mountains, following Mister McKenna, who guided a feisty black gelding he called Fernando.

She debated whether trusting him was the best course of action. Regardless, she and Mister McKenna were business partners. She wasn't sure whether to mention this to him; perhaps he already knew, but the fact that Robert had hidden the claim document inside the metal box in the floor indicated that McKenna probably *didn't* know. For now, she'd keep that little tidbit to herself.

It unsettled her that she was being watched. She worried that Robert was involved in something way over his head, and now, by the simple association of being his sister, she was in the muck of it, too.

To add to it, she was going into the mountains with a man she hardly knew. She resolved to have faith that it would all work out, and if not, she had the compact Colt Derringer Robert had given her two years ago tucked into the pocket of her split skirt. It only allowed one shot, but she convinced herself that one would be enough.

She praised her foresight in secreting it away in her luggage on her first adventure alone. Traveling by stage and train from the Arizona Territory to Creede to visit her brother was the most exciting enterprise she'd done in her short life. Hopefully, it wouldn't be the last.

The rain came first as a light sprinkle. McKenna guided Fernando back to her and offered her a slicker, which she gratefully took although she was bundled in a wool coat and scarf to ward off the early morning chill. Within minutes, the sky released a deluge, and they were both drenched.

They continued trekking into the wilderness, the horses stepping gingerly as the downpour turned the trail into mud. At last, as a gray haze began to lighten the sky, a cabin came into view, buttressed by a stand of pine trees and surrounded by high rocky slopes.

McKenna halted before the structure and dismounted, gesturing for her to do the same. Her boots landed in a thick puddle of mud.

"I'll take care of the horses," McKenna said, raising his voice above the din as the heavens released heavy sheets of water. "You go inside."

Molly nodded and bundled the gear he handed her into her arms and carried it to the cabin's entrance.

Standing at the threshold, she paused to let the water drip from her so that only one spot of the dwelling would need to be cleaned. The simple, one-room accommodation was furnished with two single cots, a potbelly stove, a table with two chairs, and a kitchen workspace with a shelf above a window holding cookware and cups.

Molly deposited the gear on the floor, removed the slicker and hung it on a hook near the door, then leaned down to unlace her boots, pulling them from her feet.

Only wearing stockings, she shuffled forward and located a stack of wood beneath the kitchen countertop. She retrieved several small pieces and a large one, then set to work starting a fire in the stove. When Jake returned, she had a good flame ignited.

His large frame filled the cabin, and she squared her shoulders, suddenly aware of his presence and the tight quarters they now found themselves in.

"You started a fire." Jake grinned, removed his hat and placed it on the corner of one of the chairs, then removed his slicker and long coat and hung those as well.

"Is there some reason I shouldn't have?" Perhaps he didn't want to give away their presence.

"No, that's fine. We'll need the heat."

For some reason, the comment struck her as odd and her pulse quickened.

Did she actually *like* Mister McKenna?

To hide her reaction, she sat on the edge of the nearest cot and held her hands toward the stove in attempt to gain a bit of warmth. "Whose cabin is this? It's very well-kept."

McKenna grabbed a chair and positioned it close to the stove then sat, elbows resting on knees. "It's mine. I stay out here when I'm prospecting. That way I don't have to go to town so often."

"You have two beds. Does Robert stay here too?"

McKenna nodded. "He has."

"Do you think he would try to return?"

"The thought did cross my mind, but it appears no one has been here. The stable around back hasn't been used either."

McKenna's jet-black hair curled along the collar of his shirt, and a coal-colored stubble had sprouted on his strong jawline. When he shifted his gaze to her, his eyes put her in mind of molasses. Molly chewed on her lower lip and glanced away, lest McKenna catch her staring.

Shaking off her fascination, she asked, "How did you meet Robert?"

"In a poker game."

Molly gasped. "Robert gambles?"

McKenna chuckled. "You've already been to a whorehouse. If you wanted to remain innocent, you shouldn't have come to Creede."

Her backside stiffened. "I'm not naïve to the ways of the world."

Another grin lit his face. Her breath caught and her heart pounded more intensely. She honestly couldn't look away. She'd read about people who possessed a charm that swayed the masses and opened doors with merely a glance, but she'd never met such a person.

What was the word she'd come across? Charisma, that was it. In this moment, the meaning became crystal clear.

"Whatever you say, Miss Simms. Why did you come to Creede?"

"To visit my brother, of course."

"You came by yourself all the way from Tucson?"

"My folks believed that Robert would be here to meet me."

He nodded, his amiable demeanor slipping a bit. She took a steadying breath to quiet the knot in her stomach that never quite receded. *Please be all right, Robert.*

"My folks thought that Robert would look after me," she added, her voice muffled as rain continued to pound on the roof of the cabin. "But I assure you that I can look after myself."

"I don't doubt that. I'm at your service, nevertheless."

"For what?"

"Protection."

He held her gaze, and a frisson of awareness shot through her. She shifted her eyes to the stove. She hadn't traveled all this way to fall for the first rugged buckaroo who crossed her path, charisma or not. She had more important things to do with her life first.

"Where are you from, Mister McKenna?"

"You can call me Jake. I was born in San Francisco."

"So was I."

He raised an eyebrow. "Maybe we passed one another on the street."

"Probably not. My folks were only there to visit my Aunt Emma. After I was born, they returned to the Arizona Territory."

"So you and Robert grew up in Tucson, the land of the Apache."

"And my younger sister, Evie."

As the flames in the stove grew, Jake closed the cast-iron door and latched it. "How did Robert ever survive two younger sisters?" he teased.

"How many siblings do you have?"

"None." He scrubbed a hand over his cheek. "My folks died when I was very young. I grew up in an orphanage."

"I'm so sorry."

"About what? Life is what it is."

"So you never had a home or a family?"

He shook his head. "When I was fifteen, I sneaked onto a steamer headed for Asia and I never looked back."

"You did?" Fascinated, she stared at him.

"I grew up fast."

"So you've seen the world?"

He leaned back in the chair and stretched his legs out, crossing his arms over his chest. "I guess you could say that."

"I've been studying French, and I hope one day to see Paris."

He gave her a crooked smile. "You've a bit of the wandering spirit as well?"

"Something like that. I'd like to travel and write about it. I was hoping I could convince Robert to take me to San Francisco or even New York City." Her tone was bright, but her shoulders sagged over the possible reality of the situation.

"We'll find him, Molly Rose."

Her eyes flicked to his, the use of her given name still hanging in the air. Her throat tightened, so she simply nodded.

McKenna stood. "I can make a pot of coffee, and I've got a can of peaches here somewhere for breakfast."

Molly hadn't considered food. "I'm afraid I don't have any staples with me. How long do you think we'll be here?"

"Hopefully not more than a day or two. I've got supplies in my gear. We'll be fine, but it won't be gourmet cooking."

Molly came to her feet as well. "It would help to have something to do. Show me what you have."

———

JAKE CHECKED ON THE HORSES, mostly to give Molly a break from the cramped quarters forcing them in such close proximity to one another. Or maybe *he* needed a breather. He'd never brought a woman here before. There was no reason. And if he was looking to romance one, this wasn't the way to do it.

Not that he planned to romance Miss Simms.

He shook his head. His thoughts were wandering a lot today.

The warm smell of baking bread greeted him when he walked back into the cabin. "Did you make something?"

She glanced over her shoulder. "I managed to make a batch of very thin biscuits by covering a pan and setting it on the stove." She shrugged a shoulder toward the table. "So it'll be biscuits, peaches and boiled coffee for breakfast."

"I'm not complaining." He removed his hat and the slicker, then took a seat. His boots still dripped with rain and mud, but he left them on. He'd just be heading back out again, and it was too much effort to remove his footwear every time he entered the cabin. On the other hand, he didn't usually have a woman preparing a meal for him.

He hoped she wouldn't take offense over his manners.

Molly set the coffeepot on the table using a rag. She'd already opened the peaches and placed two cups filled with coffee beside it. She sat across from him.

"I think I can make a stew later with the potatoes and dried meat you brought."

"I guess I should've brought a woman here sooner. You've brightened up the place."

"Glad I could help." She slurped a peach off her spoon.

"Very ladylike," he remarked.

She threw him an annoyed look but continued to eat, which he was glad to see.

"Why did you follow me into Bertha's yesterday?" she asked. "Or were you there looking for company like that other man?"

It surprised him that he felt like a boy who'd been caught with his hand in the cookie jar. "I wasn't there as a customer," he defended. "I was just keeping an eye on you."

"Why didn't you just come forward and introduce yourself?"

Jake hesitated, but decided to tell the truth. "I wasn't certain if you could be trusted."

She broke off a piece of biscuit and stuffed it into her mouth. "But you do now?" she asked around the food.

"You shouldn't talk with your mouth full."

She shot him an irritated look.

"And trust has to be earned," he answered truthfully.

She swallowed. "I agree. So you won't hold it against me if I don't entirely trust *you*."

Bemused, he finished off his peaches. "At least we understand one another."

Having consumed two biscuits, a bowl of peaches and a full cup of coffee, Molly leaned against the chair and crossed her arms beneath her bosom. "What kind of trouble is Robert in?"

His eyes traveled to the ivory blouse now pulled taut across her breasts, and, for a moment, he forgot the question. A heavy wave of rain startled him, hitting the tin roof as if school kids had released a bucket of marbles.

"I already told you about Shep Lannigan. Suffice it to say, he's rather disreputable. Shep has a daughter named Bridget, and Robert has taken quite a shine to her." He didn't mention Bridget's attempts to snag Jake's attention first, moving along to Robert only after she'd failed. "Robert and I had a bit of a falling out after that."

"Why?"

"Because he started spending more and more time in the Lannigan camp, and I didn't like it. Robert wouldn't listen to reason, so for the past few months, I've been on my own, prospecting."

A clap of thunder startled Molly, but she quickly regained her composure. "And Robert prospects on his own now?"

"No, I think he scouts claims for Lannigan now."

"Robert never mentioned any of this in his letters home."

Jake drank the last of his coffee. "Which makes me wonder how far in over his head he might actually be. I find it curious that one of Lannigan's men was watching you. All I can think is that they thought you'd lead them to Robert."

"If this Shep person had just asked, I could've told him I don't know where Robert is."

"Maybe *he* doesn't know where Robert is either, and he thought you might lead him there." He settled his gaze on the attractive Miss Simms. He had to be sure. *"Do you know where your brother is?"*

She leveled a cool gaze on him. "No." Her response held a hint of annoyance.

"You searched Robert's room last night. Did you find anything?" He watched her closely for a reaction, a flinch that might indicate she was lying.

With a look of disgust on her face, she said, "So much for your high and mighty attitude of Lannigan having me followed, when you clearly have done the same." She stood and crouched near her travel satchel, rifling inside until she found a piece of paper. Returning to the table, she unfolded it and tossed it before him.

Jake read the mining claim document—similar to the dozens of others he'd filed both alone and with Robert—but this one made no sense.

The Chigger Lode. Owners: Jake McKenna and Molly Rose Simms. Filed: April 15, 1892.

*What the hell?*

The location was an area that he and Robert had never scouted.

"Why would Robert do this?" he asked aloud.

"I guess he thought you and I would make perfect partners."

But the real reason set off alarm bells in Jake's head. Robert was in trouble, and he sought to hide a claim that was likely very valuable by putting it in someone else's name. But why involve Molly? He could've just put the document into Jake's name.

Obviously Robert sought insurance by including his sister, a way to keep Jake in check. Jake couldn't blame him, but the distrust in the act sliced deeper than he would've imagined. Jake didn't make friends easily, and Robert had been the closest thing to a brother he'd ever had. When Robert had chosen a woman over Jake, it had left Jake frustrated and more than a little resentful.

Still, considering Jake's recent travails with Shep Lannigan, it showed a modicum of trust on Robert's part to slap Jake's name on a claim.

Whatever Robert wanted to throw his way, Jake could handle it, but this lode would likely spark interest from Lannigan, and that meant Molly was now squarely in the man's path.

*Dammit, Robert.*

# CHAPTER 4

Once the sun had set—and she and Jake had eaten a potato stew—Molly really wasn't sure how the sleeping situation was supposed to work, so she lay on one of the beds, fully clothed. She even left her boots on, having wiped the mud from the soles after a trip to the outhouse.

The little cabin had warmed considerably from the constant fire in the tiny stove, so she didn't need a blanket to cover her.

Lying on her back, she closed her eyes and rested her hands on her stomach.

The door opened and Jake entered, drenched yet again. The rain had been relentless, making Molly feel edgy and claustrophobic.

"You look like you're laid out for a funeral," he said.

She cracked an eyelid. "You've described perfectly what it's like to be with you."

He laughed, sitting on a chair and removed his boots.

She closed her eyes again, wondering how much undressing he was about to do. Soon she heard him settle onto the opposite cot. When she peeked again, he'd doused the light.

"I could sleep in the shed with the horses." His deep voice filled the space around her.

Rain still pelted the cabin, having contrived to keep them cooped up together all day...and now all night.

Molly considered his offer. It would certainly make her feel more comfortable, but if her mama ever found out that she and Jake had shared a room...

"No. I'm a big girl. I can imagine that shed is cold and wet."

"Cinnamon and Fernando have only complained a little." After a moment of silence, he said, "I've been wondering why Robert called the claim he gave us the Chigger. Does that have some significance to you?"

"It was his nickname for me when we were young. I used to chase him around and call him chicken because we had chickens, and I thought he looked like them. He didn't much like it, so he'd throw it back at me. Over time, it changed to chigger."

Jake chuckled, low and deep, and in the close darkness of the cabin, the intimacy of their predicament became more pronounced.

To combat her discomfort, Molly willed her shoulders and arms to relax, then her legs, then her feet. She often did this to help her fall asleep, especially on nights when an incident in a well reminded her that real terror was never truly forgotten. She also drank copious amounts of willow bark tea, a natural sedative. Why hadn't she thought to bring any with her from Tucson?

She breathed through the frustration of having forgotten her tea.

*I'll seek out some in Creede.*

"Goodnight, Molly."

Unable to bring herself to use his first name, she replied, "Goodnight, Mister McKenna."

MOLLY AWOKE with a start to the burgeoning light of day. McKenna's bunk was empty. She swung her feet to the floor and sat for a moment to fully awaken. The ever-present rat-tat-tat of the rain deflated her spirits. She'd hoped to get a bit of fresh air this morning. She unraveled the mess of her hair from the bun that no longer was holding its shape and ran her fingers through the knotted tresses to smooth them out, then quickly braided it and pushed the thick rope behind her.

Since she was already dressed and wearing her boots, she went to the coffeepot, but Jake had already gotten it started—it sat percolating upon the hot stove. He'd also brought a bucket of water inside—the pump was located outside—and left it on the workspace. She found a bar of soap and a rag and started washing the dishes from the previous day.

The door opened behind her. "Thanks for making the coffee," she said without looking up.

"Who the hell are you?"

Screaming, she dropped the tin cup with a loud clang.

"Jesus, Boom," Jake said from behind the giant man filling the doorway. "Are you trying to scare my guest?"

"Apologies." The towering man took off his hat and entered the cabin, looking a bit sheepish.

Molly leaned down and retrieved the cup, her heart racing.

Jake came inside and shut the door behind him. "Boom, this is Molly Rose Simms."

"Are you Robbie's wife?" he asked, clearly perplexed.

"No, his sister." She fought to steady her breath as she extended a hand to the man who could easily break her in half if he chose.

He awkwardly took it, then quickly released it. He nodded and smiled, and she exhaled.

"Sit down," Jake instructed the man. "You're bigger than most trees. I think you're making Miss Simms uncomfortable."

Molly cleared her throat. "Would you like some coffee, sir?"

The giant laughed, loud and hearty, then shook his head. "You don't have to call me sir. No one calls me that out here. You're much too kind. It's such a pleasure to meet Robbie's sister. You look a lot like him."

"I'd say she's prettier than Robert." Jake caught her eye before sitting on the edge of his cot.

Her face heated from the compliment, and she busied herself with grabbing the just-washed cups, filling them with the dark brew then bringing them to the men.

"Thank you," Boom said.

As McKenna took the other cup from her, his fingers brushed hers. She pretended it didn't happen and instead pulled the other chair closer to the stove, acting as if she was cold. In truth, she sought to give McKenna and this man a semblance of privacy. She would've gone outside, but the rain still came down in sheets.

"Got any news?" McKenna asked.

"I saw the smoke from the stove, so figured you were here. I came to find out if *you* had any news."

"Would you happen to know where Robert is?" Molly blurted. So much for staying out of the conversation.

"Nah. Are you lookin' for him?"

Molly nodded.

"You came all the way to see him and you can't find him?" Boom asked.

Molly silently agreed again.

"Huh. That don't sound like Robbie."

"No, it doesn't," Jake admitted. "I'm thinking he might be out in the hills."

Boom thought for a minute. "I did see him about ten days ago, give or take some. He was with that Winston fella and another one... I think his name was Jones. They're Lannigan men."

"Yeah, I know." Jake took a swig of coffee.

"You think he's in trouble?" Boom watched expectantly.

"Maybe."

"You should go see Pedro."

A derisive snort escaped McKenna. "The last time I saw that crazy Mexican, he tried to shoot me."

"Who's this Pedro?" Molly asked, trying her best not to intrude but failing miserably.

"He lives across the ridge," Boom replied. "He might know what's happening in the backcountry. He just don't like The Jackal."

"Who's The Jackal?"

Boom nodded toward Jake and grinned. "Him."

She looked at McKenna. "Why are you called that?"

"Long story. Maybe I'll tell you sometime." He turned his attention to Boom. "You're welcome to stay the night in the shed."

"With you?" Boom's eyes widened as he shook his head in mock disgust.

Molly's face heated again. She stood and busied herself with whatever dishes and potatoes she could find. Would Jake admit that the two of them had shared his cabin the previous night?

"Yeah," Jake drawled, "with me."

Had Molly imagined his reluctant response? And why did his words fill her with disappointment? She tried to ignore the fact that spending the night with Mister McKenna—definitely taboo for a proper young woman—had been an exciting experience. She imagined sharing the details with her friends Ellen and Polly back in Tucson. They'd roll their eyes and demand all the particulars, but there really were none. Mister McKenna had been a perfect gentleman, and the only thing to report was that he snored. She'd finally been forced to poke him to get it to stop.

She needed to look at the bright side. At least she'd get a good night's sleep with The Jackal in the stable with Boom.

JAKE WAS glad when the rain finally cleared in the afternoon. Boom offered to help him fix a leaky corner in the shed.

Boom hauled a piece of lumber from the ground and handed it up to Jake. "You've never brought a woman here before."

Kneeling on the slightly tilted roof after a boost from Boom, Jake grabbed the wood and fit it into an empty slot. "I think Lannigan's having her followed. I was worried about her safety."

The horses nickered from inside while munching on hay.

"She's right pretty," Boom remarked.

Jake took a nail from the corner of his mouth and pounded it in two hits. He nodded and made a noncommittal sound.

"Is she spoken for?" Boom lowered his voice a notch, apparently worried that Miss Simms might hear, or maybe the horses.

Jake grimaced. "I don't know." Hell, he hadn't considered that.

"Well, not many fine ladies come to these parts. I've been thinking it might be time for a missus. She's young and sturdy, and fair to look at, too. If you could put in a good word for me...unless you think Robbie'd be mad."

Jake pounded another nail, then another, whacking each with only one swing. The words *Hands off!* caught in his throat, but he swallowed them back. "I'm sure she has a beau back home, Boom. I wouldn't get your hopes up."

He shrugged. "You're probably right."

Jake needed to seal the roof again with linseed oil and turpentine, but that would have to wait until he was back in town for supplies. There'd no doubt be more rain, but, hopefully, the leaking would be less now. He and Boom would need to bed down on the other side of the shed.

He preferred to stay in the cabin with Miss Simms, despite the impropriety of the situation. It was certainly warmer and drier and more comfortable. And, the truth was, he needed to be near her in case they had any trouble.

But it wasn't right to do it in front of Boom, at least not for Miss

Simms' reputation, and while the man was harmless enough—and had aided Jake and Robert in more than one scrape—he'd better not catch the burly Russian pressing his charms on the young woman.

---

THAT EVENING, Jake sat on the edge of the cot that would remain empty tonight while Boom and Molly sat at the table. They ate a potato and beef stew, along with more thin biscuits that Molly had prepared.

"Why are you called Boom?" Molly asked. "Is that your real name?"

"Nope. It's Boris Orlov."

"Did you come all the way from Russia?" she asked, an awestruck look on her face.

Jake was about to mention that *he'd* been to Russia but instead shoved another spoonful of food into his mouth.

Boom nodded. "I did. It was some years ago. I'm from a town called Kislovodsk, at the base of the mighty Mt. Elbrus, a place not much different than here. I struck out to America to find my fortune."

"And have you found that fortune?" Molly inquired.

Boom gave a hearty laugh. "Some, but I can always use more. I'd like to take a wife soon—"

Jake coughed loudly and stood, reaching for another biscuit from the table.

"Are you all right?" Molly pinned her gaze on Jake, concern etching her face, and her blue-green eyes watching him like deep pools of jade.

He pounded a fist on his chest twice. "I'm good."

She turned her attention back to the Russian who, unbeknownst to her, was attempting to woo her. "Do you have a woman you fancy?"

"It's funny you should ask—"

Jake dropped his tin cup. The crash startled everyone and sent coffee across the floor.

Molly jumped up and grabbed a rag then knelt before him to clean the mess. He retrieved his cup, bumping into her shoulder as he did.

She glanced up at him. "I hope you're not becoming ill."

"Just clumsy," he muttered and shrugged.

"If someone asked me to describe you, that wouldn't be it." Her eyes caught his and for a moment he held her gaze, warmed by the compliment she seemed to be paying him. Confusion played across her face and she broke the contact. She stood and set the rag on the kitchen counter then returned to her meal. "You never told me how you got the nickname 'Boom,'" she said to Boris.

He chuckled and scratched his chin. "Well, I'm very handy with dynamite." His eyes flashed as his hands mimicked an explosion. "Ka-boom."

Molly tensed. "That sounds dangerous. Does Robert use a lot of dynamite?"

"Nah," Jake cut in. "Hardly at all." It wasn't entirely true, but there was no reason to needlessly worry her. "We can find a lot of claims by digging and picking."

She nodded, but he could tell she wasn't entirely convinced.

"Why are you called The Jackal?" she asked.

"He looks like one, don't he?" Boom said, slapping Jake on the shoulder.

"Thanks." Jake ran his spoon around his bowl to scoop up a few potato pieces stuck to the side. He swallowed the last of his meal and wiped the back of his hand across his face in case he'd been sloppy. For some reason, Molly Rose Simms rattled him.

"I was in a caravan heading out of Marrakech and into the Sahara," he said.

"Where's Marrakech?" Molly asked, interest sparkling in her eyes.

"Morocco," he replied then added, "North Africa."

Her face registered recognition.

"We had just come through the High Atlas Mountains when a sandstorm hit. Somehow, in the confusion, I got separated from everyone. When the dust finally cleared, I was on my own."

"What did you do?" she asked.

"I headed in the wrong direction, and the search party couldn't find me. In the end, I was on my own for over a fortnight."

"How did you survive?"

"The jackals. There was a band I came across, and I started shadowing them. I managed to occasionally steal some of their kills, and they knew where water could be found. By the time the caravan found me, the other men claimed I'd become one of the critters."

"The animals accepted you?"

"I wouldn't quite phrase it that way. They'd come to tolerate me."

"So you're a tolerable jackal," she teased.

"Most of the time," he murmured, enjoying the look of bemusement in her sea-green eyes.

"What's Morocco like?"

"Old villages filled with locals—they're called Berbers. There's a lot of date trees and the unbelievable aroma of rose plantations."

"What do they like to eat?"

"There's an old Berber dish called a tajine that I frequently ate —lamb cooked in a shallow earth pot flavored with spices."

"Sounds delicious. What's it like for a woman there?"

"They remain covered from head to toe for religious reasons. Women can't do anything on their own. Their father controls their life until they marry, then their husband has control over them."

Molly frowned. "They have no say over their lives?"

"No. It's very different than it is for women here."

"We still don't have the right to vote, except in Wyoming, and I don't know many women who'd want to go there."

"Why would a woman want to vote?" Boom asked. "Seems like a waste of time."

Jake glanced at Molly and noticed the change in her posture along with the strain that had settled in the room.

"We do have opinions, Mister Orlov," she said simply and quietly, "and contrary to what some men might believe, we also have brains in our heads."

Boom laughed again. "Oh, don't mind me. I like smart ladies."

She appeared to relax, but not entirely.

Jake couldn't help but hope that Boom had officially lost any headway in trying to court Miss Simms. And that made him very happy indeed.

"We best turn in," Jake said.

Molly stood and gathered the dishes. Jake stacked the plates and carried them to the counter.

"I can bring you a bucket of water," he offered.

"Thank you." She bustled around him. "I'll heat a bit on the stove and get this all cleaned up."

"Thank you for supper, Miss Simms," Boom said.

"You're welcome." Molly gave a curt nod.

"I'll see to the horses." Boom left the cabin.

"Will you be fine in here alone?" Jake asked.

"Of course." She pushed the dirty dishes into a pile on the counter.

He went outside to the pump and filled the bucket then brought it inside.

Molly was wiping the table when he entered.

"Do you need any help?" Jake asked.

"No." She paused, hands on hips, her breath a bit ragged. "Just to be clear—I won't be a burden. I can cook and clean, and even sew if need be. I can also tend a horse and shoot a gun as well as any man. I don't expect to be coddled."

Jake suppressed a smile. "I understand. No coddling. Your beau is a very fortunate man."

"I have no sweetheart." She straightened her arms then bent them again, hands back on hips, shifting from foot to foot. "Well, then." She nodded to emphasize her words. "I'll see you and Boom in the morning."

"Sleep well, Molly Rose."

"Goodnight, Jake." She glanced at him then flicked her gaze away, her cheeks awash in a faint blush.

It was the first time she'd used his first name, and the sound of it snagged a space in his chest, causing it to swell with some unnamed emotion.

*I have no sweetheart.*

Once outside, he couldn't wipe the grin from his face.

## CHAPTER 5

Molly's horse trailed behind Jake's in search of this person, Pedro, that Boom had mentioned. According to Jake, the man had a cabin over the next ridgeline.

Boom had left them first thing that morning. She liked the big Russian man, but she suspected she'd offended him with her prickly attitude regarding the vote of women. Molly had grown up surrounded by strong women, from her mama to her Aunt Tess, and her Aunts Molly, Emma and Claire.

Her folks had been keen on education, and once the Plaza School in Tucson had opened when she was ten years old, Molly had dutifully attended, learning literature, history, Latin, algebra, and bookkeeping, as well as studying the nature of alcoholic drinks and narcotics and their effect on the human system.

Molly had managed to convince her mama and papa to allow a woman in town to tutor her in French. The resourceful, well-informed Mrs. Haynes—who had traveled extensively through Europe—had whetted Molly's appetite for the world at large. Mrs. Haynes had urged Molly to read such books as John Richard Green's long *History of the English People*, poetry by Elizabeth Barrett Browning, and *Silas Marner* by George Eliot.

If women were intelligent enough to travel and write books about the world around them, then they surely possessed a sound mind to vote in the communities in which they lived.

She wondered if Jake was upset with her behavior, but, in truth, he'd been quite agreeable all morning.

A blue sky and sunshine was welcome after all the rain. Despite the chill, she was heartily glad to be outside. She suspected Cinnamon was happy to stretch his legs as well.

Molly inhaled the clean, fresh air suffused with pine trees and the budding signs of spring. It was late-April, and winter still touched the land with patches of snowpack. Despite that, the area was bathed in a lush anticipation of new life. Boulder-strewn slopes reached toward smooth pinnacles, and Molly wondered at the beauty of it. She could well understand why so many people flocked here because in addition to the riches of silver and gold present in the terrain, there was also a richness of nature almost beyond comprehension.

Was Wyoming half as beautiful as Colorado? If so, perhaps she should consider living there one day, if only to experience the right to voice her opinion in the form of a vote. Although rumor had it that those in charge of such things only granted that right to lure women to the state. Apparently, men in that wild country struggled to find a wife.

Molly wrinkled her nose. In Wyoming, she might have the right to vote, but she'd be pressured to marry. Actually, matrimony would be an issue if she stayed in the Arizona Territory as well. And right now, marriage didn't fit into her plans, not if she hoped to travel to places like Morocco.

Where else had Jake been?

She could learn much from him.

In the afternoon after a steep descent down into an adjacent valley, they rounded a bend, and Molly saw a dilapidated cabin built right into the mountain. Up ahead, Jake pulled the rifle he kept in a saddle scabbard and rested it across his thighs. Molly tensed, glancing around. He was too far ahead for her to ask what trouble he sensed. She had her derringer close, but it would only be useful in an up-close encounter.

Jake slowed his horse. As Molly caught up to him, the door to the cabin opened. A wiry Mexican wearing a floppy hat appeared and pointed a shotgun at them.

"Hold it right there, McKenna!"

Jake raised one hand, palm out, while resting the other on his rifle. "Easy, Pedro. I'm just here to talk. You can put the gun down."

"You gonna apologize for your thievery?" Pedro spoke with a thick accent.

"I didn't steal your gear over in Landry's Valley last month. And you're one to talk. You help yourself to other people's stuff all the time."

"You don't know what you're talking about."

"Can we just agree to set our differences aside for a bit? I need to speak with you."

"Who's that girl?" Pedro waved the barrel of the gun in her direction.

"She's Robert Simms' sister. We're looking for him. Have you seen him?"

Pedro growled out several colorful phrases in Spanish, and—having grown up in Tucson—Molly understood every one of them. He lowered his weapon, and she started breathing again.

Pedro shook his head and relented. "I saw him a few days ago in the valley to the west. He was with Winston, but I suspect you knew that."

Jake swung down from Fernando, his rifle in hand, and walked back to her. He motioned for her to dismount, and she obeyed. He stepped close, which caused her to bump into Cinnamon, and the brim of his hat cast a shadow over both of them. "Would you rather stay out here?"

"No, I'm fine." At such close range, a faint golden glimmer was visible around the edges of his dark, dusky-brown eyes.

"If I thought he was really dangerous, I wouldn't have brought you here. He's a lot of bluster."

She nodded, trying to act as if the close presence of a man like McKenna didn't affect her one whit.

"But that being said," he continued, "stay close."

*As close as you are to me now?*

Not trusting her voice not to betray her, she gave another silent agreement.

He took one last look at her then turned away, and Molly felt as if a gust of wind had just knocked into her, leaving her a bit giddy and shaken.

She led Cinnamon to the hitching post and secured him beside Fernando, then climbed the two uneven steps into Pedro's cabin. Once inside, she had to step around the mess that greeted her, putting her in mind of Robert's room at the boardinghouse. Were all prospectors so unkempt?

Jake's cabin hadn't exhibited such disarray. The tolerable Jackal was apparently more neat-as-a-pin than his brethren.

"You keep the place so tidy, Pedro," Jake remarked.

"I wasn't expecting visitors." The Mexican—the same height as Molly—had wrinkles bunching at the edges of his eyes, but up close it was clear he wasn't old. In fact, Molly was struck by his almost-handsome features. He reached his hand out to her. "I'm Pedro Elizondo."

"I'm pleased to meet you. I'm Molly Simms."

"Robert's *hermana*, huh?"

"Yes."

Jake cleared off a stool and offered it to her to sit on. She settled herself while Jake scanned piles of rocks covering a corner of the cabin. "Find anything?"

"Don't think for one minute you'll get squat out of me regarding my claims." Pedro adjusted his scowl to a more pleasant expression when he turned back to her. "What's happened to Robert?"

"We were hoping you might know," Molly replied. "He was supposed to meet me at the train station three days ago when I arrived for a visit. Can you say exactly how many days ago you saw him?"

Pedro thought for a minute, scratching the side of his nose, his fingernails rimmed with black dirt. "*Lo siento.* I can't recall exactly." He glanced toward Jake, who knelt and handled several of the ore pieces. "You're so damn meddlesome, you jackal."

"These specimens are shit. Why do you have them?"

"I don't have to explain anything to you."

Outside, the horses nickered in agitation. The sound of a shotgun being cocked registered in Molly's mind just as a man yelled, "Elizondo, you scummy prick. We can see the horses. We know you're in there. Get your ass out here."

Jake grabbed Molly's upper arm and yanked her from the stool, pushing her to the back of the cabin and into a crouch. "Stay down."

He shuffled along the wall to peek out the window. "What've you done now, Pedro?" he murmured.

"Take your pick. It's been a busy week." Pedro grabbed his shotgun.

Jake readied his rifle. "It's Winston and Jones. They were last seen with Robert."

"We know you took ore from our claim," one of the men yelled. "Come out here and apologize like a man!"

"You're lying," Pedro hollered, his body taut with anger. "That was my claim and you know it!"

"You need to stay where you belong, you little Mexican degenerate. Don't say we didn't warn you!"

Gunfire erupted.

Pedro and Jake dropped to their knees as shots pelted the cabin and splinters flew. Molly covered her ears and sank lower on the floor, desperate for a way to escape, but the only way in or out was the front door. Jake and Pedro returned fire through the one and only window.

Her derringer was useless, so Molly scanned the piles of ore and mining tools for a weapon.

Nothing.

Lying on her stomach, she attempted to slide to the right, but the rug beneath her caught on something. She rolled to the side and yanked at the ratty woven cloth. It popped free, revealing a metal latch.

*Prospectors and their hidden compartments.*

She flipped the rug back, exposing a trapdoor.

"Where does this go?" she said, keeping her voice low so the men outside didn't overhear.

Pedro glanced back at her. "Oh hell no."

Jake glared at Pedro. "Now I know how you disappeared after you drank all my whiskey last month. Can we get out that way?"

Pedro's lips thinned. *"Sí."*

Molly unlatched the door and pulled it upward. The odor of damp earth engulfed her as she stared down into black nothingness. A new panic began to rise that had nothing to do with the bullets splitting the wood above her head. Slivers sprayed into her face, causing her to duck repeatedly, but she couldn't move.

"Go, Molly," Jake demanded. He turned back and continued to fire.

"I can't," she said in a hoarse whisper.

She attempted to bring moisture to her parched throat, licking her dry lips with a tongue that had turned to cotton. Her heart beat so hard that she thought it would explode at any moment.

"Molly, go!"

The anger in Jake's voice made her jump. Limbs trembling, she swung her legs into the opening and struggled to find the wooden ladder with her feet. Time stretched itself like honey dropping from a spoon as she floundered, and there was no end in sight for her terror. Her boot snagged a cross board. Slowly, she lowered herself one rung at a time, her arms threatening to fail her with each desperate grip.

When she finally hit the bottom, she stepped back and glanced upward.

The door crashed shut and absolute darkness consumed her.

———

JAKE CLOSED the trapdoor above him and descended the ladder. In the pitch black, he felt his way along the wooden slats until his feet hit the dirt. Pedro remained in the cabin—the crazy coot insisted he had important items to gather, and he didn't want Jake present when he did it.

*Where's Molly?*

And where was the light? Pedro had said there were candles and lucifers in the tunnel. Jake hesitated, the air in the tunnel thick.

A whimper came from his right.

"Molly?"

He barely heard her response. In the dark, he held a hand out for the tunnel wall, his fingers meeting moist earth. His feet bumped into something soft. He leaned down and pulled her to stand. Beneath his hands, she shook like a frightened animal.

"What's wrong?"

All he heard was gasping.

Jake had seen this before—an uncontrollable panic in men when faced with life or death situations. There was no reasoning when the brain crumbled from the terror. The shoot-out had knocked the balance out of her.

He tried to calm her, rubbing his hands up and down her arms then cupping the side of her face while he leaned his forehead to hers. "It'll be fine. I won't let anything happen to you."

But his words had little effect on her.

Guided by instinct, he sought to calm her with touch since they could see nothing in the complete darkness of the tunnel.

He leaned forward and kissed her.

She went still. He held his lips to hers, letting the contact slowly ease her fear, but when she stiffened, his misgivings began to rise. He'd been certain she'd felt the same spark between them that he had.

He'd been wrong.

He began to pull away.

She shifted toward him and joined her mouth to his, her lips hungry and searching and desperate. Jake didn't hold back, drinking her in, and the world fell away as he deepened the contact, aware only of the softness of her lips.

Desire flared, fierce and intense, and he held her closer. With the force of a sandstorm, longing swept through him and nearly knocked him to his knees.

*My God.* He'd had no idea that behind his fascination with her lay this.

He had the oddest feeling that it had *always been her.*

Light poured over them and Molly jumped, her eyes wide as she stared at him.

"Run, you *idiotas!*" Pedro yelled.

His mind spinning, Jake released her and scanned the ground for the candles. He knelt and struck a lucifer. Pedro—a knapsack hanging from his shoulder—yanked the rug just as he shut the trap door in an effort to hide it, then scrambled down the ladder. He took the candle from Jake and scurried away.

Jake looked back at Molly, her stunned expression still visible in the waning light of the candle. He sought to ignore the acute need of his body that merely kissing her had ignited.

He clasped her hand. "We need to go."

"Jake," she whispered. "I can't."

"Why? What's wrong?"

"I freeze in confined places."

He brought a hand to her cheek. "I wish we didn't have to do this, but we have no choice. Take a deep breath and keep a hold of me. We'll get through it together."

He dragged her behind him—and it *was* dragging—and caught up to the light Pedro's candle was emitting.

The tunnel narrowed and Jake was forced to his knees. Since he had to release Molly's hand, he pushed her ahead of him. If he didn't, he was afraid she would stop where she was and refuse to move.

He removed his hat, and dirt sifted into his hair. Molly ducked and threw her arm over her head as the tunnel closed in on them. They emerged from the narrow passageway, and sunlight greeted them, blocked only by the dark outline of Pedro's body.

They'd reached the end.

Pedro struggled out of the exit, then pulled Molly free.

As Jake took a welcome inhale of fresh air, he froze.

Winston, Jones, and three other men had them surrounded, guns aimed.

"Your tunnel ain't much of a secret, Pedro," Emmett Jones sneered.

# CHAPTER 6

Molly sat in a chair, her arms bound behind her and her legs tied at the ankles. Winston and his men had brought them to what appeared to be an abandoned homestead on a flat valley floor.

Across from her, Jake and Pedro also sat trussed up in chairs.

Whenever her eyes met Jake's, a warmth greeted her, and she felt he was still trying to calm her down, as he'd attempted in the tunnel.

*He kissed me.*

Her stomach flip-flopped over the memory.

Even more shocking was how she'd kissed him back, like a starved lunatic in the desert. There'd been no time to explain her terror, her panic...and the symbol of safety and distraction he'd represented.

Her heart pounded—as much from the sudden, powerful connection to Jake as the dangerous predicament in which they now found themselves.

"I hope you know what you're doin', Winston," one of the men murmured.

Molly's focus jerked to the fair-skinned, red-haired man who was clearly in charge. Winston shot his colleague a threatening look.

This must be James Winston, the man who'd told Mabel that Robert was dead.

She was shaken over the rough treatment of their capture and the heap of guns the gang of five possessed, but now she was mad. "I understand that you were recently with my brother, Robert Simms."

Winston narrowed his eyes at her. "You're Robert's sister?"

Somehow she suspected he already knew that. "I am, and I find this detainment to be unacceptable."

Mock surprise crossed Winston's face. "Then you shouldn't associate with men like McKenna and Elizondo."

"Let her go," Jake cut in. "She's got nothing to do with whatever has you so cross."

"Tell me what happened to my brother," Molly demanded.

Winston shrugged. "How should I know? Maybe he ran off and joined the circus in Denver."

At that, all Winston's comrades snickered.

Winston turned toward Jake. "I know it was you who broke into the stock office, destroyed legal documents, and stole money."

"And what proof do you have?" Jake's gaze was unflinching.

"You shoulda been arrested, but the Marshal was a coward. And now we find you in the company of this low-life." He nodded toward Pedro. "What do you have to say for yourself, Elizondo? You trespass on claims that aren't yours and steal from good, hard-working prospectors, such as these men here." He swept the room with an outstretched arm. "And you haul sham samples to Charlie."

"Who's Charlie?" Jake asked.

Winston opened his mouth to answer but turned his head toward the sound of an approaching rider. He pulled his gun from the holster and stepped outside, closing the front door behind him. Once the rider arrived, the sound of muffled voices could be heard, escalating quickly into an argument.

Winston entered the house abruptly, followed by a tall older man with a mustache, graying hair visible beneath the brim of his hat, and a slight belly that pressed tightly against his vest. He wore a fine wool jacket, far better dressed than the five ruffians currently holding them hostage. His gaze swept Jake and Pedro but settled on Molly.

"I understand you're Robert's sister. I must apologize for this misunderstanding. I'm Shep Lannigan." He extended a hand to her.

She stared at him, making no effort to hide her disbelief. How could she shake his hand with her wrists bound?

"Untie Miss Simms," Lannigan demanded.

One of the men stepped behind her and sawed through the rope with a knife until her hands were free. He knelt before her and did the same with the binding at her ankles.

Molly rubbed her right wrist, which chafed the most. "Where is my brother?"

"He seems to have lost track of time while in the mountains. I have no doubt he'll turn up soon. I must insist that you be my guest at my ranch. My daughter Bridget will be very happy to have another young woman in residence. You can both await Robert's return. It's only a matter of time before Robert and Bridget announce their engagement."

Winston tensed. Why was he disturbed by that statement?

Jake had told Molly that she'd been followed by a man who worked for Shep Lannigan. If Lannigan suspected she knew where Robert was, then he clearly didn't know himself. Her gaze met Jake's. She had only known him a short time, but already she could read his expression. *Stay quiet.*

Molly raised her chin a notch. "I appreciate your offer, but I'm afraid I won't leave Jake and Pedro."

"I wouldn't concern yourself with those two," Lannigan said, then turned to face Jake. "You're such a thorn in my side, McKenna, always sticking your nose where it doesn't belong."

"I could say the same for you," Jake replied.

"You tried to steal *my* claim, remember?"

"Bullshit. I filed the Shanghai first, then your men re-staked it."

"You can always hire a lawyer to follow up on your fabricated version of events."

A muscle in Jake's cheek flexed. "You push enough men around, and they'll eventually rise up against you."

"Empty threats from a desperate man. And now you're dragging an unmarried woman around the countryside." Shep gestured towards her. "How typical of you to ignore the rules of civilized society."

"Creede is hardly civilized," Jake retorted with a smirk. "Men like you make certain of that."

"Men like me are trying to bring enlightenment and culture. Who builds the schools and the churches?"

"At what cost? You swindle and ruin men, then sweep them aside like nothing more than an ant pile."

"And a man like you is the answer?" Lannigan shook his head. "You believe you can take matters into your own hands, and that makes you the most dangerous kind out there. What is it that you're called? The Jackal? I can well imagine the underhanded deeds that earned you that name."

"You have no idea." The threat in Jake's voice sent a shiver through Molly.

Lannigan stepped back to Molly's side, his lips spreading out beneath his mustache. "I appreciate that women find McKenna quite charming. It's all an act, I can assure you, Miss Simms. You wouldn't be the first female in this town to fall for it. I feel it's my duty to look after you as if you were my own daughter." He reached a hand out to her.

She didn't take it. "I don't know you, sir."

"I understand," Lannigan replied. "You boys can vouch for me, can't you?" He swung his gaze to the five men currently holding them hostage.

"Yes, sir," Winston said, as did the others.

Molly wanted to throw it back in Lannigan's face. She wasn't a ninny. The hypocrisy of the situation all but choked the air in the room, but fear held her in check.

"I can wait for my brother in town." She kept her voice low to hide her nervousness.

"You could," Lannigan agreed, "but Robert's first stop will no doubt be my ranch. He'll want to see Bridget the first chance he gets, and, of course, you. I know he'll be happy if I offer you a place to stay."

While Lannigan attempted to keep this exchange light—giving the impression that Molly had a choice—she sensed the iron command underlying it. Shep Lannigan had no intention of letting her go.

Her stomach clenched, and she hoped she wouldn't lose the last meal she'd eaten.

"What will happen to Mister Elizondo and Mister McKenna?" she asked.

Lannigan adjusted his hat. "Oh, you don't need to worry about them. My men will see that they account for their misdeeds then make sure they get home."

"And what misdeeds are those?" she asked. "I seem to have lost the gist of that during the conversation." She felt Jake's glare upon her. He wanted her to remain quiet. Was it for her own safety, or was he really as unsavory as Lannigan implied?

"These aren't topics for a refined young woman." Lannigan nodded to Winston, who stood behind her.

The man had the gall to slip his hands under her armpits and haul her to stand.

She gasped and yanked free of Winston. "Don't touch me. I demand that you let them go." She nodded toward Jake and Pedro.

"I understand your passionate response," Lannigan said to her as if she were a child, "but you've no idea the trouble these two have caused. You best stay out of it, Miss Simms." His gray eyes held her in a steely vise. "I really must insist."

For the second time, fear snaked down Molly's spine, but she maintained her outward composure, not wanting any of them to know how much all of this spooked her.

"Molly, you should go." Jake's voice cut through the tension holding her legs rooted to the floor.

*No.*

"I'll come visit you in a few days," he added.

Lannigan shook his head but said nothing.

Molly gave a stiff nod. "Fine." She tugged at the hem of the fitted jacket she wore, straightening it. "I'll go on one condition."

"And what might that be?" Lannigan asked, as if he meant to indulge her.

Molly suspected he wouldn't, but she had to try. "Your men won't hurt Jake and Pedro. Because I'll find out. And I'll go to the Marshal about it." She swung around and pinned James Winston with a hard stare. "I know what you look like." She shifted her gaze to Emmett Jones, his long face covered in a sheen of sweat. "And you." She took in the other three men—they didn't need to be aware that she didn't know their identity. "All of you."

Lannigan laughed, a forced response. "My men aren't outlaws, Miss Simms. We don't go around murdering and pillaging. I'm sorry if we gave that impression, but you must understand that we have business with these two. There's no reason you need to be a part of it. My men retrieved your horse. It's time we were on our way."

Molly glanced at Pedro—the Mexican hung his head and muttered obscenities under his breath. Her gaze snagged Jake's. For one wild moment, she wanted to kiss him, hard and long, but it wasn't lost on her that he could be as dangerous as Shep Lannigan.

She'd do well not to trust any of them.

She walked out of the cabin.

# CHAPTER 7

J ake watched Molly leave.

It was for the best.

If there was to be trouble—and there would be—she didn't need to be in the middle of it.

He settled a dispassionate gaze on Lannigan. "If you harm one hair on her head, you'll have me to answer to."

Shep pretended to dust off the sleeves of his jacket. "I have never, nor will I *ever*, answer to you, McKenna." He turned to exit the house, then paused at the threshold. "And just so we're clear, the Bluebird is mine."

So that's what this was about, the elusive Bluebird lode. Steeped in legend and myth, Jake had searched for it along with nearly every other prospector in town, but Lannigan had staked a territory around it—just as mythical, in Jake's opinion—going as far as stealing claims. But Jake had little proof. Someone had doctored the claim he'd filed on the Shanghai two months ago. Taking Lannigan to court over it would prove pointless, and Lannigan knew it.

Yet another divisive point between Jake and Robert.

"No one knows where the Bluebird is, *estúpido*," Pedro cut in.

"I will. And soon." Lannigan departed, a smug look on his face.

No one spoke or moved until the staccato of hoof beats faded into nothingness.

Winston grinned at Jake. "Payback time."

"Is this over the money you lost at the Orleans awhile back?" Jake had managed to strip Winston of a nice chunk of cash at the blackjack table one night.

"Oh, I took care of that," Winston replied, conceit in his tone.

Realization hit Jake. *That's what happened to my money.*

It wasn't Robert who'd stolen it. Winston was the thief.

Jake kept his smug satisfaction to himself when he felt the rope that bound his wrists give way. During his smuggling days in China, he had acquired the habit of keeping a small, serrated blade tucked into a custom-made pocket in his boot. Before Lannigan's men had tied him up, he'd retrieved it and tucked it into his hand. He'd been steadily sawing away at his ropes all afternoon.

As Winston came at him, Jake slid the coils from his wrist and waited until the man was nearly upon him. As he butted him in the face with his right palm, he grabbed one of the man's guns from the hip holster with his left hand, cocked the hammer and swung it in a half-circle. The other men stopped in their tracks.

"You jackass!" Winston lay on his back, holding his nose while blood seeped through his fingers.

"I've been called worse." Jake considered his assailants. His feet were still bound. A moment's distraction to extricate himself, and they'd all be on him. And Pedro was still tied up. He needed to get him free as well. "Drop all your guns, boys," he instructed.

For a moment, none of them did anything.

Jake pointed his weapon at each of them in turn. He probably didn't have enough bullets to finish them all off, and he was reluctant to do that. The end result would only land him in jail. But he also didn't want to end up dead.

He aimed more clearly for Emmett Jones, since he was the next in line of command with Winston down. With a look of disgust,

Jones pulled his gun and set it on the floor. The others slowly followed suit.

"You too, Winston," Jake said.

The man pushed his second gun along the smooth wooden planks toward Jake, a lethal rage flashing in his eyes, the only thing visible on his bloody face.

"Back up now, boys." Jake waved the tip of the gun for emphasis.

They did as they were told, but Jake knew he didn't have long before they contemplated jumping him. He scooted his chair to the side then back, hoping to catch a glimpse of the blade he'd dropped.

Still watching the men, Jake leaned to his right and swept his hand on the floor until it hit the sharp weapon. Grabbing it, he worked it quickly against the ropes around his ankles. Once he was loose, he went to Pedro, freed the man's hands, and handed the blade to him. The Mexican got loose of the last of his bindings and stood. He grabbed two guns while Jake picked up a second one.

Pedro cocked both hammers and pointed the guns at two of the men. "Let me shoot 'em before we go."

"They're not worth it, *amigo*." Jake scowled. "But get more rope. I'm always happy to return a favor."

---

THE RIDE with Shep Lannigan didn't take as long as Molly thought it would. He'd pushed hard, and she'd had to concentrate to keep her horse on target behind him, so there'd been little conversation.

She hoped she was doing the right thing.

She wished fervently that Robert would appear soon, safe and sound.

Robert had left their home in Tucson two years ago, eighteen years old and eager to make his way. Their mama had held her tongue, but Molly knew she hadn't wanted him to go. Her pa had been annoyingly supportive.

Molly had been heartbroken. Robert was her brother, her friend, her nemesis. She'd grown up seeking his approval, while at the same time railing against his sometimes-controlling ways.

When he'd sent word that he'd finally settled in Colorado, she'd hatched a plan to visit him almost immediately. Waiting until she was eighteen herself had been in deference to her folks, and convincing them to let her come alone had been hard-won.

They'd agreed after her stubbornness and relentless begging had worn them down but stipulated that Robert had to look out for her.

And now he was nowhere to be found.

Her body tensed. She would need to write to her mama soon. She couldn't put it off much longer. What would she say?

*Please be all right, Robert.*

It was her chant, repeated over and over.

If Robert truly was sweet on Lannigan's daughter, then Molly had to believe that coming to the Lannigan ranch was the best and most sensible course of action in locating her brother.

*But Jake…*

Worry gnawed at her, adding to her unease.

A large ranch came into view as the sun dipped low on the horizon. South of Creede, the flat, open area was near a part of town she'd heard referred to as Jimtown. Molly shook her head over the unoriginality of the name. Why didn't the townspeople refer to the entire area as Creede? Likely, a collection of men couldn't come to an agreement.

A rider greeted them at a gate, the name SHEPHERD'S PASS spelled out in dark gray metal on an archway above. As soon as they passed through, the man latched the gate and locked it. This didn't bode well.

Her horse trailed Lannigan's as they passed a large corral and various buildings to their right. The main house came into view, and

Molly couldn't help but be impressed. Lannigan's wealth was plain to see in the large two-story structure and wide porch.

A young man exited the front door and came to greet them.

"Hi, Pa."

"Archie, this is Miss Simms. She's Robert's sister, and she'll be staying with us. Please help her with her things, and then get her horse settled in the barn."

Molly dismounted as the youth nodded and approached her. His head continued to bob up and down, and he smiled too much. Her mama's voice rang in her head—*people like that see the world at a different speed than we do.*

She held out her hand. "It's nice to meet you, Archie."

He took it, glancing off to the side before briefly meeting her eyes with a bashful peek. He couldn't be more than fifteen or sixteen and was a bit short for a boy his age. Archie hadn't inherited the height of his father or his dark features; freckles covered his face, and a mop of straw-hued hair went in wild directions atop his head.

"I'll bring your things inside." Archie's gaze remained downward.

Despite her reservations about Shep Lannigan, Molly couldn't help but like his son. "Thank you."

"Is your sister here?" Lannigan asked Archie.

The boy nodded and continued to do so as he departed with the horses.

Molly followed Lannigan up the wide steps to the porch, then entered through an ornately decorated glass door. The entryway was filled with polished dark wood and plush carpeting.

"Bridget?" Lannigan yelled in no particular direction, then removed his hat and hung it on a hook.

"Coming," a distant female voice answered.

A young woman with auburn hair and a slim figure descended the staircase, her ankle-length plaid skirt swaying atop a pile of petticoats. She stopped before them, her blue eyes guarded as she looked at Molly.

"This is Robert's sister, Molly Simms."

Bridget's gaze brightened. "I'm so happy to finally meet you." She pulled Molly into a brief, awkward hug. "Did you come all the way from Arizona?"

"Yes."

"Alone?"

Molly nodded, struck by the comeliness of Bridget Lannigan.

Bridget laughed. "You're so brave. Does Robert know you're here?"

"It would seem he doesn't," Lannigan interrupted. "So please get Miss Simms settled in one of the guest rooms. She'll be staying with us for now."

"Of course," Bridget replied.

Molly accompanied Bridget upstairs, feeling a bit conspicuous in the dark wool skirt, cotton blouse, and dusty fitted jacket she wore, all sorely in need of laundering. "Do you know where Robert is?"

Bridget's cheery countenance softened. "I'm afraid I don't."

They walked down a long hallway, passing several doors, and then Bridget finally led her into a bedroom.

The room wasn't large, but the accommodations were certainly fancy with a large four-poster bed, a tall mahogany wardrobe, and a sofa. Molly stepped inside and sighed audibly. "Your home is beautiful," she said quietly.

She hadn't traveled much—mostly long trips to Texas to visit her Aunt Molly and Uncle Matt, although she sometimes stayed with Aunt Em and Uncle Nathan.

"Thank you," Bridget replied. "You must be tired. Did Papa pick you up at the train station?"

"Something like that." Molly didn't know how much she should say about Shep Lannigan's tactics in front of his daughter. "Was Robert with James Winston?"

Bridget's eyes widened in surprise. "You know James?"

"Only briefly."

"Well, yes, sometimes my pa sends Robert and James out together." Her brow pinched in a crease. "I'm not really sure why Robert's so delayed this time." She wrung her hands and glanced to the side.

Molly was certain she didn't imagine Bridget's discomfort. She waited for the woman purported to be Robert's sweetheart to say something more.

"I'm sure he just forgot that you were coming," Bridget said, but her tone was half-hearted. "I'm confident he'll be along any day now."

"How long have you and he..."

Bridget fidgeted, and for some reason, that was reassuring. It made the woman seem more real. She hated to think that Robert had fallen for someone who lacked heart.

"Not long. A few months now."

"I'm afraid he never mentioned you in letters home, or else I would've tried to contact you sooner." A little white lie, but had Jake McKenna not intervened—and had Molly not been followed, probably by a Lannigan man—she liked to think she would have.

"How did you hear about us?"

"Jake McKenna."

Bridget made a guarded sound. "Just a word of caution. I wouldn't necessarily believe everything Jake says."

*Jake?* The sound of his given name on Bridget's lips annoyed Molly. "So you're telling me he lied about you and Robert?"

"No, no." Her voice sounded strained. "Look, I'm the first to admit that Jake is very fascinating, but he uses that to take advantage."

Molly's irritation kicked up a full notch, her heart pounding in her chest. She was beginning to think that Jake and Bridget had an amorous history, and the very notion set her nerves on edge. Was Bridget not only a rival for her brother's affections but Jake's as well?

"Mister McKenna didn't take advantage of me," Molly replied. But hadn't he? He'd kissed her in Pedro's tunnel, when she'd been in no shape to fend him off. But safeguarding herself from him had been the furthest thing from her mind. She'd kissed him back. A wave of shame washed over her as she viewed the indiscretion through the lens of Bridget's assessment of Jake's character, but she would never admit the incident to the other woman.

Feeling deflated, Molly wished to be alone. "I'm very tired. It's been a long day."

"Of course. I'm sure your things will be brought up shortly. Is there anything I can get you?"

"Some water?"

"I'll have Stella bring a pitcher up for you. She's our housekeeper." Bridget moved to each window and pushed the curtains aside to let in the last remnants of the setting sun. "Supper is at seven. I'll come for you a few minutes before so I can show you where the dining room is located."

Molly nodded her thanks.

Bridget left, closing the door behind her.

Alone at last, Molly breathed a sigh of relief. She unbuttoned her jacket and removed it, setting it on a chair, then moved to the window.

She looked out over the empty holding pens and corrals behind the house. Several men milled about. Lannigan's men. If Jake was right, none of them could be trusted.

Had she done the right thing in coming here?

A knock at the door made her jump. When she opened it, Archie greeted her with his head bobbing in a steady rhythm.

"I have your bag, Miss Simms."

"You mean the veins dried up?"

"No. I filed them, but the recording office no longer has them, and when I go to the claims, the stakes have been pulled. In some instances, a new boundary has been erected, similar to your Shanghai." Pedro's gaze was lethal. "Those bastards won't drive me away. I'll blow their cocks off."

Jake had no love of Pedro—the Mexican was volatile and paranoid. It was a combination best left alone, but Jake sensed the man might be in over his head. Hell, maybe he was too. He'd thought of leaving when his partnership with Robert had broken down, but something had kept him in town.

Payback for losing the Shanghai.

His missing money.

The mountains themselves, perhaps.

No, it was the elusive Bluebird vein that tugged at him, stoking his determination and wanderlust. He would take great satisfaction in yanking it from Lannigan's arrogant grasp.

And then there was Molly Rose Simms.

*When had she entered the equation?*

The moment he'd laid eyes on her.

"Be careful, Pedro." Jake meant it, surprising himself.

The Mexican guided his stolen mount away and shook his head in disgust. "*Adios,* you louse-ridden polecat."

So much for a moment of sentiment.

Jake dropped his horse at the livery, then he walked to his tiny house that sat on a narrow plat of land up against Willow Creek. A small kitchen and sitting area were divided by a single bed with a curtain. Nothing fancy, but it was home. A shared outhouse was located across the street.

He shucked his jacket and sat on a chair to remove his boots.

A slight creak alerted him.

In an instant his gun was in his hand, pointed at the curtain. As the fabric was brushed aside, Jake swore and quickly released the hammer, lowering the weapon.

"Sonofabitch, Robert! I could've shot you!"

Robert swung his feet to the floor. "Sorry. I didn't mean to startle you. Where've you been?"

"Where the hell have *you* been?"

"It's a long story," he replied wearily, shaking his head. Dark circles shadowed his eyes, and he scratched at the stubble on his cheeks. As he moved, his ripe odor wafted toward Jake.

"Molly's here."

Robert's gaze jerked up. "She is? I thought she wasn't supposed to visit until next month."

"Well, whatever the case, she arrived earlier this week, and she's been looking for you ever since."

"You've seen her?"

"Yep."

"Where is she?"

"Lannigan took her to his ranch today."

Robert balked. "Why?"

"Well, you are Lannigan's newest lapdog. Guess he thought he'd tighten your leash with her under his roof."

Robert shot him an icy stare and swore under his breath. "You were right, you know."

"About what?"

"About Lannigan, about Bridget. I was a fool, and I almost died because of it."

"What happened?"

"I overheard Shep and Bridget talking, about how she was supposed to romance me to bring me into the fold. But I guess that's what you were trying to tell me back then. I was just too bull-headed to listen." Robert glanced at him. "She tried it on you first, didn't she?"

Jake didn't answer.

Robert laughed but it was laced with disgust, maybe even a hint of despair.

"I never touched her," Jake said. "She doesn't suit me."

*But your sister does.* He doubted Robert was ready to hear that.

Robert accepted Jake's explanation with a flagging resignation, running a hand through his brown hair.

Jake took little joy in Robert's enlightenment. The look in the man's eyes told him how deep the disappointment lay. Women certainly had a way of muddying the waters and messing with the very sanity of a man. "Where have you been?" he asked.

"Well, despite knowing that Bridget was just stringing me along, I couldn't simply walk away from Lannigan without a reason why. I was scheduled to go into the hills with Winston and Jones, so I went. I needed time to think, anyway. I was trailing them along a precarious ridgeline when the pathway gave out. I landed in a steep ravine. My horse was killed. And those two bastards left me."

"Are you injured?"

"No, nothing that won't heal on its own."

"How'd you get out?"

"Sheer desperation. You'd be surprised how that can motivate you up a slick granite wall." He laughed. "And luck. I fear mine will run out eventually. I've used up too much."

Jake hesitated but went forward anyway. "Your sister found the claim in your room for the Chigger. What the hell is that?"

Robert let out a good-natured huff, and then became serious. "Molly. Shit. She's so damn nosy. So here's the thing. Lannigan has been using me to find claims for him."

That was hardly a surprise. Jake and Robert had been pretty successful in their own scouting ventures. Lannigan using his daughter to lure men in was underhanded, but Jake supposed the blowhard saved it for the ones who simply wouldn't budge. He and Robert had been in that group until Robert fell utterly to the charm of Bridget's womanly bait.

Jake really couldn't blame him. If it had been Molly Rose throwing succulent crumbs his way, how long would *he* have held out?

Why couldn't he stop thinking about her and that hungry kiss in the tunnel?

"I wanted to hide that one from Lannigan," Robert said.

"Then why not just put it in my name."

Robert leveled his gaze at Jake. "I know you. Molly evens the odds."

"You *are* a sonofabitch. You should know that when Molly arrived into town, I caught Chip Westfield following her."

Robert quietly considered that news. "Then I can't leave Lannigan's compound just yet. I won't put Molly in danger."

"I think you may have already done that when you put her name on the Chigger. What's the lode look like?"

"High-grade silver exposed."

The tinge of excitement in Robert's voice set off alarm bells in Jake's head.

"Holy hell," Jake murmured. "You think it's the Bluebird."

Robert watched him, his gaze dark.

"Is there any gold?" The lore of the Bluebird included nuggets of gold, scattered on the ground like a field of California poppies.

"Not that I saw, but I didn't have a lot of time to explore."

Excitement thrummed in Jake. He leaned forward, grinning like a schoolboy. "Where is it exactly?"

"To the east of Mammoth mountain, near Ivan's place."

"No shit? Well that explains it. We never looked there."

"No one does. The only way in is through a narrow, steep rocky pass. I didn't have much time. I didn't want Winston to find me. I quickly staked out a claim and grabbed a few samples, but the yield was low. I need to return."

Jake stood and began to pace. "I'll go. You shouldn't be anywhere near it. Are there any other claims in the area?"

"No."

Jake stopped and stared at him. The gravity of it didn't escape him. "We need to find the apex."

"Exactly. I have one condition though. If you switch the claim, Molly's name stays on it."

"Why don't you just add your own."

Robert shook his head.

"Did you sign something with Lannigan?" Jake asked.

"I get forty dollars a month and a one-eighth share." Robert's tone dripped with sarcasm.

"It's not a bad deal." Except if the Bluebird was anything like the Amethyst—currently the biggest vein in Creede—then Lannigan would become very rich at the expense of everyone else involved. "But you know there's a problem in the claims office, right? I didn't lie about the Shanghai. Winston filed the Mystery Box claim on Lannigan's behalf *after* I filed. They overlapped *me*, not the other way around."

Robert sighed. "I'm sorry I didn't believe you before. Where's the Chigger claim now?"

"Your sister has it," Jake said.

"Then I'll head to Lannigan's."

"You really ought to clean up first. You look like hell."

Robert nodded. "Let's keep what happened with Winston and Jones between us for now."

Jake released an uneasy chuckle. "Pedro and I had an incident with them recently, so they'll be detained for a bit, but I doubt it will last for long. I imagine I'll be higher on their hit list than you...for the time being."

"Do I wanna know?"

"Probably not." Jake sat in the chair again. "Molly was with us."

Robert's back straightened, eyes wide with alarm. "What?"

"That's how Lannigan got his hands on her."

"She wasn't hurt, was she?" Robert demanded, scowling.

"No, she's fine. In some ways, she's probably better off under his roof, but you'll need to determine that for yourself."

"How is she?"

"A lot like you."

Robert narrowed his gaze. "How's that?"

"She's got stars in her eyes and the stubbornness of a mule."

Robert let out a belly laugh, the first spark of life Jake had seen in him in a good long while. "I can't wait to see her," he said.

*Neither can I.*

---

MOLLY ATE THE HAM, potatoes, and creamed corn with a gusto that surprised her. The day's events had left her ravenous. Shep Lannigan sat like a king at the head of the table to Molly's right, while Bridget and Archie faced her across the dining room table.

Molly had changed into a green cotton dress, even though she had little clothing with her in her satchel, having left the remainder of her belongings stored at Zang's Hotel when she'd fled in the night with Jake. She would need to retrieve them. Better yet, she hoped to return to her rented room as soon as she could.

Lannigan leaned back to let Stella—an older woman with a stern countenance—remove his plate. "We've had the pleasure of getting to know Robert these past few months. I'm sure he'll be very happy to see you."

Molly nodded and took a sip of water from a glass goblet.

"How long do you plan to stay?" Bridget asked.

"A few weeks." It was the truth, but what if Robert never appeared? What if something truly awful had happened? She resolved to remain as long as it took to find him. "And you're certain that none of you know where Robert is?"

"We're just as in the dark as you are," Lannigan said.

"Has Mister Winston returned?" Molly asked.

"No," Archie cut in. "I haven't seen him."

"Well, there you have it." Lannigan watched her as if she were a deer he was about to slaughter. "He's probably still with Robert." The lie slid easily from his lips.

Stunned, Molly sat motionless until rage began to burn away the chill in her bones.

She sought to hide her reaction, knowing that she hardly had the upper hand while in the man's house. Concern for McKenna coiled tightly in her belly.

A knock at the front door drew Stella from the room. Molly halted the path of the goblet to her lips, listening to the rumble of voices beyond.

Robert!

Without waiting for permission from Lannigan, she stood and ran to the parlor then flung herself into her brother's arms. "I've been so worried." Holding tight to him, she squeezed her eyes shut to staunch the flow of tears.

"I'm sorry I didn't meet you," he said into her hair. "I had my days mixed up."

"Robert," Bridget said, entering the room. "Thank goodness."

Molly stepped back so that the two sweethearts might have a heartfelt reunion, but when Bridget leaned close, Robert pecked her cheek with little warmth.

He appeared freshly bathed and shaved, but his eyes were dull with fatigue. Molly wanted to ask more but not with a Lannigan audience.

"You look very tired," Molly said.

"A little." He smiled at her. "How's Ma and Pa, and Evie?"

She couldn't hide how very happy she was to see him. "They're fine."

Lannigan strode over to them, his face pleasant, but his eyes as hard and cold as diamonds. "Robert, it's about time you showed up. I expect a full report."

Robert nodded.

"But first, come inside and get something to eat," Lannigan added.

Archie followed them back to the dining room, bounding after Robert like a puppy. "Did you find the Bluebird?"

"No."

Robert sat beside Molly as the others resumed their seats.

"What's the Bluebird?" she asked.

"It's a famous and mysterious mineral vein," Archie answered enthusiastically, his eyes wide and his head back to bobbing. "Everyone is looking for it. They say it will be worth millions."

"That's a lot of money," Molly remarked.

"My pa will find it." Archie speared his fork into a potato and deposited it into his mouth. "He has lots of men looking."

"Perhaps I should search myself," Lannigan said. "It would seem all those men are finding nothing." His eyes landed on Robert.

"The origins of that lode are murky, Shep," Robert said. "You know that. It takes a lot of time and patience. Where's Winston?"

"He's not here," Bridget replied.

"Taking care of other business," Lannigan said over Bridget's words, shooting her an irritated frown.

Molly tensed, as much from Lannigan's chastisement of his daughter as to knowing the *business* of which Lannigan spoke involved Jake.

"Such as?" Robert asked, his jaw set in a hard line.

"Thieves who won't keep to their own claims." Lannigan shifted so that Stella could place a plate filled with apple pie before him. "I'm certainly glad I don't have to include you in that group."

Robert chuckled. "If you're talking about McKenna, he's not in the hills. I just saw him in town."

"You saw Jake?" Molly asked before she could stop herself.

Robert pinned her with a curious look and nodded.

At Lannigan's grunt of contempt, Molly tore her gaze from

Robert and her desperate need to interrogate him, and stared at Lannigan's scowl of disgust.

Robert leaned back in his chair. "Why am I getting the feeling that Winston was with McKenna earlier today?"

"You did the right thing, breaking ties with that no-good upstart," Lannigan said. "Our partnership will be far more profitable for you in the end." He shifted his attention to Molly. "It's best to avoid the likes of McKenna from now on."

"I tried to tell you that," Bridget added quietly.

Molly wanted to spit nails. She was getting damn tired of everyone telling her how awful Jake McKenna was.

Lannigan turned back to Robert. "After supper, meet me in my study."

Robert nodded and dug into the plate of food Stella set before him.

The talk turned to other matters—the train depot Lannigan was lobbying to have built on his property, a women's town meeting, and the struggle between three counties to claim Creede as its own.

Despite the less-than-ideal circumstances surrounding her reunion with Robert—and her worry over Jake—Molly closed her eyes and sighed with blessed relief. Robert was alive and well. Thank the Lord for that.

# CHAPTER 9

Molly tossed aside the copy of *Frankenstein* that she'd been half-heartedly reading and leapt from the bed at the sound of a soft tap on the door. It was Robert.

She beamed and let him inside, squeezing his hand. She released him and shut the door, and then sat upon the sofa at the foot of the bed. He settled beside her.

"I'm sorry about the mix-up and not being here when you arrived," Robert said.

"I've been a bit terrified for you." She kept her voice low. "What's going on?"

Robert rested against the sofa, his body sagging with a sudden release of tension. He still wore the crisp, white shirt from earlier although the vest hung open and the collar was unbuttoned. "It's nothing."

"Why do I now own a mining claim with Jake McKenna?"

Robert sobered. "Sorry about that. I'm just trying to keep everyone in check."

"Don't you trust him anymore? I thought he was your friend."

"He is." Robert exhaled heavily. "I guess being with Lannigan has made me paranoid."

"You do know that I was with Jake earlier today, when Winston took us hostage?"

Robert's face hardened. "Hostage? Jake neglected to mention that." He muttered an obscenity.

"I'm fine, but I was forced to leave Jake and a man named Pedro Elizondo with him. You said you saw Jake? He's well?"

"Yeah. You don't have to worry about McKenna. He can take care of himself."

Molly quieted, clamping down on her desire to know more about the man. She changed the subject. "Are you in love with Bridget Lannigan? Her father has you all but engaged."

Robert looked away. "I thought I was. I'm beginning to think it was all just a silly game."

Molly reached out to touch his shoulder. "I'm sorry." She cleared her throat and removed her hand. "So now what? I'm scheduled to return home in a fortnight. Do you want me to transfer the Chigger back to you? I should mention that the claim document I took from you is no longer in my possession. My guess is that Winston searched my bag and took it. He probably gave it to Lannigan."

Robert went silent, then finally said, "Jake thinks someone in the claims office is helping Lannigan jump them. It may not matter that your name was on it, if he steals it." Robert shook his head in frustration. "Jake plans to go back to the claim and get a better handle on it. You don't need to worry anymore. We'll take care of it."

"I should go with him."

Robert raised an eyebrow and looked at her as if she were a two-headed rooster.

"I'm half-owner," she said, defending herself.

"You don't know anything about prospecting."

"How hard can it be? You climb around in the hills and search for gold, right? Or do you pan in the streams?"

Robert ran a hand across his face, clearly exasperated.

"Something like that. But we rarely find gold. It's silver everyone's after."

She nodded. "Got it. We're searching for the shiny gray stuff."

"You need samples to bring back to the assayer's office. They melt the ore down and extract the metals. A good sample will give you an idea of what the vein might hold."

"Bring back rocks. I can handle that."

Robert sighed. "Molly, you're not going anywhere."

"Well, I sure as hell don't want to stay here."

"Quit cussing."

"Then can you at least help me move back to Zang's?"

Robert leaned forward. "I know you don't want to remain here, but I think you should for now. I plan to break from Lannigan, but not yet, and I won't while you're here."

"Then let me go back to the hotel."

"I'll do it when you leave town. Maybe you should go back to Tucson tomorrow."

"No!" The heated rebuttal hung in the air. She took a calming breath, brought her knees up, and hugged them. "I've come all this way to see you. I'm staying. Figure out what you need to do, and then we'll both go. I came here to ask you to travel with me, Robbie. We could go to New York City. You know Mama and Papa would never let me venture there alone, but if you were with me, they'd probably say yes."

Robert smiled. "You still have dreams of wanting to see the world? I really thought you'd outgrow that. You ought to think about getting married."

Molly grimaced and shrugged. "There's time enough for that." She glanced at him. He was different now, certainly older, but the carefree sparkle in his eyes was gone. "I love you, Robert."

He grinned and flicked a finger against her knee. "I love you too, Chigger."

THE NEXT MORNING Bridget appeared at Molly's door with a gift. She entered and laid a deep blue gown upon the bed.

"What's this?" Molly asked.

"It's for you. My pa is having a dinner party this evening, and I thought you'd look very lovely in this color."

Molly's heart sank. The gown was, by far, the fanciest she would ever have the opportunity to wear, but she didn't want to spend the evening at a party. However, she plastered a grateful smile on her lips. She'd be the dutiful sister and play nice with her brother's sweetheart and her family although from her conversation with Robert the previous night, it would seem that the courtship between he and Bridget might be coming to an end.

"It's beautiful. Thank you."

Bridget handed her a matching pair of velvet shoes. "Hopefully these will fit you. Stella can help you dress later."

Molly nodded. "Can I ask you something?"

"Of course."

"Why does your father have armed men guarding the ranch?"

"It's just for protection. Doesn't it make you feel safer?"

"I suppose. What if I want to go into town? Am I a prisoner here?"

Bridget appeared affronted. "No. Would you like me to go with you?"

*Not particularly.* But that was rude, so Molly silently agreed.

Later that day, Molly and Bridget rode into Creede, accompanied by two of Lannigan's men. Since Molly could hardly act on the real reason she had wanted to take the excursion—to see Jake McKenna and determine for herself that he was well—she had to settle on retrieving her remaining belongings from the hotel, followed by an amiable lunch with Bridget at a restaurant in Jimtown.

One thing did surprise her—it wasn't an altogether unpleasant afternoon. Bridget Lannigan might not be the girl for her brother, but, against Molly's better judgment, she was beginning to like the woman.

---

JAKE ENTERED the hotel and approached the clerk behind the counter, a young man with bright eyes and an efficient demeanor.

"I'm looking for one of your guests and was hoping she might be here," Jake said.

The clerk watched him expectantly.

"Molly Rose Simms." Jake rested a hand on the counter and glanced around the sparse lobby.

"Oh, you've just missed her. She was here with Miss Lannigan to retrieve her belongings. I would imagine she's staying at Shepherd's Pass. Perhaps you should look there."

Jake's gaze settled back on the boy. "I'm afraid you're not much help." He held little hope of Lannigan ever letting him on his property.

"I heard them speak of a party," the clerk added.

Jake considered the information. "At Lannigan's?"

"Yes. This evening. Perhaps you can catch up with her there."

Jake nodded at the boy then stepped out of the hotel onto the bustling street. He'd held back from checking out the Chigger for only one reason—he wanted to see Molly Rose Simms again, and it bothered him that she might depart for home before he had a chance to return to town.

A social gathering at Lannigan's ranch opened up possibilities. He needed to pay a visit to Henry and Esme Patterson.

---

Molly returned with Bridget to Shepherd's Pass in the afternoon. As they handed off their mounts to the stable hand, Molly spied Archie. "Would it be alright if I had a look around?"

"I really need to have Stella work on my hair for the party," Bridget replied.

"Maybe Archie can give me a tour."

Bridget looked over her shoulder as her brother hauled water into a stall. "I suppose that would work," she murmured under her breath then called her brother over. He appeared once his chore was complete. "Archie, can you show Miss Simms around the ranch?"

He hooked his thumbs into his suspenders and stared at his boots. "Yes, I certainly can," he said, his voice quiet, almost bashful.

Bridget's eyes caught Molly's, and the entreaty was clear. *Take care with my brother.*

Molly gave a reassuring smile. "I won't keep him long."

Bridget left them. Molly untied the straw bonnet on her head and carried it in her hand as Archie showed her each and every stall in the massive barn.

"My pa likes to breed horses."

"The animals seem strong and in fine form."

Archie's gaze swiveled toward her then slid back to his boots. "Do you know about horses?"

"A little. But I grew up in town. My pa ran a flour mill. You're very lucky to live out here."

"I am. I am lucky." His head bobbed up and down.

Molly couldn't help but smile. There was something sweet and innocent about Archie Lannigan. She hoped that his pa treated him well. She had sensed Bridget's protectiveness, and it further warmed her heart in regard to the woman.

"You're fortunate to have Bridget," Molly said. "I can tell she loves you very much."

Archie stopped outside a stall and gripped the railing of the gate. Beyond was a magnificent jet-black steed munching on hay, his tail flicking in a steady repetition, back and forth. "Do you have a sister?"

"I do. She's about the same age as you. Her name is Evie."

"Do you love her?"

Molly laughed. "Yes, of course, but she borrows my dresses and hair ties without asking, so we fight sometimes."

A grin tugged at Archie's mouth. "Bridget and I don't share dresses."

"That's good."

He laughed, a bit too loud, but his enjoyment was infectious.

"My sister is very smart," Molly continued, "especially at arithmetic. She wants to study astronomy."

"What's that?"

"It's the investigation of the stars in the sky."

"That seems a strange thing to learn about."

Molly rested against the stall gate. "It is, I suppose, but there is so much beauty in the world. It's up to people to see it and share it with others."

"I like animals," Archie said, watching the horse.

"I bet you're very good with them."

"They make me happy." Archie leaned forward, grasping the gate with both hands. "Don't tell my pa, but sometimes I sneak out. I want to see the animals. Sometimes they're hurt, and I help them."

Concern swelled in Molly's chest. "You should be careful, Archie. Wild animals can lash out sometimes. You could get injured."

He shook his head, his attention on the stallion enjoying a respite. "I know how to do it."

"How to do what?"

"How to approach animals. I can hear them."

"So you climb over the ranch's fencing in the middle of the night?"

He peeked up at her. "No. I have a key to the padlock."

JAKE KNOTTED the dark tie at his neck and put on the black jacket. He didn't usually dress this fancy in Creede, but a party at Lannigan's merited it. He'd bathed and shaved and combed his hair. He had a strong need to look presentable, and it had nothing to do with Lannigan or any of the other men who would be in attendance.

*Molly Rose will be there.*

He exited his cabin and walked to Fernando. The horse waited at the hitching post, the livery boy having delivered the animal, saddled and ready. Jake mounted and headed south toward Jimtown.

He passed through downtown—Kinneavy's Saloon already bustling with customers—then navigated the business district. He finally approached a two-story home as a couple emerged, headed to a carriage hitched to a single horse.

Henry Patterson waved. "You want to ride with us, Jake?"

"No thanks. I'll be fine." He tipped his hat at Henry's wife. "Esme, you look lovely as ever this evening."

She laughed, the lines on her face deepening. "You're such a charmer, Jake."

The Patterson's were his way onto Lannigan's property, and it was one more debt he owed Henry. The elderly man had befriended him just after Jake had come to town, and it was Henry who'd grubstaked Jake's first foray into the mountains. Henry and Esme had become like family, even going as far as trying to find a suitable wife for him, which he had successfully evaded at every turn. Until now.

Esme had watched him with a shrewd gaze when he'd described Miss Simms and her arrival into town to visit Robert. With a gleam in her eye, she'd prodded Henry until her husband had insisted Jake accompany them to Lannigan's ranch that evening. She wanted to meet the girl herself. Jake knew matrimony was on her mind, but subjecting himself to some matchmaking was a small concession if it got him near Molly.

Henry helped his wife into the carriage then looked at Jake. "I sure hope Lannigan doesn't throw you out on your very charming backside."

"I plan to stick close to Esme. She's my insurance plan." Jake turned serious. "I appreciate you letting me tag along, Henry."

The stout old man grunted. "A lot of us tolerate Lannigan because we don't have a choice, but I'm also of the mind that you don't poke the bear, and you've done more than your share of that." Henry shook his head. "You're here because of Esme. She's determined to see you enjoying wedded bliss. Don't say I didn't warn you."

Esme leaned out the carriage window. "I've never kept my matchmaking intentions a secret."

"I wouldn't have it any other way," Jake said.

Henry watched Jake as if he'd lost his mind then shook his head in resignation.

Jake moved his horse closer to the carriage window. "I owe you a kiss, Esme, for letting me accompany you both this evening."

Esme tittered and waved the lace kerchief in her hand. "I'll collect."

"Like hell," Henry grumbled, seating himself on the bench beside her. "How old are you, Esme? A hundred now?"

"I'm too old to still be married to you."

Jake suppressed a grin.

"She was always a tart," Henry added, donning a hat over the shock of gray hair that covered his head. "That's why I married her."

Jake smiled in acknowledgment, but the gesture went flat as thoughts of Henry's health crept in.

Henry was well over seventy years old, and even though he still went into the mountains with the surveyor to assess claims, Jake worried that he didn't have the stamina to keep up the pace of his life. What if he fell ill from overexerting himself?

Henry represented investors from as far away as New York City while also bankrolling from his own funds. He'd arranged the sale of three of Robert and Jake's most promising claims—the Lucky Dog, the Arabian, and the Sit Down. He would likely have been involved with the Shanghai if Jake hadn't lost it.

If the Chigger panned out...damn, it could possibly be the find of a century. He and Robert would need Henry's help if they did indeed come to own the Bluebird.

Correction, he and *Molly* would need assistance. The legalities of the situation could be simple or complicated, depending on how it all played out.

Jake guided his horse beside the Patterson's carriage as the road wound out of town. At the base of the mountains sat Lannigan's Ranch, Shepherd's Pass.

As blue sky melted into gray, Jake tugged his jacket tight to ward off the chill. A line of guests amassed along the road to the main house, a collection of carriages, buckboards, and riders atop horses, everyone dressed in their finest attire. Lannigan was known to throw extravagant and well-attended parties.

Jake had only ever been to one gathering, near the end of last year following the sale of the Lucky Dog. That had put him and Robert on the map as players in Creede's prospecting game. Back then, Bridget Lannigan had been a big flirt, and for one brief, crazed evening, Jake had found himself the object of her attention. She was certainly pretty, and nicely rounded in all the right places, but he still praised whatever god took residence up high that he hadn't done something stupid. She was cut from the same cloth as her father, and a man needed to stay a mile away from it.

He'd tried to tell Robert.

It hadn't worked.

Jake brought Fernando near the house entrance and

dismounted. A young man took the horse, along with another mount, and led the animals toward the stables. Jake recognized several gentleman and nodded while he made his way to the Patterson's carriage. He hadn't been joking when he'd said he planned to stick close to Esme.

Lannigan would throw him out if given the chance, but Jake was counting on the fact that the man wouldn't dare upset the party or any of the female guests.

Jake gently grasped Henry's elbow as the elderly man stepped down the carriage steps.

Henry shook his head and pushed Jake's hand away. "I'm not an invalid."

"I just want to make sure you're out of Esme's way." Jake held a hand out to Esmeralda Patterson.

"My knight in shining armor." She let him help her to the ground.

"Always, Esme," Jake replied and tucked her hand into the crook of his elbow.

Henry moved away from them and shook another man's hand. "John, it's good to see you." He was soon lost in discussion with several gentlemen.

Jake guided Esme to the steps leading to the porch, slowing his steps to keep pace with Esme's much shorter stride.

"We've only just arrived, and he's already doing business," Esme lamented.

"It's all for you, Esme."

"I know. I'm a mighty lucky lady. You don't have to tell me."

"He's mighty lucky to have you, as well."

Esme smirked. "I do tell him so every day."

"I'm sure he appreciates that."

Jake removed his hat as he and Esme entered the crowded parlor. Shep Lannigan immediately honed in on him. Jake held the man's gaze, challenging him. Shep finally turned away.

Several people greeted Esme. While her attention was diverted, Jake scanned for any sign of Molly or Robert or even Bridget, but didn't see them.

He received several curt nods from guests milling past him, who were no doubt surprised to see him in attendance. The issue with the Shanghai and Mystery Box claims was no secret.

Esme's popularity soon had several ladies guiding her away from Jake, freeing him to roam. He deposited his hat on a side table then slipped from the parlor and headed to the dining room, where an array of food was laid out for the guests to help themselves.

A mouthwatering feast of glazed ham, veal cutlets, steak, and pork tenderloins occupied one half of the table, while corned beef hash, boiled potatoes, and various other vegetables presented a colorful counterpoint on the opposite side. Jake grabbed a fish cake and popped it into his mouth.

He savored the flavor, silently acknowledging that Lannigan had one hell of a cook, and turned to explore a crowd of people in another room.

Shep stepped in front of him "What the hell are you doing here?" He leveled a lethal gaze at Jake, his voice low.

"I'm with the Pattersons. They were gracious enough to let me tag along. I'm guessing my invitation was lost in the mail."

"I'll tell Stella to lock up the valuables."

Jake smiled, a mocking action meant to goad Lannigan, then he dropped the façade and pinned Shep with a cold stare. "Don't ever send Winston after me again."

Lannigan's dark eyes never flinched. "Someday your luck will run out, McKenna, and there won't be anyone to help you. I won't throw you out because Esme Patterson is a nice old lady, and for some reason she likes you, but I've never made that mistake."

"I'm crushed. I always thought we were friends."

A rotund man Jake didn't recognize clapped Lannigan on the shoulder. "Where the hell is all the bourbon, Shep?"

As Lannigan became engulfed once again by his guests, Jake came face to face with James Winston.

"That's quite a bruise on your nose." Jake didn't bother to hide the sarcasm in his voice.

"Go to hell." Winston's red hair was combed back, and he was dressed as fine as any of the men present, but Jake knew full well he carried an iron somewhere on him.

Jake had his trusty knife tucked away, just in case.

Robert appeared from the throng of guests.

"There seems to be a lot of riffraff at this party," Winston said. "I could smell it a mile away."

"You know, James," Robert remarked, looking a sight better than when Jake had seen him yesterday, "I think you owe me a horse."

"It's not my fault you can't stay upright when you're in the hills."

Robert settled an icy gaze on the man. "Yeah, thanks for your assistance."

"I just assumed you sneaked off to prospect on your own. I'm not your keeper."

"You're not Bridget's, either."

A cocky smile appeared on Winston's face. "I think that's up to her."

Winston wanted Bridget? Damn, that girl was popular. Jake hoped Robert didn't do something stupid for her sake.

Robert uttered a colorful phrase under his breath, nodded at Jake, then moved across the room to Bridget's side. Her ivory dress stood out like a beacon. Jake suspected she intended it to.

"I think you owe me five thousand dollars, James," Jake said.

"Is that so?" Winston watched him with a cocky gleam in his eyes. "I'll tell you what, I'll write you an IOU."

"And I'll take it straight to the bank," Jake mocked.

Winston pushed aside his jacket just enough so that Jake caught sight of the gun tucked in a side holster, then he walked away and grabbed a snifter from a side table, downing it in one swallow.

Jake grimaced. He should've let Pedro shoot the asshole when they'd had the chance.

As Jake contemplated getting a good stiff drink himself, he glanced to the staircase and froze.

Molly descended slowly, her eyes cast downward as she lifted the front of the ornate gown she wore. The dark blue material showcased a figure her clothes had only hinted at before, and her hair swept away from her face into an array of curls that made Jake itch to bury his fingers into the tresses. Her bosom peeked enticingly from the ruffled edge of the gown, the creamy hue of her skin reminding him of a full moon in the warm embrace of a starless night.

His legs carried him closer to the bottom step as his eyes remained fixed on her, his heart racing. He hadn't been this nervous around a woman since...well, ever.

He'd lost his virginity at age sixteen with an experienced madam in Casablanca, and from that moment on, women had been a pleasant diversion, nothing more.

Molly glanced up, startled by his presence, then an elated smile spread across her face. She hurried toward him but tripped on the gown and flew into his arms.

Jake caught her just in time before she hit the floor. "Too much sherry?" He gently eased her to her feet, holding her a tad longer than appropriate.

With a flushed face, she stepped back from his support and laughed, smoothing her hands down the gown. Her gaze swept around them and she cleared her throat, then she looked at him. "This dress is too long," she whispered. Then she gushed, "I'm very happy to see you."

Her enthusiasm jolted right through him, and his mind went blank as he basked under her attention. It was far more potent than he'd recalled, and he'd been doing nothing but *recalling* everything about her since they'd parted ways...her eyes that shifted from sea-green to the deepest azure depending on the light, her heart-shaped face, her stubborn tenacity in standing up to Lannigan, and her obvious deep love for Robert. He'd even missed her sarcastic wit. She'd been on his mind almost nonstop.

"I'm glad you didn't forget me," he murmured.

"I've been worried ever since I left you and Pedro...I didn't think I'd see you tonight. Does Lannigan know you're here?"

Jake recovered himself. "He does. It'll be fine. I doubt he'll make a scene—there are too many witnesses."

Molly tugged at the bodice of the gown, then at the tiny sleeves.

"Stop fidgeting," he said. "You look beautiful."

"I do?"

Bridget strode up to them. "Mister McKenna, Papa didn't tell me you were here. Have you been introduced to Robert's sister?"

"Yes, we're acquainted."

Bridget snagged Molly's gaze and raised an eyebrow. Subtlety wasn't Bridget's strong suit.

"Splendid," Bridget said. "Molly is visiting from Arizona."

"I know."

Bridget's nose crinkled in frustration. "Then you won't mind if I borrow her so that she has the opportunity to meet some of our other guests."

Bridget hooked an arm into Molly's and dragged her away but not before Molly cast a glance over her shoulder. Jake wanted to think it was filled with longing from having to leave his company, but he suspected she just wanted to escape Bridget.

He exhaled his disappointment over the brevity of the encounter and tried not to gawk at her retreating backside.

He needed a whiskey.

It was going to be a long night.

# CHAPTER 10

"You live in the desert?"

Molly nodded. She was trapped in a huddle of women, all curious about the Arizona Territory.

"Is it as wild as they say?"

"Who says it's wild?" Molly asked in return.

"Why, the papers do," said a woman in a brown dress that matched her brown hair although it was streaked with gray. "They say it's still quite lawless down there."

Molly sipped at her glass of sherry, the liquid robust and fruity, uncertain what the woman wanted her to say. By all accounts, Creede was a more dangerous place to live than Tucson. She swung her gaze to the side and nearly choked on the wine. Jake stood across the room talking to two other men, but his eyes met hers, and his bemused expression sent a thunderbolt right through her.

She coughed to hide her stunned response, swaying slightly from a wave of dizziness; it dawned on her that she may have drunk too much. Ladies didn't usually imbibe in public, but the well-heeled guests at Lannigan's party had seemed to relax that standard. At eighteen years old, it was the first time Molly had been treated as a full-fledged adult.

She rather liked it.

"Molly dear, do you have a sweetheart back in Tucson?" a nice woman named Beatrice Perkins asked her.

"No."

"Well, I hope you'll let me introduce you to my son, Carl. You're so pretty and sweet. I just know he'd fancy you."

"Oh no, not Carl," said Esme Patterson, shaking her head.

Of all the ladies she'd conversed with, Molly liked Mrs. Patterson the most. And now, even more so.

"I disagree, Esme." Beatrice shook her head. "Carl will make a fine husband. I would love for Miss Simms to meet him." She swung her gaze to Molly. "I could invite you to tea. How about next Tuesday?"

"I've already made prior arrangements with Miss Simms for Tuesday." Esme winked at her, and Molly suppressed a smile. "And I have it on good authority that there is already a suitor in the picture," Esme added.

Shocked, Molly stared at the elderly woman.

Beatrice looked at Molly, her eyes bright and inquisitive. "Who?"

Molly had no idea what to say and glanced at the group of women now watching her with avid curiosity. Too late she realized her mouth was agape.

"Jacob McKenna," Esme said.

The women all shifted uncomfortably.

Molly frowned. Why would Mrs. Patterson say such a thing? She'd told no one about the kiss in the tunnel. Had Jake shared it with her?

It had become clear earlier during the conversation that Esme Patterson had a fondness for Jake and spoke highly of him. One of the few, Molly had noticed.

Unsure what to say, Molly blurted, "I'll only be in town a short time." The squeak in her voice annoyed her. "I don't really think it would be wise to create any unnecessary attachments." Even with McKenna, although her heart rebelled at that thought.

"Just a word of advice," Beatrice said, her voice lowering. "Jake McKenna is a scoundrel. I've heard rumors that the man doesn't abide by the law. You'd do well to steer clear of him. But my Carl, he's as true and loyal as they come. He'd make a fine husband. You two might suit," she pressed. "You never know."

"Pshaw." Esme waved a hand for emphasis. "You said it yourself, Bea. The talk about Jake is just that—rumors—and those are often couched in fabrications." Esme focused on Molly. "The law in these parts is questionable at times. Jake McKenna is a good man. You can mark my word on it."

Molly paused, unsure how to respond. Finally, she plastered her most sincere smile upon her face and lifted the glass of sherry to her mouth, dismayed to see that it was empty. "I think I could use a bit of fresh air. If you'll excuse me."

She stepped away before any of the women could stop her, and then made her way to the kitchen. As she passed a young worker carrying a tray filled with goblets of a red liquid, Molly snatched one and kept walking, her goal a quiet niche on the back porch where she could be alone.

She slipped out the rear entrance and found a spot between two posts, an opening that would easily seat two people, but her puffy gown consumed the extra space.

With her legs dangling over the edge of the narrow porch, she shivered, wishing she had a wrap, but getting one would mean returning to the party, and, for now, she didn't want to. She watched the crowd of horses in the corral beyond, milling about, antsy and releasing agitated snorts and neighs. Clearly, tensions were high from all the new and unfamiliar animals stuck in one place together.

*I understand.*

Who would want to be cooped up with creatures you didn't know nor particularly desired to know?

She sipped her drink—the flavor signaling that she had grabbed a different wine this time. She took another taste.

"Aren't you cold?"

Molly jumped at the sound of Jake's voice, holding the goblet away from her gown so the fluid didn't spill. "A little."

He strode toward her, removed his jacket, then placed it onto her shoulders.

Immediately she was engulfed in McKenna's smell—musky and wild and distinctive. "Thank you." A wave of longing swept through her, primal and fierce. It was as if she were a coyote who'd just caught the scent of her mate...*or a jackal*.

He sat beside her although the post holding the railing divided them. His white shirt all but glowed in the dark night that embraced them. He loosened his tie and undid the top button.

Molly watched from the corner of her eye, trying not to stare.

How could she even consider some boy named Carl when she'd already met a man like Jake?

She took another gulp of wine and stared straight ahead. Had Esme spoken the truth? Was Jake courting her?

"Go easy," Jake said, his voice a caress in the night air.

"Why?"

"Because you'll regret it tomorrow."

She considered his advice then stared at the corral. "Did you tell Esme Patterson that you kissed me?"

"No. Is she spreading rumors?"

His voice sounded amused, which emboldened Molly to move forward. Or was it the alcohol? "There seems to be talk that you... and I...that we..."

She glanced at him, and his tenacious gaze caught her attention. She couldn't look away.

"That we what?" His voice, deep and hypnotic, washed over her like a warm rainstorm.

She shook her head, suddenly bashful. "Never mind." She was

being silly. Jake McKenna wasn't courting her. She needed to remember his reputation. Swallowing another sip of wine, she forged ahead. "You apparently have the distinction of being a scamp around these parts. I was cautioned to avoid you, by more than one woman, I should add."

"I'm a what? A scamp? That's a new one." Shaking his head, he chuckled. "What do you think, Molly Rose?"

"I don't think anything. I don't know you."

"Don't you?"

Confused, she reiterated, "No, I don't. Isn't that what I just said?" Her muddled thoughts swirled in her head. Damn the wine.

"You don't have to be afraid of me, you know."

"I'm not."

He grinned. "I spent some time in Istanbul, and while I was there, I studied a poet and philosopher named Rumi. He was a great observer of life, of how important the smallest thing can be. *What you seek is seeking you.*"

She watched him, perplexed.

"Maybe we've been searching for each other," he added.

She laughed, but it was more of a snort. Embarrassed, she straightened, trying to sound indifferent as she asked, "Is this how you sweet-talk women?"

"No. Just you."

"I think I've had too much to drink."

He reached over and took the goblet from her. His fingers brushed hers, sending a shiver through her, and, for a moment, she thought he might kiss her again. Did she just swoon toward him?

As he downed the remainder of the liquid, she stared at his mouth. "How did you get away from Winston?"

"I'm The Jackal."

A smile stretched clear across her face before she could rein it in. "You're full of bluster, just like every other man."

His expression sobered. "And how many men have you known?"

"Some. A few." She nodded. "Some. Beatrice Perkins has me all but engaged to her son Carl."

Jake's eyes narrowed. He tensed and turned his face from her. She didn't like it. Had she offended him? She lifted her hand to touch his arm, but when he swung his gaze back to her, she hid the gesture by pretending to swat at a nonexistent fly.

"I want to check out the Chigger. Since you're my partner, do you want to come?"

She giggled. Heavens, she needed to curb her drinking. "How scandalous. You'd really let me go with you?" *Don't sound so eager, Molly. Act like a woman.* She sought to compose herself.

"Yes. You can stay with Ivan and Pearl Krupin. They have a place in the hills."

"Where will you be?"

"I'll use the Krupin's place as a base to go scouting. I'll see you every night."

"Can I scout with you? Will you teach me?"

He nodded, his gaze softening. "Yes, I'll teach you."

Molly had the oddest feeling that they spoke of more than just prospecting. "Should I tell Robert?" she asked softly.

He hesitated. "Probably. He'll worry if you don't."

"You think he'll stop me?"

"I think you're his sister, and he loves you very much. He'll always have a need to keep you safe and sound."

She considered the situation. "How long would we be gone?"

"Not more than a few days."

"Alright. When do we leave?"

"I can get horses and supplies together tonight," he said. "But I'm not sure how to get you out of this house."

Archie came to mind. "I think I might have a way. I'll meet you at the dip in the road beyond the entrance to the ranch."

"When?"

"Before sunup," she answered.

He nodded. "Should I ask how?"

"No."

Jake's body exuded warmth and Molly swayed. He was a heady combination of rugged male physique—broad shoulders, rolled sleeves revealing muscled forearms, a freshly-shaved chiseled jaw. She had to force herself not to reach out and touch the smooth skin of his cheek.

"You're not that irresistible." Had she just uttered the words aloud?

He grinned. "Are you sure about that?"

*No. I'm not sure at all.* "Why did you kiss me in the tunnel?"

The amusement left his eyes, replaced by a penetrating gaze that awakened an ancient feminine part of herself, always present but never acknowledged. Until now. Until Jake. *The Jackal.*

"Because I wanted to."

---

"I'm going with Jake to the Chigger claim," Molly said to Robert.

It was late in the evening, and many of the guests had already left—Jake included—and Molly had finally found privacy with her brother, huddled in a corner of the parlor.

Robert sighed and rubbed the back of his neck. "I suppose me saying no is pointless."

"Probably," she replied, her voice quiet. "He said I could stay with the Krupin's. It won't be like at his cabin."

"What are you talking about?" Robert's face became stern. "What happened at his cabin?"

"Nothing," Molly said hastily. "He was trying to help me—and you, I might add. We were in the cabin alone, but he behaved like a gentleman."

"Hell," Robert muttered under his breath, swiping a hand across his chin.

"You know I can take care of myself." She glared at him. "And don't be so high and mighty with me. I know that you gamble and visit women like Mabel at Bertha's Saloon."

Molly reveled in the shocked expression on his face. She raised an eyebrow in response.

"What will people in town say?" he asked.

Incredulous, Molly released a bark of laughter. "About you? Probably nothing. As for me, no one is a paragon here. There are so many places of prostitution in town, I've lost count, and every woman at the party tonight was drinking."

"Including you?"

"Yes, dammit."

"And are you plannin' to become a fancy girl as well?"

"No, of course not."

"Then I'll only say this once." Robert leaned in close. "If McKenna compromises you, I'll hold a gun to his head until he marries you."

Molly suppressed a gasp. "You wouldn't." The thought mortified her. As fascinating as she found Jake, forcing his hand in marriage would place her in a category of women she refused to occupy.

"Try me."

She narrowed her eyes. This side of Robert had always aggravated her. "I knew I shouldn't have told you."

He grimaced. "Fine, you have my very reluctant blessing, but I'll be along in a few days."

"Why? Do you think Jake is going to hold me captive and ravish me?" The very thought made her face flush with warmth.

His gaze pierced her like the sharp clang of the blacksmith's anvil. "Don't tell *anyone* about the Chigger, not even the Krupins."

"But Lannigan probably already knows."

"Maybe. I can throw him a bone to get him off your scent. And while I may not trust Jake with your virtue, I do trust him with your life."

The statement sank deep into Molly's bones, alerting her. "What's so important about this claim?"

"Most likely—nothing. But there's a chance it's a find like no other."

The awe in her brother's voice triggered gooseflesh along her arms and shoulders, causing her to shiver. She wished she still had Jake's jacket. Already she couldn't wait to see him again, but Robert didn't need to know that. "I told Jake I'd meet him before sunup. I thought to ask Archie to help me get past Lannigan's locked gate. He said he has a key."

Robert shook his head. "He'll talk. Go upstairs and change, and then pack your things. We'll leave right now. With all the guests coming and going, it'll be easier to slip out. Lannigan's guards will be lax tonight."

"Should I tell Bridget I'm leaving?"

"No. I'll say later that I took you back to Zang's. Meet me out back in twenty minutes."

Molly hurried upstairs, but, unfortunately, she couldn't remove the gown by herself. Frustrated, she wondered how she could get Stella to come up when a knock sounded at the door. On the other side stood Bridget.

"I wondered where you'd gone." Bridget wrinkled her lovely forehead. "Did you enjoy the party?"

"Yes." Molly spoke the truth. The entire reason was Jake McKenna. "Would you help me out of this gown? I'm ready to turn in."

"Of course. It is awfully late." Bridget stepped into the room, and Molly shut the door.

Bridget moved behind her and began to unhook the two-dozen buttons on the backside of the dress. "There were several gentlemen who inquired after you. I think we could arrange visits if any of them have caught your eye."

"That's very flattering, but I can't say that I'm interested."

"Can I ask you something?"

Molly tensed, wondering if somehow Bridget knew she was about to flee Lannigan's compound and run into the hills with The Jackal. She gave a curt nod over her shoulder.

"What was Robert like when he was younger?"

Molly released the breath she'd been holding. "He was very black and white, Bridget."

"What do you mean?"

The dress gave way, and Molly pushed it down her hips then stepped out of it, still wearing three layers of petticoats. She pulled the straps of the camisole onto her shoulders and faced the other woman.

"He was always straight up. Sometimes a little righteous, but mostly fair, and a believer in doing the right thing."

Bridget's face turned to stone, and she looked away.

"But like many men," Molly added gently, "he's let go of some of his lofty ideals. He must really care about you."

Bridget's hooded gaze met hers, and Molly knew the woman understood. The Lannigan's likely never did the right thing.

"Be honest with him," Molly said. "If you love him, then tell him."

Bridget chewed her lip and nodded.

———

IN THE HOURS BEFORE DAWN, Jake approached his small house and recognized Robert's horse tethered outside. When he entered, he was surprised to see Molly Rose there as well.

He shut the door and dropped the bag of supplies he carried. "How'd you get her out of Lannigan's?" he asked Robert, but his eyes slid to Molly. She was dressed plainly and bundled for warmth, but her face was bright with anticipation. A smile tugged at her mouth, and his heart raced in his chest.

"It wasn't that hard." Robert stepped forward and pushed the curtain aside on the front window, then glanced outside. "Everyone was drunk."

"I know," Jake answered, grinning at Molly. She grimaced, clearly remembering her own inebriated state earlier.

Jake hadn't minded. He'd enjoyed seeing her with her guard down. But, while he'd definitely wanted to kiss her again, he'd held himself in check for that reason. He wanted her of sound mind when he next took her in his arms. He was feeling a little territorial that way. There'd be no thought of any of those other men she knew, whether back home or from the nosy biddies in Creede trying to pair Molly up with one of their sons.

He also hadn't kissed her because they were at Lannigan's ranch. Jake desired more privacy. By taking Molly into the mountains, he suspected he was about to get it, but Robert's presence filled the room with tension.

"I've got most of the supplies together," Jake said. "One benefit of this town never sleeping."

"You should leave now." Robert let the curtain fall back into place. "I don't want anyone following you. I'll meet you at Ivan's place in a few days."

Jake nodded. "I need to get another horse from the livery for your sister. Molly, pack your things in here." He handed her an empty saddlebag.

While she knelt and began shifting her belongings from the satchel, Robert leaned close to Jake. "She's my sister." His low voice was edged with warning. "Not a plaything."

"I can hear you," Molly murmured from her spot on the floor, her eyes fixated on her task.

Robert stared at Jake with an unflinching gaze. Jake had only ever seen this side of him when it came to Bridget, at least in the beginning when Robert had become involved with Lannigan's daughter.

"I'll guard her with my life." Jake meant it.

Molly stood. "Are you two done trying to one-up the other? I'd like a gun, since I'm pretty certain James Winston stole my derringer."

They both looked at her.

Robert shifted his attention to Jake. "You still got that Colt Lightning?"

"Yep. Think she can handle it?"

"I told you I can shoot," Molly said matter-of-factly.

Robert gave a nod. Jake retrieved the weapon from his gear and handed it to Molly, placing the grip into her palm. She took the weight, released the cylinder, eyed the empty chambers, then popped it back into position. "Do you have cartridges?"

Jake found a box of .38's and handed it over. She went to the table and proceeded to load the gun.

Robert's attention landed on Jake. "Maybe I won't have to worry about you tarnishing my sister's reputation after all." Robert smiled, but there was little humor in the gesture.

Jake had never had a woman shoot him.

There was always a first time for everything.

# CHAPTER 11

Molly guided her horse out of town as the sky began to lighten on the edges of the ridgetops, trailing behind Jake's mount and a mule loaded with supplies—a canvas tent, blankets, slickers, food for both humans and animals, basic medical supplies, and mining tools. She only knew this because she'd quizzed Jake before they departed. After their prior hasty run into the mountains, Molly wished to be more prepared this time.

Once clear of town, she was able to move side-by-side with Jake. "How far is it to the Krupins' place?"

"We should be there by nightfall, depending on how well you hold up."

"I'll be fine."

"You've had no sleep, and you had a bit too much sherry. If you need to stop and rest, just let me know."

Fortunately, Jake had rented Cinnamon once again for her to ride, which made Molly very happy. She patted the gelding's neck. "I'll only stop if the horses need a break."

"We can work on your liquor tolerance. I've got a bottle of rye whiskey from Pittsburgh, Pennsylvania, that's over fifty years old."

"So you're taking me into the wilderness to get me intoxicated?"

He laughed. "No. But on a cold night with the wolves howling and bears grunting in the distance, sometimes the only remedy is a bit of liquid gold."

"Bears?"

"Most are probably still hibernating, but a few could be out early. Don't worry, even if you're only an adequate shot, you can easily hit one."

"My pa made sure I was more than adequate." And her cousin Eli—while four years younger than her—had fine-tuned those abilities while staying with her family two years ago. Living on the plains of Texas had honed his skills to pinpoint accuracy. Either that or it was his determination to best their cousin Lucas. Her money was on Lucas. When she'd spent the summer with her Aunt Molly and Uncle Matt seven years ago, the two boys had been annoyingly competitive, and they'd only been eight years old at the time.

"I hope one day to get down to Arizona. Maybe I'll have a chance to meet your pa."

"If you do, you probably shouldn't mention kissing his daughter in a tunnel or camping in the hills with her."

A smile tugged at Jake's mouth. "I'll remember that."

The sky shifted to light gray as sunrise approached. Although they'd left Upper Creede and entered the mountains along the same path as their previous excursion, once in the hills they'd diverged east into a new area. For now, the way was flat, but beyond Molly could see they would soon begin climbing out of the valley they now traversed.

Jake slid a glance at her. "Why don't you like tunnels?"

She tugged the brim of her hat down and tightened the scarf around her neck—a challenge with the leather gloves on her hands. "When I was young, I fell into a well. I wasn't found for quite some time."

"How old were you?"

She cleared her throat. "Seven. I can't seem to quell the fear, even now." Embarrassed, a part of her wanted to hide the incident from Jake. It was hardly a tragic event that she'd experienced, but she nevertheless relived frightful echoes of it whenever she was in a tight space, which, blessedly, wasn't often, since she made a point of avoiding them. Seeking to change the topic of conversation, she asked, "When you lived overseas, what did you do for employment?"

He considered her question. "You may not like my answers."

"Were you a criminal?"

"Not if I could help it, but sometimes life isn't so simple."

Sitting astride Fernando, he held himself with a dispassionate demeanor, but Molly was beginning to realize that it was a pretense. She could almost smell the survival instinct wafting off him.

"Give me an example," she prodded.

"When I was eighteen, I was a salt smuggler in Shanghai."

"Why salt? Wouldn't opium make you more money?"

He laughed, and Molly liked that she could prompt such a response in him.

Shooting her an amused look, he asked, "How would you know about opium?"

She shrugged. "We've got Chinese immigrants in Tucson. There are opium dens in Old Chinatown."

"I hope you don't go into any of them. It grabs hold of people and robs them of their soul."

Molly wondered if he spoke from personal experience.

"At the time, I decided that salt was less dangerous. The government regulated who could buy and sell, which hurt everyone. In situations like that, smuggling becomes a necessary evil."

"But it's still dangerous."

"Only if you get caught." The rogue in him emerged. Was that why he was so compelling?

"The Jackal Smuggler." She swung her gaze to encompass the

surrounding splendor of the mountains of Colorado, afraid her fascination with this man was all too apparent.

"Has a nice ring to it, doesn't it? But I did get caught although not by the police. One night, a group of us was off-loading a shipment down at the docks when we were jumped by another gang. They killed two of us then grabbed me and three others. We were taken to an abandoned warehouse and interrogated. They wanted all our contacts."

"Did you tell them?"

"Yeah, I did." His light-hearted tone faded. "I was only eighteen and I wanted to live. It was just salt smuggling, after all, not worth dying over, but my contacts weren't too pleased. I managed to get away but had to go into hiding, at least until I could get out of China. I ended up on a boat headed to Vietnam and landed right in the middle of a war between China and France."

Her heart beat a rapid staccato in her chest, and her breath was shallow. As if she were with him in that time, she worried over his safety. It was such an odd sensation. He was healthy and well and alive not three feet from her, but it took a moment for her mind to accept that logic.

She hadn't lost him. In fact, she hardly knew him. Was there some grand design of the universe that had caused their paths to cross? Was her attraction to him something more?

Her head spun from the possibilities.

Her mama's voice whispered in her ear. *It's God's plan.* Mary Simms believed firmly in a higher power, most especially after Mary's younger sister—Molly Hart—had been resurrected from the dead ten years after everyone had thought her brutally murdered. It was difficult not to speak of it without using the words *miracle* and *fate.*

Molly had never thought overmuch on the topic, but now she wondered if Aunt Molly had ever felt Providence murmuring in the recesses of her soul.

Slowly her tension dissipated, replaced by relief. "I'm glad you have a knack for staying alive."

Jake grinned. "Me too."

---

By late afternoon, Jake halted the animals beside a trickling stream so they could rest and drink. They'd spent the last several hours climbing out of the valley and deserved a break.

"Are there many prospectors back in these hills?" Molly asked as she led Cinnamon to the frigid water.

"There can be." Jake untied the mule's lead from Fernando then pulled his Winchester from its scabbard. All the animals busied themselves with quenching their thirst. "Stay here. I'll be back."

He adjusted his hat and moved up the trail, seeking a vantage point. He noticed tracks in the dirt. Mountain lion?

He stopped and listened. The wind funneled down the high granite walls and caressed the trees. Birds twittered; a good sign. In his experience when a threat was present, animals became silent. He walked quietly for a time, avoiding the occasional snowy patch, his boots sinking into the soft ground. He scanned the surroundings, his instincts alert.

Nothing was more reliable than his own gut feeling, a hard-won lesson from his Shanghai escape.

He and Molly Rose weren't alone. That much he knew.

He halted at the sound of panting, trying to determine the location, but in such a narrow ravine the echoes could be deceiving.

An animal burst from the bushes and leaped for Jake. Jerking around, Jake recognized the mutt at the last second and lowered the barrel of his rifle. The dog bounded up to him and planted his front paws on Jake's chest, desperately seeking a face to lick.

Jake scratched the dog's ears and leaned forward so the animal could get his kisses in. "Grom, it's good to see you." The dog's straight, brown hair was a bit ratty, but otherwise he was well-cared for by his owners.

"There he is." Ivan Krupin's stocky frame burst through the brush, holding a shovel in his hand. "I knew it had to be someone we knew, the way he took off. Either that or he'd found a sweetheart."

Jake laughed as Grom settled back on all fours, wagging his tail like a cowpuncher swinging a lasso. "I hope I'm not Grom's sweetheart."

Ivan sighed. "I think you're all he's got. Pearl and I don't get many visitors." He tugged at the black fisherman's cap atop his head and watched Jake with his left eye—the right one was covered with a patch, thanks to a dynamite debacle years ago. With the man's swarthy complexion and scruffy beard and mustache, Jake had always thought he looked like a pirate.

Jake shook Ivan's hand. "You're a little far from home."

Ivan shrugged. "Just a few hours. Been digging up a few pilings. You here to steal all my hard work?"

"Nah. I'll stay out of your hair. I've been wanting to explore a valley near here."

"Which one?"

Jake sidestepped Grom as the dog rubbed against his leg. "I'll let you know when I find it."

"Prospectors and their secrets," Ivan groused, but then he laughed. "You shouldn't go alone."

"I'm not. I have a partner."

Ivan raised an eyebrow. "You and Robbie make up?"

"Of a sort. I've got his sister with me."

"Don't pull my leg, McKenna. Pearl would give her left arm to see another woman."

"Then Pearl will soon be armless."

Ivan let out a hearty bellow. "Damn, what are we waiting for? Show me this elusive female before I'm convinced you've gone loco from too much tarantula juice."

"Speaking of which, I've got a bottle of rye you're gonna like." Ivan clapped him on the back. "You're the son I never had."

The sentiment was sincere, and also filled with heartache. Ivan and Pearl had lost their only child—a boy—many years ago.

---

MOLLY LIKED IVAN KRUPIN IMMEDIATELY. Upon introduction, he'd scooped her into his arms in a boisterous hug, and his dog Grom had nearly knocked her to the ground with his bouncy antics. Ivan had no horse, so Jake walked beside him while leading Fernando as they continued farther into the wilderness. The mule didn't care for the dog but finally started moving once Ivan directed Grom to run ahead.

With a shovel resting on one shoulder and a knapsack on the other, Ivan angled his body so that Molly could hear him from where she sat atop Cinnamon. "Robbie's a good boy except for keeping company with that hooligan, Winston."

"If it's any consolation," Jake said, "I don't think Robert does it because he likes the man.".

Ivan shook his head. "Then I hope he knows what he's doin'. You know I owe you one."

"And I've come to collect." Jake lightly clapped the man on the back as they resumed walking.

"Name it."

Jake threw a glance back at her. "Can Molly Rose bunk with you and Pearl while I go searching in the hills?"

Ivan let out a whoop. "Of course she can. Pearl will squeal like a pig in mud." He looked at her. "You're always welcome in our home, miss."

"My thanks," Molly said. "Why do you owe Jake a favor?"

"I'm almost too mortified to say." Ivan shook his head. "But I will, since Jake saved my hide. I was duped by that no-good Winston into buying stock in a bogus company. Jake recovered my money along with the incriminating paperwork."

"So Winston was right when he accused you of stealing," she said to Jake.

"Guilty as charged." He didn't appear remorseful.

Ivan looked at Jake, concern in his gaze. "Hope you didn't have any trouble over it."

"Nothing I couldn't handle."

Jake caught her eye and held it for a moment. It was clear he didn't want her to elaborate on what had transpired between him and Winston.

It was a bit of a trek, but after several hours, they approached a cabin, small corral, and shed nestled under a copse of trees. Smoke spiraled from the chimney. Grom bounded forward, ears flopping.

A tall woman with a trim build came onto the porch and waved. An apron covered a faded wool skirt and shirtwaist, the sleeves bunched at the elbows.

Molly dismounted and strode forward for an introduction.

"I know who you are." Pearl engulfed her in a hug, much the way Ivan had done.

Molly enjoyed the warm embrace, marveling over the affection the Krupin's had for complete strangers, and then faced the woman again. "You do?"

Eyes as green as the forest greeted Molly. Pearl's thin lips stretched into a crooked smile, her brown hair dappled with gray and knotted in a bun at the base of her neck. "I'm Pearl, and you're Molly Rose."

"How do you know my name?" Molly asked, awed by the woman's foresight. Pearl was like a fresh gust of wind, exuding a sense of *knowing*. Gazing into the woman's face, Molly was enveloped in a cocoon of peaceful serenity. "Have we met before?"

"You're the spitting image of your brother, and he's told us so much about you."

*Of course.*

Molly smiled, embarrassed that she had thought Pearl was some otherworldly earth mother. She was simply a woman who paid attention.

# CHAPTER 12

J ake sat at the table inside the Krupin's modest cabin, Molly beside him, along with Ivan and Pearl. They ate hearty portions of a rabbit and turnip stew Pearl had prepared. It was as if she'd known they were coming.

There were times when Pearl sometimes said peculiar things, but Jake had generally dismissed them as the musings of an old lady who spent too much solitary time in the woods. Their cabin was isolated, even by a recluse's standards, and Ivan frequently went off into the mountains alone.

"I've got three places I plan to check out," Ivan said. "I found some pilings and want to see if I can find the source."

"Near here?" Jake asked around a mouthful of food.

"Ah c'mon, you know I can't tell you that."

"Why?" Molly asked, her arm bumping Jake's. His left-handedness collided with Molly's right-handed tendency. She pretended not to notice, so Jake indulged himself by touching her whenever he could.

"Prospectors are a superstitious lot," Ivan said.

Pearl stood. "Is that what you call it?" She retrieved the

coffeepot warming on the stove and poured a cup for Ivan and Jake. "It's more like a madness."

When Pearl hovered over Molly's cup, Molly waved her away. "I won't be able to sleep."

"Everyone worries about claim-jumping," Jake said, sitting back and resting his arm on the back of Molly's chair.

Ivan drank his coffee and released a happy grumble. "Pearl, you make the best brew this side of the Rockies." His gaze settled on Molly. "While claim theft is a problem, a bigger concern is all the men who start sniffing around once you find something."

"They're all hoping to find other access points to a vein, but the most important find is the apex," Jake added.

Molly leaned back and didn't flinch when Jake's fingers brushed her shoulder. "What's that?"

"In simple terms," Jake said, "it's the beginning of the vein at the surface. If you're lucky, you'll stake your claim on it, then the law of the apex, otherwise known as the Mining Law of 1872, gives you the right to follow that vein until the end, even if it crosses someone else's claim."

"Why don't you just file multiple claims all over the area you're interested in?"

Ivan chuckled and Jake smiled.

"Working a claim is backbreaking labor," Pearl said, settling back into her seat. "In order to keep your claim, by law you must develop it. Prospectors are better off finding one or two areas to claim and focusing on them, rather than spread the work out too much."

"How big can a claim be?" Molly asked.

"Maximum length is fifteen hundred feet, and the width is three hundred," Ivan said. "You get everything that's straight below it, unless it's the apex, then you can branch beyond the boundaries of your claim. However, the discovery point has to be within these boundaries. Sometimes you make a claim, but after weeks of digging, you can't find anything worthwhile. That discovery point you thought you had turns out to be worthless."

"What do you do?"

"Find another claim, if any remain in the area," Jake replied.

Molly turned to him, her eyes a deep hue of moss-green in the flickering light of the oil lamp on the table. Her nose was reddened from the long day spent trekking into the mountains. "This all sounds very difficult."

Jake reluctantly removed his hand from Molly's chair before he gave in to the inclination to touch her again since they had an audience. "Prospecting isn't a get-rich-quick scheme."

"Speak for yourself," Ivan cut in.

Jake smiled. "I guess that's why we keep chasing it. You never know what you'll find on the next rocky cliff side."

"Are there any women prospecting out here besides Pearl?" Molly asked.

"I only prospect when I have to," Pearl replied. "But there really aren't any women out here."

"It's tedious and often-boring work," Jake said. "Don't say I didn't warn you."

"Are you headed out with Jake tomorrow?" Pearl asked.

"I'd like to." Molly pinned him with a hopeful expression.

"If you find something, then you'll have to share it." Ivan pushed his bowl aside and patted his stomach.

"There is a power in contracts." Pearl buttered a biscuit then looked at Jake, and then Molly. "There's always a purpose behind them."

Fate ran a finger down Jake's spine. He hadn't told either Ivan or Pearl about the Chigger, but, as usual, they'd managed to hone in on it, nonetheless.

"Pearl is right," Ivan said. "Take care if you plan to break one. I've never seen any good come from it."

"Point taken." Jake caught Molly's eye and found his own bewilderment reflected back at him.

A smile tugged at her mouth as she turned away and asked Pearl, "How long have you and Ivan lived out here?"

"We've been here for almost three years. At first, we lived in a tent, and Creede was nothing more than a throughway for miners coming and going from Lake City and Silverton. The growth since then has been extraordinary."

"How did you get supplies?" Molly asked.

"Whenever and wherever we could." Pearl laughed. "We've always managed, somehow."

"I can see why you'd love it here. It's so beautiful and majestic. I've never seen such a place."

"There's a feeling in these mountains like few places I've been. The powerful current of the earth itself flows strong—in the streams and the air and the trees, and even the rocks."

"You should listen to her," Ivan said. "Every time she's told me about the rocks and her feelings about them, I've found something. She's my own divining rod."

"Damn," Jake muttered. "Now I know your secret, Ivan."

"And she's all mine. Get your own secret weapon."

Jake's gaze flicked to Molly, but her attention was on Pearl.

"I have an aunt," Molly said. "Her name is Emma, and she has the ability to *know* things as well." Her voice held a hint of reverence. "For her, it was almost as if she couldn't switch off the knowing. She told me once that it was like slipping into a stream and having it rush around you."

"And now?" Pearl asked.

"She's more deliberate."

"It takes practice to enhance one's ability to *see*. For me, if I become very still and quiet, I can *hear*."

"What do you hear?" Molly asked.

"The sound of the earth and all her creatures."

Pearl's face glowed in the lamplight, and, for a moment, she appeared very young, a slip of a girl with a preternatural ability to navigate the world with extraordinary senses. It was clear to Jake that Molly was a perfect match, a spirit with the ability to grace those around her by peeling back the layers of the visible world.

*"Be grateful for whoever comes because each has been sent as a guide from beyond,"* Jake said, the words climbing from a memory long ago, a time and place etched permanently into his mind.

"Where does that come from?" Pearl asked.

"A poet I studied while in Turkey." His teacher—a blind man named Doruk Mataraci—had easily been the smartest man Jake had ever met. They'd bonded over Turkish tea and milk pudding, and a tendency to see life as a game.

Pearl beamed at him. "You *are* The Jackal—as clever and sly as the coyotes we have." She looked at Molly. "I hope you can keep up with him."

"I won't leave her behind," Jake said.

"Now, the bunch of you out." Pearl waved them off and stood again. "I need to clean up supper."

"I'll help," Molly offered.

Ivan pushed his chair back with a scrape. "You grab that bottle of rye, and I'll grab my pipe," he said to Jake.

Jake nodded.

"Give me a cup, woman," Ivan demanded.

Pearl shook her head but grabbed two clean tin cups and handed them to Jake. Grom hightailed it after them as they went outside. Jake retrieved the bottle of liquor from his gear in the shed then sat in a rocking chair on the porch, Ivan beside him. Jake poured a bit of whiskey into each cup and settled back to sip the strong brew and watch the thousands of twinkling lights crowding the night sky.

Ivan stuffed his pipe and struck a lucifer, puffing until the tobacco started to burn. "I like her."

"Pearl? I'd hope so."

"No, you scalawag, Molly Rose." Ivan took a swig of his drink then inserted the pipe back into the corner of his mouth. "What're you gonna do about it?"

"What do you mean?"

"You're not gettin' any younger, McKenna. You really ought to settle down. A good woman can make all the difference in a man's life."

"I don't doubt that."

"'Cause I can think of no other reason you'd bring her out here."

Jake downed his cupful of firewater. "Maybe she owns an important claim, and I mean to steal it from her."

Ivan stilled, his gaze pensive. "I know you've lived life on the outer reaches, son, but I also know you'd never go so far as to ruin a pretty young thing like Robbie's sister in there." He flicked his head toward the interior of the cabin.

Jake stared into his empty cup. "You think too highly of me, Ivan." Ever since Molly Rose had come into his life, Jake had been plagued with pangs of wanting to be a better man. It was a novel and unexpected sentiment. The man he was had never bothered him before.

Ivan leaned close. "For the right woman, we all strive to be a man worth his salt."

The pungent tobacco aroma reminded Jake of the men on the steamer that had taken him to Asia all those years ago. They'd been a mix of cutthroats, wanderers, and opportunists—oddly honorable men but selfish in their own pursuits. In a word, pirates. It was a tribe into which Jake had taken residence, a kinship that had fit him like a glove, but it was hardly a life that a woman like Molly Rose would long for.

"How is it that you've stayed with Pearl all this time?" Jake asked.

Ivan tapped the pipe, dumping the used contents onto the porch, then started repacking it again. "What you're really asking is how does a man hand his life over to a woman." He struck another match and lit the pipe again. "But it's really the other way around. I'd be lost without my Pearl."

Jake refilled both cups and smiled. "You do have a terrible sense of direction."

"You're a rat, but I can see it."

"See what, old man?"

"She gets to you."

Jake swallowed his drink in one gulp. *Yep.*

Grom's shadow darted beyond, chasing a rabbit or a squirrel or a mouse. Jake felt an affinity to the dog. The past ten years had been filled with one exploit after another, never keeping him in one place for long.

But he couldn't shake the feeling that kismet had just kicked him in the teeth, and her name was Molly Rose Simms.

---

MOLLY DRIED the dishes as Pearl washed. They soon had the kitchen in order.

"Jake will bed down in the shed," Pearl said. "Ivan and I don't live on a high horse, so I expect you'll bed down there as well."

"I—"

"Do you know how to avoid a child until the time is right?"

"Umm..." Molly shook her head, embarrassed, her voice clogged in her throat.

"Do you want to know?"

"I'm not sure." Molly's voice was barely more than a squeak.

"I can see the look in your eyes. When the hunger strikes, the mind stops working right." Pearl patted her hand. "I believe women should be prepared for passion, since the stakes are so much higher for them."

Molly couldn't move, frozen in disbelief. Even her own mama had never been so frank with her.

Pearl guided her back to the table and gently pushed her into a chair to sit, then settled beside her. "What God made between a man and a woman is a wondrous thing. Have you lain with Jake yet?"

Molly shook her head at the speed of a woodpecker attacking fresh bark.

Pearl chuckled. "I know Jake. He won't press you if you're not ready. He's a good sort. You can bank on that, so calm your nerves. The most important thing to remember is that when he joins with you, he can't complete within you. If he does, there's a chance you'll get with child."

Molly gulped. She wasn't quite certain what Pearl meant but didn't want to sound like a complete dolt by asking. Besides, she and Jake were nowhere near *completing* with each other. Were they?

"Jake and I haven't known one another very long," Molly murmured.

"Oh, sweet pea, that makes no difference."

Molly's head swam. She didn't know which feeling was stronger —curiosity or worry. "Why do you say that?"

"It is said that souls reach across time and place." The lines on Pearl's face smoothed away as she appeared to shine with an inner light, her dark eyes reflecting a wisdom that Molly had sometimes seen in her Aunt Emma and Aunt Tess. "And when the time is right, they find one another. The pull between you and Jake is very strong."

"Perhaps," Molly conceded.

Pearl's warmth beckoned Molly to crawl into the woman's lap and embrace her as a granddaughter might a grandmother. Molly willed herself to stay seated, but she couldn't stop her hand from seeking Pearl's. The older woman's palms encompassed Molly's right hand. "Why does he feel so familiar to me?" she asked in a rush of longing.

"Your souls are sticky."

A laugh escaped Molly. This certainly was one of the strangest conversations she'd ever had. Then, in a flash, a distant memory surfaced, and she gaped at Pearl.

"What is it?" Pearl asked.

"I'd forgotten it until now. When I was eleven, I spent the summer in Texas with relatives. I told you about my Aunt Em, about her abilities of knowing. One day, as I helped her bake bread, she asked if I would be interested in hearing about a vision that she'd recently had...about me. Of course I said yes."

"What did she tell you?"

"She said she saw me running with an animal. She called it a coyote, but now I wonder..."

"In some places, coyotes are called jackals."

Molly sat quietly then shook her head. "Is this all just nonsense and wishful thinking? Her vision could've meant anything."

"What did your aunt say?"

Molly searched her mind for more snippets. "Well, it was something along the lines of how cunning coyotes can be, how they have a strong survival instinct."

"That's true of Jake. I think that's why Ivan likes him. Kindred spirits and all that."

A shiver ran through Molly. *Kindred spirits.*

"Aunt Em said that certain animal spirits can cling to us," Molly said. "That maybe they chase us. I'll admit it made me slightly afraid because I thought it meant I'd be chased down by a coyote at some point."

"I think perhaps she saw the future. Some people can do that, but the clarity can be harder to come by."

"Do you possess this skill?"

Pearl shook her head. "No, not really. I prefer to live in the moment. There is plenty to know in the here and now."

Remembering another detail from the exchange with Aunt Emma, Molly frowned. "My aunt also said there was a letter in the vision. She couldn't read the name written upon it, but there was a Hong Kong stamp with an additional marking that said Shanghai. She admitted at the time that she didn't understand the significance of it." Another shiver. "Jake told me he was a smuggler in China."

Surprise lit Pearl's face. "Was he?" She let out a hoot of laughter. "What a devil he is. If I were as young and beautiful as you, I'd try to steal him straightaway."

Stunned, Molly was speechless.

Pearl clasped Molly's hand. "Oh no, I'm just jesting. I wouldn't trade my Ivan for anything."

Molly hesitated. "No, it isn't that. It's just...I'm not beautiful. That stroke of fate befell my sister Evie. And...Jake isn't mine to steal."

"Molly Rose, I do believe you're wrong on both counts." Pearl's voice was a quiet balm of reassurance. "Let me offer you a few more tips on alternative ways to couple without the risk of making a baby."

As Molly listened, her unease soon gave way to shock and awe. She'd had no idea there were so many variations in relations. No wonder men visited women like Mabel. The depth of a fancy ladies' knowledge must be staggering.

When Jake and Ivan entered the cabin, Molly nearly jumped out of her skin.

"Didn't mean to scare you, child," Ivan said then pinned his wife with an accusatory look. "What've you been tellin' her?"

"Important stuff, that's what."

"Jake, that usually means trouble for us men."

Jake grinned and Molly glanced away, afraid he might notice her ogling him, wondering what it would be like for the two of them to do any one of the activities that Pearl had mentioned.

"Time to turn in," Ivan said. "You two try to stay warm out in the shed."

Molly's heart pounded, and a flush of heat engulfed her, starting at her head and spreading clear down to her toes. Her mind filled with all the ways she might please Jake, and how he might please her. She was much too unsettled to be alone with him, that was for certain. *Good Lord, how did a woman manage such things?*

"If it's not too much of a bother, may I sleep in here?" Molly blurted. "I'm fine on the floor."

Pearl appeared taken aback. "Of course. Are you certain?"

Molly nodded.

Pearl smiled up at Jake. "We'll keep a good eye on her. Don't you worry."

A flash of disappointment clouded Jake's eyes. "I'm not worried. I'll bring her things inside."

Ivan and Pearl moved to the corner of the cabin while Jake stepped out then returned with Molly's saddle bag. She stood and took it from him.

He leaned close. "Will you be all right in here?"

"Yes," she answered quickly.

"Well then, I'll see you bright and early."

To her surprise, he kissed her cheek then pressed his hat atop his head.

"Good night," he added.

She met his eyes, looked away, then met his eyes again. "Good night."

His departure left her both relieved and missing him at the same time. She busied herself laying a pallet on the floor near the cook stove. Ivan let Grom inside, and the dog plopped down beside her, his dust-covered body pushing against her shoulder.

Ivan chuckled. "He'll keep you warm."

He also made her sneeze. Through the haze of a runny nose, her mind wouldn't stop replaying all the possible ways that Jake could keep her warm.

Good Lord, indeed.

# CHAPTER 13

Jake rose early and proceeded to get the horses and the mule ready. He didn't like dawdling.

As he led the animals to the front of the cabin, Molly came onto the porch. She was dressed and cleaned up as well, her hair pulled severely from her face and tucked into a tight bun.

"Morning," he said. "How did you sleep?"

"Fine."

*Fine, my ore bucket.* The shadows under her eyes told him she'd had a restless night.

"Grom twitches in his sleep," she added. Her gaze shifted to the horses. "We're taking a lot with us for just being gone for the day."

"I want to be prepared in case we can't make it back by nightfall."

A flash of panic pinched her face.

"Molly, you don't have to go with me," he reassured her although he hoped she would. She'd likely leave Creede in the next few weeks. He had precious little time to get to know her.

She watched him with an unreadable expression. "No. I'll go."

To hide his relief, he checked the cinch on Cinnamon. "We should head out as soon as we can."

"I'd like to help Pearl with breakfast first."

He gave a nod over his shoulder.

She disappeared inside, and Ivan took her place.

"I've got some time, so give me a chore or two," Jake said.

Ivan stepped off the porch and clapped Jake on the back. "You take all the time you need in those hills. You're gonna have to work at this one."

He spoke of Molly. And he was right.

"Help me feed the pigs and chickens," Ivan added, and Jake followed.

Breakfast was fried eggs, bacon, biscuits, and steaming hot coffee. Molly seemed to relax a bit more and chatted with Pearl about the birds in the area.

With full bellies, they moved to the tethered horses. Molly's gaze became guarded once again as she donned a hat and tugged it low onto her forehead, then tightened the stampede strings. Today her eyes were contemplative pools of blue, and she reminded him of an untouchable Egyptian beauty.

Jake shook Ivan's hand and gave Pearl a peck on the cheek. Molly hugged each of them in turn.

"See you soon," Ivan said.

Jake and Molly mounted their horses.

Molly clasped Cinnamon's reins in a gloved hand, her back rod-straight.

"Beware the coyotes," Pearl said, waving.

Molly frowned but returned the gesture.

Jake held up a hand of farewell and turned Fernando to a trail that led farther into the back country.

They spent the morning climbing a pass, and once at the top, Jake halted to rest. The chill in the air had dissipated as sunlight warmed the earth. He rested a forearm on the pommel and swung his gaze to Molly, indulging himself, since she'd been behind him the past several hours.

"One of the best views in the world," he said, glad they were finally alone.

"I imagine you've seen many amazing places."

"True, but it's nice to have someone to share it with."

The corners of her mouth tugged upward. "Tell me the most extraordinary place you've ever witnessed in all your travels."

He thought for a moment. "I'd have to say the Pyramids of Giza, just outside of Cairo. They're immensely tall, and it's hard to fathom how they were built. The stones are larger than any man. Did you know that the main pyramid was the tallest structure in the world until the Eiffel Tower in Paris was built?"

She shook her head. "Have you been to Paris?"

"Actually, no."

"For the past three years, a woman in town has tutored me in French."

"I'm impressed. I can't imagine there's much use of French in the Arizona desert."

She shrugged. "That's no excuse not to learn."

"Maybe one day we might go to Paris together."

Her forehead wrinkled with consternation. He searched for a reason as to why she was so grumpy, but her mood eluded him. "Or not," he muttered under his breath and swung from the saddle.

Molly dismounted and stepped away, observing the scenery as he relieved the mule of its load and picketed all the animals in the only grassy patch to graze.

Jake dug out food wrapped in cheesecloth from his saddlebags and laid it out, then sat and stretched his legs. At this altitude, the terrain was a bit barren—dirt and rock and little vegetation. Jake watched from the corner of his vision as Molly came and settled near him but not too near. He could almost hear her ruminating over how close to position herself. She didn't face him but perched with her torso at an angle, her gaze on the wide open space of Mother Nature.

He pulled a knife from his boot and cut off two chunks of cheese then held one out to her. She silently accepted the offering.

"You've been very quiet since our visit with Ivan and Pearl." He leaned back on an elbow.

She nodded, threw him a half-hearted smile and took a rather large bite of cheese, then looked away.

"Have I done something to offend you?"

"No," she answered quickly, a little too quickly. She shook her head for emphasis.

"You're lying. Spit it out, Chigger."

Her sapphire eyes snapped to his.

He chuckled. He couldn't help it.

She shifted her gaze toward the wide valley where Creede and Jimtown lay and squinted. "Nobody calls me that but Robert."

"You didn't answer my question." He broke off a hunk of bread that Pearl had provided and started popping pieces into this mouth.

"You haven't offended me."

"But..."

"But nothing. Do you always need to be coddled?"

He nearly choked on his food. When he could finally speak, he said, "No." He laughed at her. "Somehow, we've gotten off on the wrong foot today."

"You grin too much," she admonished. "Did you know that?"

He spread his lips wider. "Is that what's gotten under your skin?"

"No, of course not." She crossed her legs under her skirt and leaned forward, a slender hand scratching the back of her neck as she rested elbows on her knees. "It's just...well..." She cupped her chin in her hand and, just as swiftly, removed it, clearly agitated. "You kissed me, and...I think maybe *you* might think that there could be something..." She waved a hand between them. "That you might be expecting more, *a lot more*," she lowered her voice for emphasis, "now that we're alone out here in the middle of nowhere."

"Why would I think that?"

"Ivan and Pearl certainly did."

"Is that why you stayed in the house last night?"

"It was the proper thing to do." Her voice rose in pitch.

"So now you're worried because it's just the two of us out here?"

"If you kiss me again, you'll just be disappointed," she blurted.

Jake sat up. The conversation was making his head spin. He needed to tread carefully, and he wasn't certain in which direction the treading should take place. "I doubt that, but I won't kiss you unless you ask. Deal?"

She watched him, and the look of fear in her gaze took him aback.

"Pearl told me what men want," she said.

"Why would she do that?"

"I imagine she was trying to be helpful."

He narrowed his eyes. "What exactly did she tell you?"

Molly's face turned beet-red, and panic flashed in her eyes. "I really couldn't repeat it."

"Maybe if you told me, I could tell you if it was true."

A nervous laugh escaped her, and she turned away from him. Then she took a steadying breath. "Oh, all right." But she wouldn't look at him. "She said the best way to avoid a baby was to avoid penetration, so it was best to offer aid with one's hand, or perhaps one's mouth. She said that if penetration did occur, then it was best to withdraw before completion. The woman would need to take charge of this because the man will be lost—his mind simply unable to work any longer. She described various positions that can help either conceive a child or avoid one." She paused to take a breath. "Would you like me to continue?"

Stunned, Jake didn't know how to respond. He wasn't sure what shocked him more—that Pearl had spoken so candidly about such matters or that Molly had had the courage to say it aloud to him.

*Ivan, you lucky dog.* No wonder he was never far from his wife.

He cleared his throat. "No."

"I'm quite inexperienced in matters of this nature," she continued, still avoiding eye contact, "and since I'm sure you're..."

"I'm what, Molly?" he prodded gently.

"You've traveled the world." She picked at something on her skirt. "You've probably known beautiful and exotic women who were quite skilled at such things. I just thought you should know that I'm not."

She was far more captivating to him than any foreign paramour had ever been.

"I never once presumed you were." He leaned close, his breath causing a strand of escaped hair to flutter against her neck. "As for women I've known, I can honestly say I've *never* met one like you." He retreated to a safe distance before he did something dangerous, like nibble on her ear. He didn't want to scare her off, and he sensed that she might take off running at any moment. "And as to what Pearl said...a woman can always choose what she desires to do. Or not. And I'm not picky." He raised an eyebrow when she glanced at him. "I'd venture to say most men aren't, except, apparently, Ivan."

She gifted him with a tentative smile.

"Our next dinner with them may prove to be a bit awkward, though," he added.

He gathered up their meal, stood, then offered a hand to her. She took it, and he pulled her to her feet. "Don't be afraid to talk to me, Chigger."

She lifted her chin and met his gaze, her bashfulness suddenly gone. "I think from now on, I'll need a swig from that bottle of whiskey you have before I have any more heart-to-heart talks with you."

"That can be arranged."

She turned away, and her hand slipped from his.

Rumi whispered in his ear. *Lovers don't finally meet somewhere. They're in each other all along.*

A WEIGHT HAD BEEN LIFTED from Molly's shoulders. The uncomfortable conversation with Jake had, miraculously, eased her anxiety, along with the tension of their forced close proximity.

She sensed his desire for her—had all along, if she was to be honest with herself—but more disconcerting was her own yearning. She'd never felt this way before. She needed to keep her wits about her.

As they navigated a downhill path into a valley crowded with pine trees, she watched Jake atop Fernando ahead of her.

It dawned on her then why Pearl had said such things to her. The clever woman had meant to use it as a cautionary tactic, and it had worked.

And while recounting Pearl's words to Jake had been deeply mortifying at the time, his reaction had served to lessen the fear that had penetrated into Molly's bones. He would leave her be unless she invited him to her. *I won't kiss you unless you ask me.*

The thought caused a pleasant flutter in her stomach. If this incident had taught her anything, however, it was to take such matters slowly.

*But I don't have much time with Jake.*

Still, it wasn't a reason to run blindly forward, led only by the heart.

By late afternoon, they came to a rocky impasse.

"We'll camp here tonight then enter the valley beyond by foot in the morning," Jake said.

Molly nodded and set about helping him make camp. He erected two canvas tents while she dug out a fire pit. She gathered wood—hunting for dry pieces—then started a fire. She positioned an iron tripod over the flames and hung a pot of coffee to boil. While it heated, they ate the remainder of the cheese and bread that Pearl had given them.

"Where will you go next?" Molly asked, determined to keep her attachment to Jake McKenna to a minimum.

He swallowed water from a canteen. "Well, I've never been to Canada." He bent his knee and rested a forearm on it. "Where will you go?"

"Back to Tucson. But maybe I might tour through Europe soon."

"And how do you plan to do that?"

It was true that money and resources were a problem, but an idea had recently occurred to her. "I could become a nanny to a wealthy family and travel with them."

"But then you'd be stuck caring for someone else's children."

She shrugged. It was a small accommodation to make. Unfortunately, she didn't know any wealthy families with children who were about to embark on a trip overseas.

"It's much easier for a man," Molly said. "Have you ever thought to write about your adventures?"

"No. I doubt I'd have the patience for it."

"But you studied that Rumi poet. I assume his work wasn't written in English."

"It wasn't. I had a rather pushy teacher named Doruk during my time in Istanbul. He was blind, but he insisted I learn Persian."

"Why was he pushy?"

"He decided that I would become a renaissance man."

Molly broke off a piece of bread. "What does that mean?" She popped the food in her mouth.

"Basically that I should be awakened. That I should stop my heathen ways and find enlightenment."

"Did you?"

His eyes lit with mischief. "Can't a man be both?"

She couldn't resist and took his bait. "So you slip your way past the law, while being fully aware of what you're doing?"

"Something like that." He pulled an apple from their gear and took a bite, then handed the fruit to her.

She stared at the gaping hole he left. "Thanks for leaving some for me." She bit off a much smaller chunk. Once she'd swallowed the food, she said, "This period of enlightenment must've taken a lot of time."

"I had plenty." Jake removed the coffeepot from the tripod with a long stick then set it on the ground. "I was very ill."

"With what?" Her chest tightened. There it was again, that unnatural grip of concern for Jake's welfare.

Jake grabbed a burlap rag to shield his fingers from the heated handle then poured coffee into two cups. He handed one to Molly. "Malaria."

"Isn't that fatal?" she asked, alarmed.

"As you can see, I managed to survive. Once I got past the vomiting and endless fevers, I was as weak as a kitten. It took me quite a while to feel myself again."

"How close to death were you?" she asked quietly, abandoning the apple.

Jake reached over and took it from her. "Met the grim reaper face-to-face." He finished what remained of the fruit and set the core aside. "We should save these for the horses."

"What's it like to almost die?"

He sipped his coffee then said matter-of-factly, "At first you fight it. Then there's despair. And finally, you make peace with it."

"God's will?"

"Something like that."

"Or God's grace."

He paused, staring into the fire. "I've never told anybody..." He ran a hand across his cheeks. "When I thought it was the end, I had an encounter. I'm not sure what else to call it. I think it was my folks." His eyes flicked to hers. "They told me it wasn't my time."

"That's a wonderful vision."

"I guess. I'll admit it was nice to know they were still with me."

"You'll have to meet my Aunt Emma. She has an ability into those *other* pathways."

"I'd like that." His gaze sent a frisson of anticipation through her. He didn't want their acquaintance to end here, and she was glad. But as the silence lengthened, her head filled with visions of Pearl's descriptive intimate activities between men and women, and she began to fidget.

Jake broke the spell. "That reminds me of a tale I once heard while I was in Turkey. It was the story of the wolf-bride."

Molly willed herself to relax as he spoke.

"There was a man who had a son, so he sent for a wise elder to cast the boy's horoscope. He was told that his son was fated to be torn to pieces by a wolf. So the father built an underground chamber and hid his son away. When the boy became a man, it was time to take a wife, so the father arranged for a bride to be brought to him. His father's brother had a daughter that would suit. The wedding celebrations lasted for seven days and seven nights, and at the end, the girl was brought to the chamber. As soon as the man and his new wife were alone, she turned into a wolf and tore him to pieces. Then she turned back into a girl, having no idea what had happened."

Molly frowned. "That's a terrible story."

Jake laughed. "It has to do with fate. Whatever is to be, will be. You can't fight it."

Molly shook her head. "I don't believe that."

"It certainly makes a man think twice about matrimony."

"Only if you marry the wrong woman."

"Yes, but a man has little choice. He's fated to only marry *one* woman."

Molly chewed on her lip. "I suppose that's one way of looking at it. I prefer to think we make our own paths. You certainly did that when you left the orphanage at fifteen."

"Haven't you ever felt yourself pulled toward something?"

"Yes, sometimes. Did something tug you out of that orphanage?"

"Besides that it was an unhappy existence and there was no family waiting out in the world for me?" His face hardened. "I'm always wondering what's over the next horizon."

"So it's the unknown that drives you forward. I suppose I feel the same. There must be more to this world, and I long to experience it."

"I've seen a great deal. It can be exciting at first, but in the end, it's the people you remember." His gaze rested on her, the hardness from the moment before receding. "Sometimes you wish for that person you can be yourself with. The person you were meant to be with."

Her happiness over his attention gave way to frustration. "There you go again with this idea that people are fated to be together, that by some magical chance their paths will cross. What if they don't? What if people are just people? Imperfect and mundane." She refused to be swept up by his charm.

He looked at her as if he were a child and she'd just stolen his last molasses cookie. "Haven't you ever experienced magic in your life, Molly Rose?"

Perhaps. She felt it even now, with Jake. But she wasn't ready for this. She wasn't prepared for a connection with him that would alter her life. Maybe in a few years, but not now.

"Have you?" she shot back in an effort to avoid his question.

The possessive flash in his eyes told her what she already knew but was doing her best to ignore.

"We hardly know each other, Jake."

He grinned. "Ask me anything."

Reckless, she plowed ahead. "Have you ever been in love?"

"No. Have you?"

"No. Do you have any children?"

He chuckled. "No. Do you?"

She pursed her lips. "Of course not. I think I'd know if I did."

She set the coffee aside, not wanting a sour stomach before bedtime. "Have you ever been in prison?"

He paused. "Define prison."

She glared at him. "An incarceration for breaking the law."

He considered her words. "I guess you could say that's a yes although both times the charges were trumped up, so I didn't really deserve to be there."

She raised her eyebrows in expectation, waiting for an explanation.

"Oh, you want details." He prodded the fire with a stick, sending sparks upward in a flurry of chaos. "The first time was in Casablanca. I was seventeen and had purchased two camels that I planned to use to scout out local wool providers. My goal was to broker the wool for shipping to Europe, but I was soon arrested for camel theft. The man who'd sold the animals to me double-crossed me. I spent twelve days in jail until it was proven that I didn't steal them.

"The second time was a year later after I'd fled Shanghai to Vietnam. I was captured by the Chinese and accused of being a spy for the French. They were fighting at the time for control of an area called Tonkin."

"Were you?"

His attention swung back to her. "Was I what?"

"A spy."

"No, but I had befriended a few French officers and shared knowledge of shipping activities I was privy to."

Dear God. This man had nine lives. "How bad was your imprisonment?"

"Thankfully it didn't last long. China and France signed a peace protocol, and I was released just a few days later."

"What if that hadn't happened?"

"I might still be there, I suppose."

Firelight illuminated the sharp lines of his face, and she craved to touch him. "Were you afraid?"

"I'm always a little afraid, Molly. I'm just a man, imperfect and mundane." Amusement danced in his gaze as he repeated her words. "And I really want to kiss you."

The treetops swayed, a low rush of wind accompanying the spectacle. The horses snorted beyond in the dark as they grazed. Starlight flickered overhead, the heavens yet one more mystery in this world that Molly was so curious about, a mystery much like the man beside her.

"Yes," she replied, her voice barely audible.

He clasped her hand, pulling her to him as he moved forward to close the gap separating them. Before she had her bearings, his right hand cupped the side of her face, and his mouth—wearing the faintest hint of a smile—took hers decisively.

They fit perfectly as his lips molded to hers, and longing swept through her for everything his touch promised. The intense desire she sensed from him mixed with her own, shooting straight to her abdomen...and lower. She sank into him, tasting coffee and apples, and her free hand slipped under his arm and she grasped his shoulder, tugging him closer.

She turned more fully to him, and his arms encircled her, his hand bracing behind her head as he deepened the kiss. She opened herself to him, relieved to finally know him this way. She hadn't fully enjoyed the previous kiss in the tunnel and had done far too much imagining since—it was nearly driving her mad.

His mouth moved along her jawline and to her neck, and she tilted her head to give him better access. His hand came between them. He slipped it inside the flap of her coat, resting it just above her breasts. She kissed him in response, holding nothing back, and buried her fingers into his hair. He ran his palm lower and explored her, despite the clothing she wore.

Her breath hitched, and she pressed herself closer to him, aching to bring him atop her.

He resisted her. "Damn," he whispered against her mouth, "this is moving faster than I thought it would."

"I won't tell Robert." Her lips found his again.

He stopped and tilted his head down, resting his forehead to hers, his breath heavy. "As much as I'd like to make love to you, we shouldn't."

His words triggered visions of Pearl's audacious descriptions from the night before, but instead of trepidation, an odd surge of confidence filled her. Jake wanted her, and it made her feel bold.

She leaned forward to kiss him again. "I told you. I won't tell my brother. I won't tell anyone."

He released a strangled laugh and put a few inches of distance between them, just enough to look her in the eye. "Am I really that much of a cad?"

"No, of course not."

"But you're perfectly happy to let me seduce you and not tell a soul we've become lovers."

Molly tried to clear the fog from her head, a difficult task with all the newly-awakened desire coursing through her. "Yes," she replied, exasperated.

He withdrew. "No."

"What do you mean *no*?" She reached to yank him back, but he evaded her.

"I want you to be more certain."

"I am."

A shadow of doubt crossed his face.

Embarrassment engulfed her. "Is it because I'm so inexperienced?" she asked in a rush. "If you'll just tell me...how... well, how it works, I promise I'll try my best."

"No, that's not it. You're perfect just the way you are. You're absolutely the most beautiful woman I've ever seen."

The sincerity in his eyes and the raw truth in his voice galvanized her. How could a woman hold out against such a confession? She would strip her clothing away and give her body to him in a heartbeat. All he had to do was ask. For a brief, wild moment, she considered doing it anyway. She could seduce *him*. Couldn't she? A sliver of hesitation held her back.

"I want you to be sure, Molly. I don't want to steal your heart. I'd rather you gave it to me freely."

"Is this the enlightened heathen talking?" she asked, finally finding her voice.

"No. Just a sincere jackal."

She shook her head. "I'll bet you were much more fun when you were eighteen."

He flashed her a smile filled with his roguish charm. "You're eighteen. I know full well the recklessness in your blood."

"I'm no salt smuggler or French spy," she said, her tone cheeky.

"Never say never." He laced his fingers with hers and brought her hand to his mouth, brushing his lips across her knuckles.

The gesture left a shiver of wanting that spread from her sensitive breasts to her limbs, finally settling in the one place she'd hoped to keep Jake out—her heart.

# CHAPTER 14

J ake awoke with a start to the ashen haze of early morning. He rolled to his side and draped an arm around Molly's slumbering form. She was facing away from him, so he indulged nuzzling behind her ear. He settled against her, enjoying the feel of her soft backside and wondered at the irony of it all. This was the second night he'd spent with her, and, once again, he'd behaved like a gentleman.

It was very unlike him.

He could have had her. He knew full well how to woo a woman —what to say, where to caress and inflame, how to make her feel special with just a look.

And God knew he wanted her. For one frantic moment last night, he'd almost taken everything she offered and to hell with the consequences.

But she'd wanted to keep their relationship a secret.

Why the blazes did that bother him so much?

He had reined in his desire, determined to prove to her that he was more than a scamp, as she'd called him at Lannigan's party. And although they had ended up in his tent—despite that he'd pitched two—he'd restrained himself to the occasional kiss and simply snuggled with her to keep warm.

His hand rested on her hip, and he envisioned removing her clothing, baring her to him, and loving her until neither of them could remember where they were. He pushed away and sat upright.

It was too tempting to remain beside her.

Jake jammed his boots on and left the tent.

The sun wouldn't be visible for a few hours since they were in a valley surrounded by high mountain peaks. He tended the horses and the mule, then started a fire and set a fresh pot of coffee to boil.

Jake laid out his mining picks in various sizes, along with several shovels and a sledgehammer he'd acquired from a blacksmith, to decide which items to take with him. As he checked the sharpness of one of the picks, a muffled noise caught his attention. He cocked his head, expecting Molly to emerge from the tent, but was disappointed when she didn't appear.

That's when he saw them.

Two men, on foot, moving beyond in the distance, hugging the edge of the tree line. He didn't recognize them, but they had the look and demeanor of prospectors. They'd no doubt seen the smoke from his fire, but they moved away. For now. Jake would need to keep an eye out.

Molly crawled from the tent.

"Good morning," he said. "How did you sleep?"

"Better than I thought I would." She stood and arched her back into a stretch. He enjoyed the curves she managed to keep hidden beneath a jacket much of the time.

He shifted his gaze but still kept her within his range of vision.

"And you didn't snore," she added. "At least, not that I remember. I do recall dreaming about a terrible storm. I'm glad to see it's clear this morning. This mountain air is very refreshing to the lungs, isn't it?"

He suppressed a laugh. It wasn't her lungs he'd been thinking about.

He bridged the distance between them in two strides and kissed her. "You'd best eat something and dress for climbing. I'd like to head out as soon as we can."

She clasped his arm and held him to her, bringing her face close to his. "We could just crawl back into the tent and spend the day there."

"I can see you're going to be a huge distraction," he murmured against her lips.

"So says the biggest distraction I know."

He laughed, kissed her, then retreated a safe distance. "Get ready to do some prospecting."

She nodded, watching him.

He turned away before her languid countenance lulled him into a trance and cast a spell on him. Prospecting had never been so much fun.

---

THE CLIMB into the valley took the better part of the morning, and Molly found herself facing a fear of heights she'd never known she had. As the sun rose, so did the heat and both she and Jake abandoned their coats. With knapsacks on their backs and canteens hanging across their chests, Molly followed Jake up a steep, nearly-sheer incline. As Jake climbed, he pounded three separate anchors into the granite and looped the rope through them as a precautionary measure to catch them should they fall. He wound the rope around her waist and then her legs for added safety. Molly squinted and ducked every time Jake's pounding sent stones and dirt pelting down on her, even though the brim of her hat shielded her.

When they finally reached the top, Molly gratefully sat down to rest and consider what she'd just accomplished.

"Is all prospecting like this?" she asked, still winded.

Jake took a long swallow of water from a canteen, a sheen of sweat covering his face. "No. That's what makes the Chigger so special. No one prospects here."

"This is crazy, Jake. I'm not sure I can climb down."

"It'll be easier going back. I'll rig a pulley and let you down myself."

Molly took in the view, trying to calm her reservations. They were utterly alone, the expanse of mountains reaching to the horizon. Jake offered her bread and salted pork, and she gratefully ate, her muscles feeling shaky after the climb.

"You ready?" he asked.

She nodded and stood. He shouldered the rope he'd retrieved from their climb, along with the knapsack—his was much heavier, since it held a pick ax, a shovel, and a large hammer—and began down a makeshift path into the hidden valley. Molly took a fortifying breath and followed.

Thankfully this slope wasn't as steep, and they were able to pick their way down without the use of the rope. As they descended, Jake stopped periodically to scan the countryside with a scope he kept in his knapsack.

"Bullseye." He scrambled along a horizontal pathway, and Molly did her best to keep up.

When she finally reached him, he was stopped near a pile of rocks.

"Is this a marker?" she asked.

"Yeah." Jake removed all the gear draped upon him and immediately dropped to his knees to inspect under a flat ledge. "This was Robert's way of defining the boundaries of the Chigger."

"What are you looking for?" She set her pack on the ground and glanced around. They were located on the side of the mountain, about halfway into the narrow valley filled with a smattering of pine trees along with bare patches. Chunks of snow dotted the higher ground, and a narrow stream flowed on the valley floor.

"The vein."

Lying on his stomach, Jake tossed his hat aside and crawled on the ground, inspecting the rock as he went. Molly sank to her knees beside him.

"How can you tell if a claim is good or not?"

He pointed to an area with a shimmer. "Mineralized rock is usually a good sign. There's a fair amount of it here. I need to gather samples to take back to town. Then I'll move higher to see if I can trace the vein to its starting point."

"Is that all silver?" She indicated the horizontal layers he studied.

"Probably, and also quartz and galena."

"Is there any gold?"

"There can be, but the yield in the Creede area has been pretty low. What you really want is high-grade ore with silver. Lots of it."

Jake sat upright, so Molly did the same.

She leaned her head back to look upward. "This slope is awfully steep. Will you stake out more claims here?"

"Maybe one or two. After the samples are assayed, Robert and I can decide where to sink the first shaft." He pushed to his feet and scanned the area where they stood. "Although that's gonna be tough at this angle. We probably need tunnels."

"You're going to dig out a tunnel?" she asked, skeptical.

"Nah, that's what dynamite is for."

He reached a hand out to her. She clasped it, and he pulled her to her feet.

"That seems unsafe in a location like this," she said.

"Robert and I sell our claims before it gets to that step."

"So you'll do the same with this one, right?"

He bent over and scooped up his hat. "If this is as lucrative as it seems to appear, I might hang on for a bit. Selling out too early could cost thousands of dollars—if not tens of thousands."

It suddenly dawned on Molly the implication of what he was saying. "You mean to say that because I'm half owner of this claim, I could make a lot of money?"

A smile tugged at his mouth. "We'd need partners—investors— but yeah, this would solve your dilemma of finding the funds to travel to Europe. But I should probably tell you that Robert thinks this could be a vein that Lannigan has been searching for."

Surprised, Molly said, "The Bluebird?"

"You know the story?"

She nodded. "Won't it anger him that we might've found it?"

A wicked gleam sparked in his eyes. "I'm counting on it."

---

Twilight was upon them when they returned to camp. Jake had been right—going back down the cliff side had gone more quickly than the ascent although no less terrifying for Molly, but she swallowed down her protests and rallied on. She didn't want Jake to regret bringing her, or even worse, regret being her partner.

That she might have her own independent income tantalized her, giving her courage to let Jake lower her down with the rope tied around her.

Returning to the animals brought relief, but even stronger was a new-found confidence.

They dropped their gear, which was heavier now with ore samples, and Molly brushed off her hands. She stilled as two men approached, ragged and unkempt, with beards and floppy hats.

"Howdy," the one on the right said.

Jake stepped in front of her.

"We saw you both earlier," the man continued as he and his

buddy came to a stop. "Thought we'd come by to say hello. I'm Marcus and this is Jim."

"I'm Patrick," Jake said.

The lie put Molly's senses on alert, and she peeked around his shoulder, not wanting to be in the dark if trouble ensued.

"You two married?" Jim asked.

"Yes," Jake answered.

"Well, that's nice." Jim grinned. "Don't know many women that like doin' this. You both find anything?"

"Not today," Jake answered. "How about you?"

Marcus sighed. "We've been here before, but it's difficult. Most of the promising stuff seems to be up high. We brought more rope this time. Hopin' it might help. Well, just thought we should be introduced. How long you plan to stay?"

"A few days."

Marcus nodded, his eyes dropping to the gun at Jake's hip. "Well, if you need anything, let us know."

They waved and departed.

Jake turned to her. "Don't get too comfortable. They came here to scope us out. Maybe they even work for Lannigan or maybe they'll just try to steal from us. Or worse."

"What would be worse?"

"They may try to steal you."

"That's ridiculous," she replied. "Who does such a thing?"

Jake retrieved a bag of oats and headed toward the horses. "You'd be surprised what a man will do, sometimes for no other reason than he can."

Molly focused her attention on the men who were now moving specks in the distance. Exhausted, she had hoped to rest a bit before making supper, but her fatigue was of little concern now.

JAKE BROUGHT the animals closer to camp and picketed them. Their agitation would be a sign if anything came near—predator or prospector. He considered what he'd pocketed earlier while scouting for the apex to the Chigger. It was a game-changer, and he wasn't keen on their new friends, Marcus and Jim, making their way into the valley and snooping around.

He hadn't told Molly about the new claim he'd staked above the Chigger. Her energy had been flagging and she'd let him scale the higher areas alone.

As they ate a supper of more salted pork with boiled potatoes, his discovery was on the tip of his tongue, but something held him back. Molly looked dead tired.

Jake had told Robert he would place any new claims in Molly's name, and he understood that, in essence, he was partnering with Robert and not her. Still, if what he'd found played out, there would be much money involved. And that changed people, not always for the better. Robert had brought Molly into the fray, but Jake sensed it was an act of desperation and not a well thought-out action. Things could get messy.

After being burned by Lannigan's theft of the Shanghai, Jake felt the need to examine this new turn of events before proceeding recklessly forward. Glancing at Molly, her face aglow from the firelight, an ache in Jake's chest twisted deep inside. The more time he spent with her, the more the strange wanting grew. While it was filled with a hungry, carnal need, there was more to it than that.

He'd never really understood the underlying sentiment of Rumi's work, that a beloved existed as the perfect complement to another's soul. A part of him itched to run. He didn't need this kind of attachment, this potential heartbreak. When his folks died and he lived in the orphanage, he'd learned to ignore the pain of abandonment, the grief of losing a touchstone in life.

Molly disturbed that wound.

And it scared the hell out of him.

At the same time, he wanted nothing more than to wrap himself around her and let her soothe the anguish, but if he got close to the flame he danced around like a moth—let himself bask in its heat—would he be able to survive without it?

"Are there many bears here?" Molly asked.

"Some," he answered, grateful for the idle chitchat, "although not any attacks that I've heard of. They're just as cautious of you as you are of them."

"Are we going back to the Chigger tomorrow? We have a lot of samples already."

"Maybe I'll climb back up early and do additional scouting. You can stay here." He wanted to examine more of the terrain around the new claim to make certain he'd staked the best area.

She nodded.

Concern about Marcus and Jim crossed his mind again. "Make sure you keep that Colt I gave you handy. You look about ready to sleep sitting up. I'll clean up. Go to bed, Molly."

Her gaze met his. In her weary state, she didn't hide the raw longing in her eyes, bringing him to full awareness.

"Can I stay in your tent again?" Her husky voice kicked his heartrate up a notch.

Anticipation heated his body. "Yes." He added a slight smile to let her know how much he cared. It mattered to him, that she know. It mattered a lot.

She crawled into the confines of the shelter, and he stoked the fire while waiting for the raging desire in his body to burn down so he could bank those coals. He couldn't lie beside her until he had himself under control.

Sucking in air, he scrubbed a hand through his hair, seeking a peace that was proving damn elusive these days.

He wanted her.

But he wouldn't take her. Not yet.

Not until he was sure—of her. But mostly, of himself.

MOLLY AWOKE WITH A START. The quiet darkness enveloped her as the fog of sleep slowly cleared.

Where was Jake?

She sat up and scooted to the tent flap.

The fire had died down. Jake was nowhere in sight.

A shiver of fear ran down her spine. She grabbed her heavy coat and shoved her feet into her boots, then grabbed the Colt Lightning from her gear.

Leaving the tent, she slowly walked the perimeter of their camp, careful not to trip in the dark. The animals acknowledged her then returned to sleeping.

Jake was gone.

Had something alerted him?

Or worse, was he in trouble?

She needed to find him.

JAKE CREPT upon the camp of the two prospectors.

He'd been unable to sleep. The implications of the new claim he'd located wouldn't stop swirling in his head like a swarm of bees. Added to it was the relenting need for Molly Rose. Staying outside the tent hadn't doused that fire in any timely fashion, so he'd grabbed his Winchester and disappeared into the night, looking to work off the anxious buzz in his blood.

As his senses became attuned to the darkness, his muscles flexed and stretched. Sometimes The Jackal simply needed to move before he gnawed off his own leg in frustration.

Nothing but a smoky plume emanated from the prospector's fire, and two dark figures slept beside it, wrapped in blankets. A soft snore echoed. Three mules stood vigil nearby, so far unaware of Jake's presence.

Nothing out of the ordinary.

He waited in a natural depression in the ground.

He stilled at a slight rustling sound behind him, but silently exhaled when he saw the cause.

*Molly.*

Hunched over, she crept to the left of him, about ten yards away. Suddenly, she tripped and fell and released a soft cry. He quickly moved to her and placed a hand over her mouth, but when he saw what she'd fallen against, laying in a ditch, he froze.

A body.

Molly squirmed against him and gasped. "What is that?" she whispered.

Jake hooked an arm around her waist and hauled her back, then leaned forward to check the man. He had a bad feeling when he saw the shirt peeking from beneath the dirt that had been tossed over him and a hand that was partially visible.

He dug handfuls of soil away from the head, his heart sinking when he could see the face more clearly.

*Pedro.*

He glanced around then grabbed Molly's arm and dragged her to stand.

He pressed his lips to her ear. "We need to go."

They moved quickly over the uneven terrain, their breaths expelling in white puffs from the cold air. Once they reached their camp, Jake immediately pulled all the blankets and bedrolls from his tent and started dismantling it.

"We're leaving now?" Molly whispered.

"I think it would be wise, don't you?"

"Did they kill that man?"

She hadn't recognized Pedro. Better that she didn't know. He nodded. "It would appear so. I don't think we should wait around until morning to figure it all out."

She agreed and helped him pack. In short order, he saddled the horses and secured all the gear. Soon they were picking their way out of the valley, the dark night making travel slow.

Jake couldn't shake the fact that Pedro's presence in this area—and his unfortunate death—had something to do with the Chigger and the new claim Jake had staked.

He thought of the float he'd found earlier that day while he'd been scouting alone above the Chigger. It was safely tucked into his coat pocket. The shiny gold nugget hinted at the possibility of a vein rich and thick. He'd staked a new claim, but who knew what lay deeper once the discovery samples were gathered and an exploratory shaft sunk. Once word got out, men wild with mining fever would descend like vultures.

It would appear the boundaries were already being positioned, and violence had become an immediate fallback position.

The need to shield Molly from the ensuing battle compelled him to get her off this mountain and back to the Krupin's—and to Creede—as soon as possible.

# CHAPTER 15

As they rode through the night, Molly struggled to remain awake. She sagged in relief when they finally approached Ivan and Pearl's place, amid the chirping and warbling of birds as the expanding sunshine warmed the landscape and brought the earth to life once again.

Had those two prospectors killed that man?

She shuddered, and a thick fear twisted in her belly.

Did this have something to do with the Chigger?

As they stopped in front of the cabin, Ivan came on the porch, securing suspenders onto his shoulders.

"You're back sooner than expected." Ivan squinted his one good eye.

"Change of plans." Jake dismounted.

He came to Molly and helped her from Cinnamon. She leaned into him, craving his strength.

"You look tuckered out," Ivan said. "Did you ride all night?"

"Just about." Jake held Molly's hand as he led her toward the cabin.

She limped slightly, her ankle bothering her. She must have

twisted it during the night when she'd all but fallen over the dead body.

"Are you hurt?" Jake asked.

She gave a shake of her head. "It's nothing."

"Come on inside." Ivan opened the door.

The aroma of fried eggs and ham smelled heavenly. Molly smiled gratefully at Pearl standing near the stove as she hobbled to a chair, only then releasing Jake's hand.

"Ivan, I need to talk to you," Jake said.

Would he tell the older man about the body they'd found? An ominous feeling settled over her. She hoped Jake wouldn't do something foolhardy.

Once the men had stepped outside, Pearl pinned Molly with a concerned glare. "What happened?"

Molly debated what to say, but her mind, waning from fatigue, couldn't muster up a good excuse. "We found a dead body."

Shock crossed Pearl's face. "Where?"

"In a ravine about fifteen miles north. That's why we left during the night."

Pearl wiped her hands on her apron. "You did the right thing."

"I'm afraid of what Jake might do now."

"You think he'll go back?"

Molly nodded.

The door opened and Ivan stepped inside.

Pearl leveled a gaze at him. "You aren't going with him, are you?"

Ivan silently agreed.

"Why don't we go back to Creede and get the Marshal?" Molly cut in.

"There's no time," Ivan said, then looked at Pearl. "Get some supplies together. Jake is winnowing his down so all he needs is Fernando. Molly will stay here."

"But—"

"Pearl," he said, cutting Molly off, "you know about the safe place. You might consider the two of you going there. These men may get past us and end up down here. I want you both out of harm's way."

Pearl remained silent.

"Maybe you two should head down to Creede now," he added.

"You know I won't do that," Pearl replied.

He sighed. "I know."

Molly limped to the door, and Ivan moved aside so she could go outside. Jake stood near Fernando, securing his gear, his hat shielding his face. Cinnamon and the mule were gone, already in the corral.

She stepped off the porch. "Why are you going back?"

He checked his rifle then slid it into the scabbard hanging from the saddle. "I'm curious."

"Why didn't you check it out last night?"

"I didn't want you there." He secured his saddlebag as Fernando ate oats from a bucket Jake had placed before the animal.

"What if I told you not to go?"

Jake finally settled his attention on her. He approached, moving with a confidence and subtle swagger that made her pulse race. Her thoughts veered, as they often did of late, to what it would be like to be with him, his naked body pressed against hers, his lips planting heated kisses upon her skin, his hands... She wasn't sure if she should be upset that he hadn't made love to her or glad that he'd showed restraint.

As he stood before her, his eyes shone with amusement.

"You think this is funny?" Try as she might, she couldn't keep the accusation—or panic—from her voice.

"Are you worried about me?"

"You worry about me. Isn't that what partners do?"

He stood very close now, his broad shoulders casting a shadow over her, blocking the world beyond. What if something happened to him? He'd certainly had near misses before. She held herself steady as a rush of desperation gripped her.

*Don't go.*

She shoved the plea down before she spoke it aloud, aware that her extreme uneasiness over his welfare might, in the end, scare him away. Letting her gaze slide from his, lest she drown in his deep mahogany eyes, she took a fortifying breath, striving to get herself under control.

She lifted her eyes, fixating on his collarbone. His shirt was open at the neck, revealing tanned skin and a bit of dark chest hair. She wanted to touch him.

*Blast it.*

Clasping her hand behind his neck, she pulled him to her and kissed him, hard and direct.

His response was immediate. His arms wrapped around her, bringing her flush against his body as his lips sank onto hers. She responded to his hunger with her own, the kiss deepening and her inhibitions flying away on the breeze.

Jake tore his mouth from hers. His hot breath against her cheek sent shivers of pleasure through her. "You're really determined, aren't you?"

"What do you mean?" She rubbed her nose across the stubble on his cheeks, enjoying the sensation and the intimacy.

"To drive me mad."

She smiled, pleased down to her toes that he found her so compelling.

The door opened behind them, and Jake released his grip on her.

Ivan cleared his throat. "Not sure now is the time, you two."

Reluctantly, Molly stepped back, embarrassed that Ivan had seen them. Jake grabbed her hand, keeping her close.

"You gotta take it when you can get it," Jake said.

"True," Ivan replied. "Pearl, come here, woman."

Pearl's voice drifted from inside. "Oh, no you don't."

Ivan entered the cabin and shut the door.

"You've got the Colt," Jake said, his possessive gaze warming her. "Keep it close. Stay inside and don't let anyone in. We won't be long, maybe a day. If we don't return by then, take Pearl back to Creede. And don't stay with Lannigan."

Molly frowned. "So many instructions. Are you always this bossy?"

"Only with you." He leaned down and kissed her softly. His hand slid down her spine, and he indulged a pat on her backside, eliciting a muffled response from her.

"Be careful," she breathed against his mouth.

He broke their contact and adjusted his hat, a gleam in his eyes. "I've been in worse situations."

"Just because you're called The Jackal doesn't mean you can rest on your laurels."

He grinned. "Maybe you can rest on them?"

She gave him a playful shove.

He climbed atop Fernando. "Come on, Ivan," he yelled.

Ivan's horse stood saddled and ready beside Jake. The old man exited the cabin, plopping his hat atop his head. He nodded to Molly as he passed by. "Don't hesitate to shoot any scalawags." He mounted his horse.

"Just don't shoot *us*." Jake gave her one last look, his gaze dark and compelling, then turned Fernando and headed back up the trail the two of them had so recently descended.

Ivan shook his head. "I ain't no scalawag, but I can't speak for The Jackal."

And then they were gone.

Pearl came onto the porch. Molly wrapped her arms across her mid-section, hugging herself. In silence they watched the two men disappear into the wilderness.

"WATCH YOUR STEP," Pearl said over her shoulder, dusk rapidly approaching.

Molly followed the woman down a pathway that led them a quarter mile from her and Ivan's cabin. A gust of wind slammed into the pine trees above, and Molly braced against it, then resumed the slow and steady climb. She winced as a twinge of pain shot through her ankle.

Agitated sounds from the animals drifted to them from the shed, along with relentless barking from Grom, who was locked in the cabin. None of them were happy with the impending storm. Neither was Molly. Hopefully Jake and Ivan had found a place to hunker down.

Pearl insisted they retreat to a hideout. Molly agreed, but now she wondered if this was such a good idea as they trudged farther away from the cabin.

Pearl carried a knapsack filled with food along with an old rifle. Molly had her Colt and several blankets in hand.

The trail became steeper, and Molly focused on keeping up with the surprisingly agile older woman. As they neared a precipice, a rope hung down with loops fashioned for feet. Pearl shouldered the rifle and ascended like a monkey, then leaned over and motioned for Molly to hand her the blankets, which she did. Molly grasped the makeshift ladder and awkwardly struggled to pull herself up, her arms straining. At last she crawled onto the ledge, trying to catch her breath, and lay on her stomach.

"Almost there," Pearl said.

Molly stood and froze, staring into the mouth of a dark tunnel. Pearl waved at her to enter. Molly's chest squeezed, her heart doubled its beating, and the urge to run consumed her.

"*This* is your safe place?" she uttered past the tightness in her throat. It was a mining tunnel, shored up with hole-filled timber, which hardly seemed safe to her.

Pearl came back out. "What's wrong?"

The wind blew more strongly now, the storm lashing around them.

"I can't go in there."

Pearl came to her, worry pinching her face. "It's secure. Ivan and I found it not long after we got here. There's no viable ore, but the tunnels are reinforced, and Ivan has done some work on it."

"I'll just stay out here."

"In this storm?"

"Why can't we remain in the cabin? I'm sure it would be fine there."

Pearl's shoulders sagged. "I said as much to Ivan, but he insisted we come here. I'll go in and make sure it's clear."

Pearl disappeared. Molly sank to the rocky escarpment and brought her knees to her chest, making herself into a tight ball as if she were once again a child trying to hide. Tendrils of hair whipped against her face as she rocked back and forth, attempting to ignore the swell of panic building in her body. A rumble of thunder rolled across the now-darkened sky, heavy gray clouds threatening to unleash onto the land at any moment.

She jerked at a bolt of lightning.

*I can't stay out here.*

She gritted her teeth and stood again, retrieved the blankets, clutched them to her chest, and gripped the Colt in her right hand. She'd managed to avoid places like this during the years after the well incident and had begun to believe that she was cured of her fright, but after the incident in Pedro's tunnel, it was glaringly obvious that she wasn't. If she'd never come to Creede, she could possibly have lived the remainder of her life without ever feeling this terror again.

*But then I wouldn't have met Jake.*

She forced herself to move toward the entrance.

Another bolt of lightning split the sky. She shrieked and jumped.

Closing her eyes, she entered the tunnel, battling every ounce of strength in her muscles that wanted to turn and run far, far away.

Once inside, the rush of the storm subsided. She gasped for breath and opened her eyes. The flicker of a light was visible beyond. Taking very small steps, Molly moved toward it. She glanced back to the entrance. They wouldn't need to go far into the tunnel to get out of the worst of the squall. She hoped Pearl would agree with her.

The tempest beyond was in full force now, its fury present at the tunnel entrance with debris flying past in violent gusts.

*Calm down. Deep breaths.*

A sudden upwelling of frustration consumed her. Fed up with herself and this damn fear, she threw her shoulders back and continued deeper into the inky depths, ignoring a wave of queasiness. She sought to focus amid her scattered thoughts, as unmoored as the bushes and branches being yanked from the surroundings by the storm.

A scuffle echoed from deeper in the tunnel, accompanied by a whimper that sounded like Pearl.

Alarm filled Molly.

She moved forward, her only thought to help Pearl. The woman could have fallen, could be hurt...

As she rounded the turn, she stopped, startled. There was a man in the dim light with a long, unkempt beard and a wild look in his eyes standing over Pearl who lay unmoving, face up, at his feet.

He pointed his pistol at Molly. "Drop it," he instructed.

Molly hesitated.

"Go on, now," he added.

Bending down, she released the Colt to the ground.

She didn't recognize him, but he had the look of many of the men in Creede who prospected—rumpled clothing that smelled of long-term use and a wary gaze filled with just a dose of madness.

Standing once again, Molly asked, her voice tight, "Who are you?"

"That don't matter. You two don't belong here."

"Neither do you." She glanced down at Pearl. "Did you hurt her?"

"Not on purpose." He waved his gun a bit. "Sit down."

Molly squatted and rested her backside on the uneven, rock-strewn floor. She organized her skirt and petticoat over her bent knees and smoothed her sweaty palms along the material. She searched for any sign of life in Pearl. Was she breathing?

Pearl's chest rose and fell slightly.

Molly released a sigh of relief.

Pearl was alive, for now. It gave her hope. She turned her attention to the man pointing a gun at her. "Are you a prospector? Because I think the Krupin's have this claim, so that would make you a thief."

"Just because they say they have the claim don't mean they do."

Molly tried a new tactic. "You should let us go."

He didn't respond.

"Let me take her out of here, and then you can leave." Her nerves were stretched mighty thin.

Pearl moved. The man stepped away from her, his weapon still fixed on the both of them.

"Can I please look at her?" Molly pleaded.

He hesitated then relented with a nod.

From the corner of her eye, Molly located the Colt lying on the ground where she'd put it. Could she grab it and shoot before he did? Not likely.

She crawled over to Pearl and gently touched the woman's face. Pearl's eyelids fluttered, a welt beginning to form on her forehead.

"Pearl, are you all right?"

The woman opened her eyes and stared at the man watching them.

"Can you sit?" Molly asked.

Pearl nodded and Molly aided her.

"Nine Toes Bishop, what on earth are you doing here?" Pearl admonished.

He circled until he could see them head on.

Pearl touched the welt on her forehead and grimaced. "Are you in trouble, or are you just convinced there's gold in here?"

"Is there?" he asked, his tone almost accusatory.

"Have you looked around?" Pearl's face pinched with disgust. "This claim turned out to be a dead end. Are you another fool searching for the Bluebird?"

"And what do you know of it?"

"This claim surely isn't it." Pearl gestured to Molly to release her.

"What about somewhere else?" he asked.

"My husband has been searching for well over two years and has never found nothing of such riches as the Bluebird is purported to be. I'm sorry to disappoint you. I must ask that you leave here though. This is my claim."

"Not if you ain't worked it in the last year, and I'm thinkin' you haven't, so you got no grounds to kick me out."

"Then let us leave and you can stay," Pearl said.

Unease snaked down Molly's spine. What if it hadn't been Marcus and Jim who had killed the man she had found last night? What if *this* man was the real culprit?

"Are you here alone?" Molly asked.

"I came with Pedro, but he done disappeared."

Molly frowned. "Do you mean Pedro Elizondo?"

The man watched her, distrust in his gaze. "Yep."

Was Pedro the dead man she'd found? She genuinely hoped not. While she hadn't known the man for long, she certainly never wished for him to be murdered and buried haphazardly in the wilderness.

Mister Bishop grunted and pressed a hand to his side then stood straight again.

Molly caught a glimpse of red on the fabric of his ivory shirt. "Are you hurt?"

Without warning, he sank to his knees and keeled over. For a long moment, neither she nor Pearl moved.

"Has he gone to meet his Maker?" Pearl finally asked.

Molly guardedly approached and poked at him. When he remained unresponsive, she carefully removed the weapon from his fingers then felt for a pulse. "He's alive."

She nudged him to his back. Blood seeped through his clothing near his left hip. She tugged the fabric away.

"Was he shot?" Pearl asked.

"Looks that way. What should we do?"

Pearl cursed under her breath. "I guess we can't leave him here. And if we stay overnight, he might die if we don't clean his wound."

"But what if he's the one who killed Pedro?"

Pearl's eyes locked with Molly's. "You think that man you found *is* Pedro?"

"It could be. Maybe Pedro shot Mister Bishop during an argument."

Pushing away from the wall, Pearl came to Nine Toes's inert form. "Well, hell," she muttered. "Pack his weapon away. We'll have to drag him out of here ourselves."

# CHAPTER 16

J ake brought Fernando to a halt in a copse of pine trees, grateful to find some relief from the storm.

Ivan pulled his horse beside Jake's. "We best stay here and wait this out. No sense being struck by lightning."

"Agreed." Rivulets of water rained down from the brim of Jake's hat. He dismounted and searched for the most covered area he could find, giving a shake to his rain slicker to stop it from clinging to his clothes.

Ivan grabbed food from his saddlebags, and the two hunkered down, using a tree trunk as a bench.

"What do you think Pedro was doing to get himself killed?" Jake asked.

Ivan chewed on a piece of dried meat. "I'd bet there were at least a half dozen men who had a dispute with him. I can't say I'm surprised it didn't end well. You reap what you sow." Ivan puffed his chest then sighed. "He was determined to find the Bluebird, but then, who among us isn't."

"Do you think he found it?"

Ivan shrugged but watched Jake with his good eye. "I've a feeling you've got some secrets yourself."

Jake looked down at the chunk of Pearl's homemade bread in his hand and hunched his shoulders to shield it from the rain.

"Just promise me something," Ivan said.

Jake flicked his gaze to the prospector pirate's intense scrutiny as droplets pelted them.

Ivan leaned forward. "If it comes to it, you'll let it go."

Jake understood what he was saying—that no amount of riches was worth risking one's life—but a part of him knew that if he was close, it would be difficult to back away. The heady sensation of seeking the unknown was only tempered by finding, at long last, the treasure. It was a game that Jake had played many times before, and he couldn't deny he liked the challenge.

"Could you, Ivan?"

The man muttered an obscenity under his breath and shook his head.

"That's what I thought."

MOLLY GRUNTED as she lowered Nine Toes Bishop's unconscious body over the ledge with the aid of the rope.

"I've got him!" Pearl's voice echoed from below.

Having anchored her footing from inside the tunnel, Molly was immediately drenched by the downpour as she stepped from the confines of the shaft, peripherally aware that her attention was no longer on her fear of dark, confined places. Having a distraction clearly helped. Perhaps she'd found a cure to her panic.

Slowly, she climbed down the ladder, careful not to entangle the rope still fastened around her waist. When she reached Pearl, the woman already had Nine Toes' right arm over her shoulders. Molly braced herself on the opposite side, and together they carried him down the pathway, his legs dragging in the wet, muddy ground. The ache in her ankle was barely perceptible.

Twice they stopped to catch their breath then continued on. Neither spoke; Molly didn't have the energy for it. Together they pushed forward with one goal in mind—to get to the cabin as quickly as possible.

When finally the homestead appeared, Molly willed herself to finish the trek and not drop Mister Bishop right where they stood. He did, after all, strike Pearl down and hold them at gunpoint. Was he worth all this effort? And was dragging him through the mud and rain the best course of action, considering his wound?

Muffled barking from Grom greeted them as they came to the porch, and Mister Bishop stirred, sputtering and mumbling incoherently. He slipped from Molly's grasp and fell onto the wooden planks.

"Get up, Nine Toes," Pearl demanded. "We're almost there."

With one final push of effort, Molly and Pearl hauled him to the door. As soon as Pearl opened it, Grom burst forward, yipping and jumping on them. Molly put her free arm out to push the animal back.

Once inside, Pearl grabbed a chair and released her side of Nine Toes. He sank against the seat, but Molly stayed near so he wouldn't fall.

"Let me strip the bed and put a blanket down," Pearl said and hastily did just that.

Grom whined excitedly, trying to lick Molly's face as she leaned over, water dripping from her face and clothing. Rain continued pounding the roof in what sounded like a cacophony of gunfire.

Pearl returned, and they both heaved Nine Toes' dead weight from the chair and dragged him to the bed.

"We've got to remove these wet clothes," Pearl said. "Don't want him catching a chill."

Together she and Pearl pulled the shirt over the man's head, removed his boots, then trousers. Beneath his long underwear, which was soaked as well, there was a bright, red stain on his left side.

Pearl sighed. "It's all gotta come off."

Molly readied herself and nodded. While the thought of undressing Jake down to bare skin held great appeal to her, she had no desire to see Nine Toes Bishop in his birthday suit.

Pearl grabbed an additional blanket. As they peeled the wet cotton material down his arms and still lower, Molly squinted so as to not see anything. Pearl quickly laid the blanket over Nine Toes' private parts as Molly jumped to the foot of the bed and pulled the garment past his feet. She dropped the garb to the floor, and Pearl inspected the wound on Nine Toes' side.

"Don't look like the bullet is still in there," she said. "Probably grazed him. Get me some water and the carbolic acid in the sideboard. Should be needle and thread there also."

Molly grabbed the items along with fresh rags. As the older woman cleaned and stitched the wound, Molly built a fire in the stove. Grom grudgingly settled on the floor, watching every move Molly made, wagging his tail with a loud thwap each time she stepped near him.

Pearl wrapped the wound then covered Nine Toes with more blankets from neck to feet.

"Get changed out of those wet clothes, Molly. I can't have you catching your death either."

Pearl was right. Just before Molly got the fire lit, her hands had stopped functioning as they should. It had been troublesome, to say the least. Molly had been amazed that Pearl had the faculties to thread the needle and close Nine Toes' wound.

She and Pearl stripped out of their blouses and skirts, not quite as heavy with water as when they'd first entered the cabin, and donned dry clothing. Weary, they both collapsed into a chair at the kitchen table, finally able to rest.

A purple welt had formed above Pearl's left eye.

"Are you all right?" Molly asked, indicating the spot where Nine Toes had obviously hit Pearl with the butt of his gun.

Pearl's shoulders sagged. "I'll live."

"Do you think he will?" Molly glanced at Nine Toes' inert body, the chest barely rising and falling.

Pearl scowled, watching her patient. "After all this trouble, he'd better."

"Do you think he killed Pedro?"

"If he did, at least we know that Jake and Ivan aren't in danger."

But Pearl's explanation didn't ease Molly's anxiety. What about the two prospectors—Marcus and Jim—that she and Jake had seen? What if they had done it, as Jake suspected all along?

Her gaze landed on Nine Toes. As soon as he awoke, she'd ask him exactly what had happened because she was uncertain how long she could remain in the cabin, worrying and wondering about Jake and Ivan. She suppressed the urge to follow after them... for now.

---

JAKE WOKE BEFORE DAWN, stiff from his bed of damp pine needles. He and Ivan had been forced to bed down in the swath of forest where they'd taken refuge from the storm. Thankfully, the rain had stopped although thick, heavy clouds continued to hug the sky.

Ivan groaned. "I'm gettin' too old for this."

"Maybe you should start prospecting down in the Arizona Territory."

Ivan chuckled. "I s'pose, but maybe it's you who should think about that. You've got yourself a good reason to head south."

A smile tugged at Jake's mouth. Could he give up the Bluebird and all the possibilities it offered for a woman? Couldn't he somehow have it all?

Frustration flared, then retreated just as quickly. If he tied himself to Molly Rose, would he regret it? At the same time, letting her go caused a flutter of confusion in his chest. Damn. Life would be much simpler if he'd never laid eyes on her.

He and Ivan didn't dawdle and were soon headed to the site of the body. Skirting the last location of Marcus and Jim, Jake spied no sign of their camp although an inspection showed the washed out remains of a fire pit. Jake guided Fernando to the dip in the ground where Molly had found Pedro. It should be easy to find the body. The rain had likely exposed it, but when he got to the area, nothing was visible.

Dismounting, Jake dropped Fernando's reins to the ground and walked back and forth in a grid pattern, kicking rocks and possible indentations, searching for a head or hand or foot.

Nothing.

Pacing nearby, Ivan glanced up from his search. "You sure this is the right spot?"

Jake nodded slowly. The burial spot did have a deeper depression than what would be normal, and the grass had been disturbed making him certain this was the location. He returned to his horse and grabbed a shovel then proceeded to dig in several places.

Still nothing.

Jake paused, scanning the area.

"Should I worry that you're losing your mind?" Ivan asked.

"Maybe I have. Or maybe those two prospectors dug up the body and took it with them."

"Why on earth would they do that?"

Jake wiped sweat from his face with the back of his sleeve. "So they wouldn't get caught for murder."

IT WAS early afternoon when Molly wiped Nine Toes' face with a wet cloth, and his eyes opened.

"How are you feeling?" she asked.

"Like dynamite exploded inside me." He grunted and tried to move. Molly pushed him back down.

The sound of horses approaching the house drew her attention. A glance to Pearl in the kitchen confirmed what they both thought. Molly went to the front door and opened it as Jake and Ivan swung down from their horses.

She ran to Jake, threw her arms around his shoulders and kissed him.

He grinned against her mouth. "I missed you too, Chigger."

She kissed him again, not caring about such a blatant display in front of Ivan and Pearl. When she finally slid away from Jake, he kept an arm anchored at her waist.

"Why don't I get a greeting like that?" Ivan grumbled to his wife.

"We've got a problem," Pearl replied, ignoring the question. She planted hands on her hips. "Nine Toes Bishop is inside. He was shot."

"What the hell happened to you?" Ivan asked, moving quickly to Pearl's side and touching her forehead. The welt had darkened to a deep purple and had bled under the skin, beginning to migrate around her eye.

"It was in the tunnel you told us to go to," Molly said. "Nine Toes was there and he struck Pearl, and then he collapsed. We had to drag him back here." She tilted her head to look at Jake. "He said he'd been in the area with Pedro. Did you find the body? It was Pedro, wasn't it?"

"Yeah," Jake replied, "but we didn't find anything. The body'd been moved. What did Nine Toes say?"

"He's just awoken." Pearl slipped into Ivan's arms. "I'm glad you've returned. We'd best talk to him. He's been feverish. There's no tellin' which way this could go."

Ivan nodded. "We'll get the horses settled and be right in."

Jake dropped another kiss on Molly's mouth, released her and led Fernando to the shed. Although dazed by the brief encounter, she was heartily glad to see him. How had she become so attached in such a short time?

---

"IS PEDRO REALLY DEAD?" Nine Toes rasped, weakened from his wound, barely able to lift his head from the pillow.

"I'd say so," Jake replied, arms crossed across his chest as he stood at the foot of the bed where Bishop lay. While he didn't know Nine Toes well, of late the man had been seen in the company of Pedro. "Did you shoot him?"

"No. I'm shot myself." Anger strained the wounded man's ashen face, his scraggly beard covering his neck.

"Tell me what happened."

"We was in the valley up north of here. We had an argument with two other prospectors about territory, and it turned ugly. I ran, but it's difficult, you know, with my rheumatism and losing a toe to the gout. I assumed Pedro was right behind me, but I never saw him after that." He paused to clear his throat, which caused him to wince in pain. "I found that old tunnel near here and hid out. That's when Pearl and Molly found me."

"Why'd you hit her?" Ivan bellowed.

Jake suppressed a wave of desperate rage. "And you held a gun on the women." When Molly told him what had happened, icy tendrils of terror had gripped his gut.

Nine Toes swallowed reflexively and gestured at the women who hovered nearby. "How'd I know they weren't with those men?"

"Why would Marcus and Jim bury Pedro, then dig him up?" Ivan asked.

"I dunno."

Jake pinned him with a hard stare. "What are you and Pedro doing around here?" With all the recent activity, it would only be a matter of time before one of these prospectors discovered the area surrounding the Chigger and the other two claims Jake planned to file. He didn't have much time.

Nine Toes sighed. "Prospectin'. What else?"

"He's lookin' for the Bluebird," Pearl said.

"There's no crime in that," Nine Toes defended, eyes bulging.

"But there *has* been a crime." Jake lifted his hat and ran a frustrated hand through his hair. "Pedro is dead."

"Maybe his partner killed him."

Jake frowned. Pedro worked alone. The fact that he'd been spending time with Nine Toes lately had been odd. "Who's his partner?"

"Some fella named Charlie."

"Have you met this Charlie?" Ivan asked.

"Nope. But Pedro was gonna cut me in, depending on what we found."

*Well, doesn't that make me feel like a selfish ass.* Jake glanced at Molly, standing off to his left. When she'd rushed into his arms upon his and Ivan's return, the sensation of rightness, of coming home to a place where he finally belonged, had sliced right through him. The thought of always having Molly Rose to greet him at the end of the day, to wrap her arms around him and kiss him with that special light in her eyes that she'd bestowed on him, called to him more deeply than he could've imagined. But in light of the violence occurring, he wouldn't risk her safety, and putting her name on those claims would do just that. He needed to stay the course and move forward with his original plan.

Pounding on the door startled all of them.
Pearl opened it. Robert stared back at them.

# CHAPTER 17

"You sure about Pedro?" Robert watched the horses in the tiny corral as he and Jake stood side by side, the sun sliding toward the western edge of the mountains.

"As near as I can be."

"The prospectors you ran into were called Marcus and Jim?"

Jake nodded. "You know 'em?"

"Of a sort. I heard talk that Winston had grubstaked a couple men. It might be them."

Jake considered the possibility. "Why in the hell would he do that? He's as bound to Lannigan as you are."

"I'm guessing for the same reason I didn't put the Chigger in my name. He's trying to keep his interests separate."

"Lannigan will never take this lying down."

Robert turned to him. "You think he had Pedro killed?"

"Marcus and Jim may have done it, but maybe someone else was behind it."

"Did you find the Chigger?"

"Yep. It looks good. I've got samples to take back to town."

"You find anything else?"

"I staked a claim higher up." A lie felt better if it was couched with a bit of truth. Jake had learned that during his smuggling days.

"You want me to go to the claims office with you?" Robert's tone was light, but Jake didn't miss the edge.

Jake played along. "If you like."

Robert watched him. "I think I'll go into that valley tomorrow."

"Not alone. In case you haven't noticed, it's not very safe around here."

"Fine." Robert exhaled then laughed. "Everybody's on edge these days."

"Even you?" Jake watched him out of the corner of his eye. "How's Bridget?"

Robert shook his head, resting his arms on the railing. "We had a fight. I'd say we're about done."

"You all right with that?"

Robert hung his head. "Hell no." He muttered under his breath. "I got it bad."

Jake clapped Robert on the shoulder. The same predicament had snagged him as well, but there was no reason to voice it aloud. He knew what he'd have to do to make all of this right at the end of the day, both with the Chigger—which was possibly the sought-after Bluebird lode—and with Molly. But over the years, he'd seen more than his share of plans go up in smoke. There was no guarantee of success. All of it could easily slip through his fingers.

He itched to drag Molly to the shed and enjoy everything she offered before she found a reason to spurn him, but that would make him a self-centered cad, and he was trying like hell to be the good guy in all this.

Changing the subject from their love lives, Jake said, "Let's go check out that tunnel where Nine Toes was hiding out."

"Why?"

"Just curious about something."

Molly sat at the kitchen table, writing in her journal, while Pearl mended a shirt. Grom was at her feet, and Nine Toes slept fitfully in the bed. Ivan, Jake and Robert had gone back to the tunnel where they'd found Nine Toes.

Molly paused her pencil over the parchment at the sound of a horse approaching. Her eyes met Pearl's, worry reflecting back at her.

Molly stood and closed the curtains on both of the windows. Perhaps the rider would pass on by if he thought no one was at home. It was a ridiculous hope. There were no other cabins for miles. Why wouldn't a rider stop?

She retrieved her Colt from where she'd left it by the front door when Grom stood on all fours and began to bark. Pearl grabbed the shotgun and moved beside her.

The horse stopped outside, and footfalls resounded as the rider climbed the porch and knocked on the front door.

"Is anyone here?" asked a familiar woman's voice.

Molly set her gun down and removed the slat blocking the door. As she opened it, she was stunned by the blue eyes and flushed cheeks that greeted her.

Bridget Lannigan.

Shadows bobbed on the walls of the tunnel from the lantern Jake held. When he reached the end of the shaft, the area opened up, and he lifted the light higher to scan the walls and crevices.

Robert stepped from behind him and pointed. "Look, over there."

Jake stepped closer and squatted.

"It's gotta be samples," Ivan said from beside him.

Two burlap sacks held ore pieces.

"You think Nine Toes hid these in here?" Robert asked.

"Maybe." Jake grabbed the bags. "Let's ask him."

Jake followed Robert out of the tunnel. The opening beyond revealed the last vestiges of daylight. As Robert crossed the entrance boundary, a shot rang out and he fell.

Jake dropped the bags and pulled his gun, halting just before the threshold. "Robert? Are you hurt?"

"Yep." He lay on his side, faced away. "He got me in the thigh."

"Can you scoot back? I'll cover you."

Ivan stood across from Jake, his weapon drawn as well. When Ivan gave a nod, both he and Jake released a volley of shots directed at a clump of sagebrush, the most likely position of the shooter.

Once Robert crawled back into the protection of the passageway, Jake and Ivan stopped and reloaded.

"I'm going out there," Jake said and left before either man could stop him. Ducking low, he jumped from the ledge, since taking the rope ladder would've put his back to the assailant. He winced from the jolt of pain as his feet hit the ground then rolled forward, losing his hat. Standing, he pulled a second gun and hugged the mountainside as he moved closer to whomever was trying to dump lead in them.

Motion in the bushes caught his eye. He released several rounds and ducked to hide against a rocky face. Return shots sprayed dirt a few feet from him.

He fired back and noticed a shadow beyond.

Maybe he hit the perpetrator.

For several long moments, Jake waited, listening.

He left his hiding place, estimating the location of the sniper, and ran toward it. Broken branches, smashed bushes, and a distinct boot print caught his eye, along with spent casings littering the ground. Whoever was here had fled.

Jake spied something. He knelt and picked up a round tobacco canister, small enough to fit into his palm. Only one man he knew used it—James Winston.

---

MOLLY CLOSED HER GAPING MOUTH. "What are you doing here, Bridget?"

"Can I come in?"

Pearl placed her shotgun against the wall and gently nudged Molly aside. "Of course you can."

Bridget stepped inside but stopped short when Grom bristled and growled. Bridget removed her riding gloves and held a hand out to the dog. "Well, aren't you a nice fella," she crooned.

Grom was having none of it and took two steps back.

Bridget straightened, her gaze darting from Molly to Pearl. She wore no hat or bonnet, and her hair was loose and frayed from her ride. Dirt smudged her white blouse, and dust coated her dark cotton skirt. "I've come looking for Robert."

"What makes you think he's here?" Molly asked, unwilling to confirm his presence. Maybe he'd been trying to get away from her.

Bridget hesitated. "I followed him, but he got farther ahead of me. Has he come here?"

"He did," Pearl answered. "He'll return in a bit with Ivan and Jake."

Bridget nodded then her eyes flicked to the bed. "Is that man ill?"

"He's been shot." Pearl waved her to the table. "Come on. I'll pour you a cup of coffee." She chuckled as she turned away. "I don't think we've ever had so many visitors."

Molly replaced the slat on the door while Pearl set mugs on the table and filled them.

As they all sat, Bridget said, "I didn't know you were here,

Molly. When you left the ranch, Robert said he took you back to your hotel."

"He did."

"Did Robert tell you to come here?"

"No." Molly couldn't think of a good reason to lie. "I came with Jake McKenna."

"So Archie *was* right," Bridget proclaimed. "He said you'd run off with McKenna, but I didn't believe it. I thought you were smarter than that."

Molly bit back a retort.

Bridget continued, seemingly oblivious to her rudeness. "Is there some reason you're barricaded in here? My horse is at the hitching post. I should tend to him." She paused, then glanced at the welt on Pearl's forehead. "Did someone strike you, Mrs. Krupin?"

"It's a long story," Pearl replied, then stood. "I'll see to the horse."

"I should go with you," Molly said.

Pearl shook her head. "I'll be fine." She patted Molly's arm. "I'll be quick."

"Leave the door open," Molly said as Pearl went outside. At least this way, they would hear if she needed anything, or if she called for help.

Molly shifted her attention back to Bridget. "There's been a murder."

"What?"

"A man named Pedro Elizondo. Did you know him?"

"No. Do you think the man who did it is still out there?"

"Maybe."

Bridget quieted and Molly sipped her coffee. "Why are you here? Did your father send you?"

Tears filled Bridget's eyes. "I can see why you might think that, but no, I'm not here on behalf of my father. I'm here because I need to talk to Robert. I'm here because I love him, and he doesn't believe me." Her voice caught on a sob. "And I need him to know that."

As Bridget crumbled, Molly's anger cooled to ambivalence. She ought to comfort the woman, but did Bridget really love Robert? Would he one day marry her? If that came to pass, then Molly would be forced to interact with her for a lifetime. Perhaps it was time to show a little warmth and acceptance toward her.

"I guess you can wait and talk to Robert, if he wants to speak with you."

Bridget wiped at her nose and the tears now streaming down her face. "Thank you," she choked out.

───────

UNDER THE CLOAK OF DARKNESS, Jake and Ivan shouldered Robert between them and brought him back to the cabin. As they approached, the door flung open. To Jake's surprise, Molly *and* Bridget Lannigan crowded the entryway. They both rushed forward.

"Robert, what's happened?" Molly demanded.

"Good Lord!" Bridget exclaimed. "Your leg is bleeding."

Robert's gaze landed on Bridget. "What're you doing here?"

"I needed to see you." Bridget stared at the blood stain on his trousers. "I couldn't leave things the way they were after our fight." She raised her eyes to his. "Believe it or not, Robert, you're important to me."

Ivan and Jake heaved Robert onto the porch. Once inside the cabin, they settled him onto a chair.

Pearl abandoned cutting potatoes at the table and stood. "What on earth has happened?"

"It's not as bad as it looks." Robert shook his head and grimaced. "You shouldn't have come here, Bridget."

Bridget appeared distraught, a look Jake had never before seen on a Lannigan.

Pearl wiped her hands on her apron then waved everyone off. "You all had better git so I can tend to him."

"No," Bridget cut in. "I'm staying."

Molly shifted her attention to Jake. "You're not injured too, are you?"

"No." He left the far-too-crowded cabin and stepped onto the porch. Molly trailed after him as he took the steps and headed to the back of the house.

"How did Robert get shot?"

"We had a visitor."

"Who?"

He entered the shed, struck a lucifer, and lit the lamp hanging near the entrance. "If I had to guess? Winston."

"Why would he shoot at you?"

Jake returned to the corral. "Hell if I know. We found two bags of ore samples in the tunnel. Maybe Nine Toes was leaving them there for Winston. Or maybe Pedro left them." He led Fernando and Cinnamon into the shed.

"So Nine Toes thought that Pearl was going to find them? Is that why he struck her?" Molly transferred fresh hay to each stall as Jake filled the water troughs.

"Maybe. When he wakes up, I plan to ask him."

"Do you think the shooter is still out there?"

Jake started brushing Fernando. "I doubt it. I think we scared him off. But stay alert."

They stopped talking, and Molly watched Jake's steady motions as he tended to his horse, worry gnawing in her belly. Pedro had already been killed, and now Robert had been shot.

"Maybe we should all just leave," she said.

Jake set the brush aside and faced her. "I'm not going to let anything happen to you."

"But what about you? And Robert?"

He stepped close and wound a wayward strand of her hair around his finger. "Why do you think Bridget is here?"

"She came to see Robert."

"She hasn't tried to pry information out of you, has she?"

Molly appeared taken aback. "I hadn't thought of that, but I haven't told her anything."

Jake nodded. "You do know that Winston has his eye on her."

Concern crossed her very lovely face. "Is that why you think he shot Robert?"

"Could be." They'd do well do get out of the hills and back to town, but he doubted Robert could leave tonight.

"I think she really loves him," Molly said. "She was very upset when she arrived and was beside herself to find Robert and talk some sense into him."

Jake felt a shiver run through Molly, so he shed his coat and draped it onto her shoulders. She slipped her arms into the sleeves and smiled. "Thanks."

Jake sighed. "I haven't the first notion where everyone is gonna bed down." Although nothing would make him happier than to have Molly by his side.

Not for the first time did the romantic situation nag his conscience. What *were* his intentions with Molly? Was he playing where he shouldn't?

He hadn't given much thought to where this might all lead. He enjoyed Molly's company, enjoyed the uncanny pull she exerted on him, enjoyed how much he anticipated seeing her.

But didn't she deserve the truth?

While he didn't completely stomach the subterfuge over his intention to file the new claims only under his name, he set it aside. The search for the Bluebird had taken a dark turn, and Jake would be damned if he lost Molly—or Robert—over it. But that didn't mean he wanted the claim to end up in someone else's hands—greedy, unethical ones like Shep Lannigan or James Winston. As far as Jake was concerned, he would take whatever he could from both men.

But his dishonesty about the mining claims—which was for Molly's own protection now that Pedro had ended up dead—didn't mean he should mislead her about their potential love affair.

"I'm beginning to think I'm doing you a disservice," he said, "and I would never want to do that."

"I'm not sure what you mean."

He spoke a truth that had always been a part of his agenda. "I'm not a man who's seeking to settle down, and that can be the only direction with a woman like you."

She narrowed her eyes. "Says who? You?"

"Molly—"

"How can you possibly know what's best for me?" Her quiet voice did little to hide her cutting tone. "Did Robert say something?"

Jake gave a slight shake of his head, frowning as his grasp on the situation slipped away like a fish that was too wily to catch. He was suddenly agitated, and he didn't like it.

"I've never indicated any interest in marriage." Molly's reddened face undercut her defensive posture, revealing her embarrassment, and Jake was instantly sorry he'd brought it up.

"If that concern is hanging over you," she continued, "then you can alleviate yourself of it. I have more important things to consider."

Impatience pricked him like an annoying mosquito. "Like what?"

"I plan to travel the world. I'm well aware that I can't leave a husband and children behind to pursue it. To be honest, a husband would simply drag me down at this point."

Jake had met women during his travels—self-reliant, entrepreneurial, and clearly of no mind to be controlled by a man—

and in places where the rules governing females were far stricter than in the States. And while he'd admired them, and had even been somewhat fascinated by such females, he'd never troubled himself with their welfare. They were free to live their life how they desired, or at least to navigate the rules of society how they wanted.

But this slip of a girl stirred emotions in him he'd rather not have —inspiring him to covet a future filled with hope and wonderment. The growing uneasiness spilled through him like hot molasses, heating him from head to toe, and filling him with fear that if she was in this world, and he wasn't beside her, then some important piece of the puzzle of his life would be missing. Starkly, an ache of loneliness that he'd not acknowledged since his days in the orphanage spread in his chest, piercing a place in his heart that— extraordinary as it seemed—could only be filled by her.

Stunned by the depth of his reaction to her simple statement of not wanting a husband, all he could manage in response to her words was to stare at her, dumbfounded.

When she yanked on the shed's door and fled, he wanted to call her back. He wanted to kiss her to drown out the maelstrom of emotions rushing through him, to hold her close and inhale the scent of her skin and revel in the feel of her pressed against him. He wanted to lose himself in *her*. More and more, with each passing day, that's all he'd wanted to do.

Reeling as if he'd been punched in the stomach, he braced a hand on a wooden post to steady himself.

*You have to keep breaking your heart until it opens.*

Hell of a time for the teachings of Rumi to finally begin making sense.

---

MOLLY ROUNDED the cabin and skidded to a stop at the sight of Robert and Bridget sitting on the porch steps, locked in a steamy embrace. While she was glad to see his leg wound was apparently minor, indignation and desperate envy gouged her at witnessing the two of them entwined in such ardent passion.

She nearly made a childlike sound of disgust, but she wasn't ten years old anymore. Her brother was a man, and he had wants and desires just like any other male of the species. Hence the resentment.

She wanted Jake to be that wild about her.

And apparently he wasn't.

Unsure what to do—the lip-locked pair blocked her path into the cabin, and the dark night didn't encourage wandering around in the woods—she hesitated. Her only option was to return to Jake, but pride held her back. As her indecision dragged on, she clenched her fists and wondered if there was anything nearby she could punch.

That was the only explanation for why she did just that when Jake's hand came from behind and wrapped around her arm.

She landed a solid blow.

"Ow." He staggered back, his hand covering his eye, his hat lying on the ground.

"Jake, I'm sorry." She shook her hand to relieve the pain coursing through her knuckles. "But why are you sneaking up on me like that?"

"I wanted to apologize."

He removed his hand from his face, and she saw a dangerous gleam in his eyes.

"For what?" She stood her ground. "You don't owe me anything."

With panther-like reflexes, he grabbed her wrist and pulled her back into the shadows, away from the light emanating from the windows at the front of the cabin. Surely Robert and Bridget had heard them bickering. Any moment Molly expected them to appear.

Jake brought her up against the cabin wall, and his lips found hers. This was no tame kiss—it was a steal-the-air-from-the-lungs overture, a heated and frantic act filled with longing and need and the urges of the body.

His mouth slanted fully over hers, and his tongue swept her mouth, accelerating her arousal in a flash. Her arms snaked around his neck, and he enfolded the full length of her against his body, sending a tremor from her breasts down to her abdomen. He pressed against her, his craving palpable and sharply focused upon her. Despite a frisson of fear surfacing, she arched her back, seeking to increase the contact with him.

She buried her fingers into his hair and hungrily consumed his mouth, tasting his salt-flavored skin and inhaling the earth and the wind and the sun that had taken residence in him.

His hands slid beneath the jacket she wore as his lips kissed her neck; his fingers skimming her ribcage then dropping lower to squeeze her hips. His mouth came to a breast—still covered in clothing—and lavished it with attention.

She could hardly breathe.

If it was like this with material blocking their flesh, what would it be like without anything between them?

She wanted this—she wanted him—but worry began to whisper in her ear. If she did this, if *they* did this, there would be no turning back. Jake wouldn't marry her. He'd just said as such, and she'd entirely agreed with him. But there was something else, an acknowledgement she'd refused to consider until this moment. It wasn't the ruination of her reputation that gripped her with pandemonium, it was the possible shattering of her heart that gave her pause.

*What if I can't let Jake go? What would become of me then?*

A sound in the cabin interrupted the carnal trance enveloping them.

Jake buried his face against her neck and wrapped his arms around her. Molly held him tightly, her heart pounding with uncertainty.

Moving his lips to her temple, he said quietly, "This is a problem I have no answer for."

Her mouth sought his.

Jake cupped her head with both of his hands and leaned his forehead against hers. "Are you a virgin, Molly?"

"Of course I am."

"And you should remain one for your husband."

"I told you. I don't want a husband."

"You're very young. Trust me, you will."

She sighed but it was more like a growl. "Are you an eighteen-year-old woman?" When he didn't answer, she continued, "No, you're not. So stop pretending like you know what's best for me."

Jake placed a hand against the wall, remaining close, his jaw flexing. She reached up and stroked her fingertips along his cheek, grazing the rough-hewn stubble of his whiskers, liking him in this raw, masculine state. Liking him a lot.

His eyes met hers. "I'll have to marry you, you know."

Winter flooded her body, driving out the heat, leaving her limbs and heart frozen.

"Like hell you do." She pushed away from the cabin wall, forcing him to take a step back. "Do you think I'm teasing you? Tricking you to wed me by using my body as bait?"

"Regardless, I'm caught, Chigger."

His gaze was steady which only served to unnerve her. She jammed her hands into the pockets of the coat he'd given her, her right hand immediately fumbling with what felt like a smooth rock.

"I'm not hunting for a husband," she ground out.

"I'm beginning to think I can't be a passing fancy for you."

His earnest expression had to be a trick. She turned the stone around in her hand. "What are you saying?"

"I won't ruin you. I owe Robert more than that. If the only way to have you is by marriage, then so be it."

"You just said you didn't want to settle down. Have you gone mad since leaving the shed?"

What was wrong with him?

Molly paused as understanding dawned—both about Jake's true nature and what was in her hand. It was a sample. Jake must've pocketed it when they'd been investigating the Chigger. Why hadn't he shown it to her? From the smooth texture of it, it was very likely gold or silver. And quite large.

Why was he hiding it?

Only one explanation made sense. He intended to keep it for himself.

While she certainly didn't have a stake in all of this, Robert did. Should she tell him? Should she confront Jake?

Maybe he had a perfectly plausible explanation. Or maybe he didn't. Perhaps the distrust everyone had for him was justified.

"Maybe I have gone mad," he admitted.

She pushed past him and rounded the cabin once again, confusion filling her thoughts. This time she didn't hesitate as she approached Robert and Bridget, who, at this point, was partially unclothed. It would seem Robert had no compunction about taking liberties with the woman he fancied.

*This isn't like Robert.* It only deepened her bewilderment.

They jumped as she stomped toward them and plowed right through the middle, breaking them apart. She entered the cabin, slamming the door behind her.

She immediately regretted the action when Nine Toes startled awake from where he lay on the bed.

Pearl glanced up from a seat near the cook stove, Ivan beside her. When she saw Molly, she said, "The course of true love never did run smoothly."

Molly nodded and sought to calm her nerves. She angled her body so that the Krupins wouldn't see her pull the stone from Jake's coat pocket. Just as she suspected—in her palm sat a brassy-colored nugget. She quickly returned it to its hiding spot.

"I've got imported Chinese tea." Pearl stood and headed to the kitchen. "You sit and collect your thoughts while I get you a cup."

But Molly couldn't shake the thought that plagued her the most. If Jake was hiding evidence of a new claim, was he also less than truthful about his feelings for *her*?

# CHAPTER 18

J ake awoke at first light. His slumber in the shed hadn't been altogether bad—the straw bed had been surprisingly comfortable. He'd fallen into a deep sleep, which had been a blessing, considering Robert had also slept in the shed—Bridget hadn't been able to bring herself to leave his side. Jake had put a blanket over his ears to block out the sounds of their canoodling.

It didn't help that all he wanted was to be alone with Molly. But she'd nursed her irritation from their heated encounter the previous night and stayed inside the cabin.

He couldn't blame her. He ran a hand down his face then through his hair. His behavior was new to him as well.

Robert stirred, wincing.

"Does it hurt?" Jake asked quietly.

Robert nodded, trying not to disturb Bridget curled against him.

"I'm thinking you're not gonna be able to ride today. What if I head to town and bring a doc back to have a look at your leg?"

Robert laid his head back and stared at the shed roof. "I'd say quit treating me like a fragile teacup, but it would no doubt make Bridget and Molly happy."

It would also give Jake a chance to file the new claims without an audience. Still, he voiced a worry that had been nagging him. "Can you keep Molly in Creede longer than her planned visit?"

"Why?"

"So I can convince her."

"Of what?"

"To marry me."

Robert raised his head and stared at him. "You're joking."

Jake remained silent.

"You're not joking," Robert murmured. "When the hell did this happen?"

"Honestly? The first time I saw her." It was true. Instinctively, he'd known as soon as he'd watched her exit the train that his life had taken a major turn; he just hadn't wanted to acknowledge it.

Clearly skeptical, Robert asked, "When did you decide it was time to get hitched?"

"I'll admit it was never in my plans. I just hadn't met the right woman."

"And Molly is that woman?"

"Why do you say that like it's such a preposterous notion? She's your sister. You must know how unique she is."

Robert muttered what sounded like an obscenity under his breath. His reaction took Jake aback a bit. He thought Robert would be happy about welcoming him into the family. Setting that aside, there was still one problem. "She's proving to be a bit stubborn."

"Because she won't marry you after knowing you for little more than a week? What a surprise."

"I really thought I'd get more support from you." He flicked his gaze to Bridget. "At least I'm trying to do the right thing."

Robert raised an eyebrow. "And what's that supposed to mean?"

Bridget rolled away from Robert and stretched, her eyes barely open. "We became engaged last night," she said sleepily.

"I stand corrected, then," Jake said. He shifted his attention back to Robert. "You *are* doing the right thing. You're getting a good man,

Bridget. I hope your family doesn't chew him up and spit him back out." Jake regretted the words as soon as he said them.

Robert pinned him with a hard glare. "You've got no say in the matter."

Jake exhaled in an effort to release his frustration. "You're right. My apologies. No disrespect intended, but take care around Lannigan. I wouldn't trifle with him."

Bridget watched him. "I know."

For the first time, Jake saw something in Bridget that almost resembled a mature woman. It gave him hope that Robert wasn't saddling himself with a relationship full of hardship.

Robert sighed and rubbed a hand on Bridget's shoulder. "If Molly wants you, then you have my blessing. But you two are cut from the same cloth. You won't get her to settle down, and you sure as hell don't want to settle down yourself. I don't care what you say. Molly needs a nice man in Tucson to take pity on her. That will make my folks happy."

"Why would you saddle her with a life that would make her miserable? I think I can do better for her."

"I look forward to watching that."

"You underestimate my charms."

Robert chuckled. "You underestimate my sister."

---

MOLLY ROSE from the pallet she had shared on the floor with Pearl and Grom. Ivan had reluctantly slept beside Nine Toes. Pearl had insisted on it since he had many aches and pains these days, and it wasn't proper for Pearl to share accommodations with a man who wasn't her husband.

Bridget had disappeared and never returned; Molly suspected she'd been in the shed with Robert and Jake.

Everyone still slumbered, so she quietly stepped outside on the porch to think. The day beckoned with cool, pine-scented air, and bluebirds flitted from ground to bush to tree and back. Their bright azure feathers floated in the stillness, the slight mist in the air blurring their edges, making it appear as if she viewed a dream.

Should she ask Jake about the sample in his pocket?

She'd returned his coat and the gold nugget to him last night—because surely that's what it was, surely that was why he had neglected to mention it.

Perhaps she was reading too much into it. She didn't understand the intricacies of mining or establishing a claim. Perhaps there was a good explanation.

She crossed her arms and chewed her lower lip because a bigger issue loomed.

*I'm falling in love with Jake McKenna.*

She closed her eyes. Falling? No. She was already there.

And it was very clear that while this went against her plan of getting tied down—at least in the short term—what weighed heavy on her was the knowledge that Jake would never truly love her...not the way she wanted him to.

All the talk of marriage was simply his sense of obligation to her brother, alongside the overwhelming physical pull that existed between them. As he'd said himself—he wasn't the settling down kind of man. Even if they did marry, he would likely soon tire of it. Molly wasn't sure she could handle that.

It didn't help that he'd withheld finding the nugget. It only spoke to a self-serving attitude, which he'd apparently managed to keep under wraps. Perhaps everyone in town was right about him, and she'd been too blinded by his charm to see it.

Conflicted, she debated what course of action to take.

A scratch from within the cabin told her Grom wanted out, so she opened the door and released the hound. He bounded away, tail wagging.

Jake appeared, and Molly's heart tumbled in her chest. He

stopped to pet the dog. Grom was beyond excited, spinning in circles, both tail and tongue wagging, his body gyrating in joyful twists and turns. To be truthful, Molly's insides were reacting much the same way at the sight of Jake, but she schooled her features to hide it.

It didn't help that he looked rugged and masculine—he hadn't shaved, probably hadn't bathed in any fashion at all, and his clothes had the wrinkled look of having slept in them. Molly knew hers weren't in any better shape. It didn't matter. She watched him like a half-starved coyote, and he was the meal to end all meals.

"Morning, Chigger." He grinned at her as Grom finally wound down.

She drew her brows together and kept her face expressionless. "Good morning."

"Sleep well?"

"Yes." She came down the steps. "You're up early."

"Figured I'd get a start on the day."

She stopped before him, hands on hips. "What's your plan?"

"I thought to head to town and bring a doctor for Robert. I don't think he's fit to ride just yet."

His gaze warmed her. "I agree that he should stay put until his leg heals more. I'm guessing that Bridget will want to remain with him."

Jake narrowed his eyes, the side of his mouth lifting into a smile. "What are you going to do, Molly?"

She shifted her eyes to a thicket of trees just beyond the cabin since watching him scattered her thoughts. "Why are you so difficult?"

But she couldn't stop a smile from creeping onto her face. She glanced downward in an effort to hide it, but he surprised her with a kiss. Within seconds, he'd enclosed his arms around her, his mouth angled against hers so perfectly she all but melted into him. She savored his attention, indulging the always-present need to touch him.

When he finally loosened his hold, she sighed, craving so much more.

"Jake, I found the gold nugget," she said against his mouth.

Would he lie to her? Did she even care anymore?

He pulled back and she held her breath, worried over his reaction.

His face was an unreadable mask. "You plan on stealin' it?"

"Of course not. Why didn't you tell me about it?"

The amorous spell between them began to dissipate. "You're thinking you don't trust me now, right?"

She withdrew from his embrace, but he held her hands in his large ones. "If you're asking if I searched your things, the answer is no. I found it by accident last evening when you loaned me your coat."

"The truth is, you're not equipped to deal with the fallout from any of this—with the Chigger or any other claim. I'd rather you not be any part of it. And I'm concerned about Robert. He and Bridget sealed their future last night. They're gonna get married."

Molly stilled. "They are?"

"Anything they have, Lannigan will take. Anything you have might get you killed, just like Pedro."

She considered his words. "So you're going to take all these claims for yourself? I may be young Jake, but I'm not stupid. You think you have the Bluebird, don't you?"

"Maybe."

The man staring at her wasn't the charming and romantic Jake that he so often showed her. It was The Jackal—world traveler and salt smuggler, French spy and opportunist. Could they have a life together? Longing pierced her, and she knew she wanted to try, the future be damned.

"Then marry me, and we'll call it even," she said.

His eyes gleamed with surprise. "I didn't expect you to succumb so easily."

"Are you retracting your offer?"

"No," he said, all levity gone. "I know this is fast, but I'm not playing a game. I mean to keep you, Molly Rose. Are you prepared for that?"

A gusting wind blew through the ravine, a breath from God's divine mouth. That she was taking a leap off a cliff into the unknown wasn't lost on her, but Molly wanted Jake. It was as simple as that. He'd offered himself to her, and while she might never know why he was so willing to tie his destiny with hers, it didn't matter. He was inclined to try. Molly wanted to meet him halfway. She wanted to be his wife and partner and friend. And she wanted to be his lover, his one and only.

"Yes." Her voice drifted away on the breeze.

He stepped close again and brought both hands to frame her face then kissed her with infinite gentleness.

*"Sell your cleverness and buy bewilderment."* He pressed his lips softly to hers again.

"Are you quoting Rumi again?" She wrapped her hands around his wrists, enjoying the exquisite restraint of his kisses.

"No one has bewildered me more than you, Chigger."

"I hope I'll be enough for you, Jake."

He rested a forehead against hers. "You already are."

# CHAPTER 19

"Are you sure?"

The dumbfounded expression on Robert's face shouldn't have surprised Molly, but a part of her bristled over the look he gave her— as if she'd lost her senses, as if she'd disappointed him.

"Why do you look at me as if I haven't a shred of intelligence?"

"Quit exaggerating." He crossed his arms and leaned against a stall railing. "I want you to be happy."

"You don't think Jake can do that?" It was true that she didn't totally trust The Jackal, but Molly hoped that, in time, she and Jake would grow to depend on and confide in one another.

Robert grimaced. "You're my sister. I'm responsible for your welfare. Ma and Pa will surely blame me for introducing you to such a smooth talker."

A laugh escaped Molly. "Jake's no smooth talker, and you didn't introduce us."

"Now you're just splitting hairs." He shook his head. "Fine. I can see you've made up your mind."

"As have you. I didn't warm to Bridget upon our first

acquaintance, but I'll give her a chance because she's obviously important to you."

Robert watched her, his gaze contemplative. "Who would've thought we'd fall in love under such circumstances? Can we trust either of them?"

The desire she had for Jake was overwhelming. It wasn't simply that she ached to join her body to his, it was a sense that she was innately already tied to him, mind and soul, and that it was meant to be, a sort of divine connection. Perhaps that was Robert's fate with Bridget as well.

Molly's throat clogged. "Can we afford not to?"

---

JAKE SAT ON THE KRUPINS' porch, watching the countryside come to life.

He was soon to be a married man.

The thought didn't terrify him as he'd always imagined it would.

Molly was in the shed with Robert, presumably sharing their news. He'd offered to be by her side, but she'd wanted to do it alone.

It was a fast courtship...perhaps too fast, but Jake often acted on impulse. Planning was never his strong suit. *I might need to change that.* Decisions would need to be made—when and where to marry, where to live. He imagined Molly would want to be wed with her family present, which was all right by him, but he hoped she'd be amenable to travel. There were still lands he was keen to see, places like Scotland and Spain and Italy. If all went well here in Creede over the next few months—if the Bluebird panned out—then they'd have enough money to move on, and then some.

He and Molly would have to sit down at some point and work out the particulars. In the meantime, he should get back to town and file those new claims as soon as possible, if for no other reason than to secure a future for him and Molly.

A man atop horseback approached. Jake immediately recognized Boom. He rose and met him as the man dismounted.

"I'm glad I found you," Boom said.

The urgency in the big man's voice concerned Jake. "What's wrong?"

"I'm hearing talk, and you should know."

"What kind of talk?"

Boom looped his horse's reins on the hitching post. "That Pedro's dead...and you did it."

Jake inhaled but it was more like a hiss. "Why are they sayin' that?"

Boom stilled. "So it's true? Pedro's dead?"

Although not entirely certain he should trust the burly Russian, Jake decided he didn't have much of a choice. "I did find his body, but it disappeared when I went back to retrieve it the next day." He could feel the man's shock and his wariness. "Boom, I didn't kill him. If I had to guess, James Winston was behind it, even if he wasn't the one to pull the trigger. Nine Toes is inside." Jake nodded toward the cabin behind him. "He was with Pedro and got himself shot in the process. He can vouch for me." At least he hoped. The wounded prospector had yet to awaken this morning.

Boom adjusted his hat and nodded. "I believe you. It's just that things have been gettin' a damn sight hairy back in these mountains. Lots of rumors flying about. For some reason, the deputy marshal was gonna head back here to investigate, but Lannigan stopped him."

Although Jake was glad for it, he knew Lannigan wouldn't try to protect The Jackal. "Why?"

Boom shrugged. "Maybe he doesn't want a lot of nosy lawmen back here poking around."

Boom had likely hit the nail on the head. If Jake was a gambling man—and despite his propensity to live a carefree life, he really wasn't—he'd bet money that Lannigan was somehow mixed up in all of this.

"So there's something else," Boom added. "That mysterious prospector—Charlie—apparently has let it be known he's out to kill you."

Jake raised an eyebrow. "Vengeance for Pedro?"

"Seems to be. That surly Mexican had more love than we thought."

"Where is this Charlie?"

"Maybe the next valley over. He's slippery as the devil, and I haven't been able to get a good lead on him."

Molly came around the cabin, Robert limping beside her.

When Boom saw Robert, he lifted him in a boisterous hug. "I was worried about you, Robbie. It's good to see you."

Robert laughed as the big Russian released him. "Same here, Boom."

"Why are you limping?"

"It's nothing. Really."

Boom noticed Molly and tipped his hat. "It's always a pleasure, Miss Simms."

A warm smile enveloped Molly's face. "It's good to see you too, Boris."

Jake noticed the slight blush that crept upon Boom's face. He couldn't in good conscience let the man suffer.

"Boom," Jake cut in, "I ought to let you know that Miss Simms and I are engaged."

Surprise registered, then Boom's face split into a grin. "That's a huge relief." He looked at Molly. "I plum forgot that I wanted to court you, and I've recently got myself a real nice gal. She's a laundress at the Orleans Club. I'm glad you didn't wait around for me. Jake's a handsome enough fella. I hope you'll be very happy together."

The surprise on Molly's face was hard to miss as Boom's lengthy reply tumbled out, but she recovered quickly. "Perhaps it wasn't meant to be, Boris. I hope you and your lady will be very happy together."

Robert turned to Jake. "You mean I could've had Boom as my brother-in-law instead of you?"

"Watch your tone, Simms," Jake said. "As it stands now, I'm about to become related to a Lannigan because of you."

Boom frowned as he looked back and forth between the two. "I don't understand."

"Robert and Bridget are also engaged," Molly explained.

"Well, I suppose that's not a surprise," Boom huffed. "They've certainly made no secret of their affections, but I don't think James Winston is gonna be too happy."

"Why do you say that?" Bridget asked, stepping onto the porch, Pearl and Ivan following behind her.

Boom addressed Bridget. "My lady gal said that Winston gave your pappy an ultimatum. You'd be his wife, or else he'd walk."

"Walk?" Bridget asked, clearly confused.

"He's gonna quit working for your father," Robert said.

Bridget frowned. "Why would that matter?"

"Because Winston has something that Lannigan wants," Jake murmured.

Robert pinned a hard gaze on Jake. "You think he found the Bluebird?"

"It's possible," Jake hedged. He had already found it. Maybe. So Winston had to be bluffing.

Molly watched him but said nothing about the claims he'd recently staked.

"I'm going to the Chigger Lode," Robert stated.

Bridget glared at him. "You can't go anywhere with your injured leg."

"I'm fine."

Ivan moved from the porch. "What's this Chigger you're talking about?"

Jake exchanged a glance with Robert. The cat was out of the bag. There was no going back now.

Robert sighed. "I found it a few weeks back. I think it might be the Bluebird."

Boom whistled while Ivan chuckled.

Nine Toes suddenly appeared at the front door, obviously having heard the conversation. He leaned heavily against the door frame. "I want in, too."

*Shit.* Robert had just revealed what could potentially be the richest claim Creede had ever known, but could they have any more fingers in the honey pot?

"It's about time you woke up," Jake said to Nine Toes. "Why were there two bags of ore samples in that tunnel you were hiding in?"

Nine Toes shifted from foot to foot, his brow furrowed with unease. "I didn't know about that."

"Quit lying."

"Fine. Pedro left them there for Charlie. I went to the tunnel to hide after those men started shooting at Pedro, and I...and I thought to take the samples to town."

"Where did Pedro get them?"

An earnest expression crossed Nine Toe's face. "I honestly don't know."

"Then why were you gonna get them assayed?" Ivan asked. "If there was anything of value, you still wouldn't know where the claim was."

"Yeah, but I could've held the knowledge over Charlie's head."

"Do you have any idea where this Charlie is?" Jake asked.

Nine Toes' shoulders sagged. "I can't say I do."

Jake wasn't so sure about that but decided to let it drop. He looked at Molly. "You and Bridget need to get back to town."

"Why?" she demanded.

"Because it's not safe out here."

"Jake is right," Robert said. "We'll return in a few days."

Before Molly could argue, he pulled her aside and said quietly into her ear, "I need you to get to the mining district recorder and file two claims for me." He produced a piece of paper he'd kept tucked inside his shirt and slipped it to her. "This contains a map of the claims along with a geographic description of each. It's enough for the filing."

While he knew it was inevitable that prospectors would flood the Chigger valley once word got out, he hadn't expected that day to be today. Still, there'd be plenty to go around, and he may as well share it with men who deserved it—except Nine Toes. He'd attacked Pearl, and Jake suspected he may have even killed Pedro. But Jake would let him think he was included, for now. The prospector's ragged appearance showed him to still be weak from his injury, and Jake preferred the enemy you could see opposed to the one you couldn't.

Jake just had to hope that he'd staked the Bluebird lode in the right spots. Wouldn't it be ironic if Nine Toes ended up with the apex to the whole damn thing? If the man was in cahoots with Winston, that would stink even more. Jake needed to make sure that didn't happen.

Molly raised her chin to look Jake in the eye. "So you're trusting me with your claims?"

"Did you think I wouldn't?"

"I won't lie. It crossed my mind."

Jake shifted his stance to shield her from everyone's view. "I can't tell you whose name to file the claim under. I'll leave that up to you." But he hoped that she understood what was at stake.

Her eyes gleamed with anticipation.

A wide grin spread across his face. "I'd tell you I love you, but that seems premature, and I doubt you'd fall for it."

"Love isn't a requirement for marriage."

"No, but I'll have yours before this life is up."

"You're very confident about certain things."

He gave a slight shake of his head. "You're wrong. It's not confidence. I recognize magic when I see it."

A laugh escaped her. That's when he knew she was the one. He'd suspected before, perhaps wished a tad more than was reasonable. But now he knew.

He wanted like hell to kiss her, but they had too large of an audience. He settled with leaning closer. "I'm calling the first claim the Molly Rose."

She held her ground. "And the second?"

"I think you know."

Her expression became serious. "You'd better be careful out there."

"Or what?"

"Or I'll be one very rich woman."

# CHAPTER 20

**M**olly guided Cinnamon into Upper Creede as Bridget brought her mount abreast, the town cast in shadow in the late afternoon. Pearl had opted to remain at her cabin.

"Will you return home?" Molly asked.

Bridget paused before answering. "I don't know." Worry lines took root on her forehead beneath the brim of her hat.

Without warning, a train of over fifty burros overtook them, all laden with heavy sacks of ore, and Molly and Bridget barely got their horses out of the way as the mass of animals headed straight for the train depot, several men on horseback keeping pace and hollering.

Molly considered how much work went in to extracting silver from the veins in the surrounding mountains. She needed to file two claims for Jake. With the day winding down, she had little time to waste before the claims office closed. Added to that, she didn't know where the office was located in the first place.

Taking a deep breath, Molly made a decision. "Bridget, I need your help with something."

RIDING HARD, Jake and the others made it to the same spot where he'd camped with Molly days before at the base of the steep entrance to the valley that protected the Chigger Lode. He noticed quickly that the journey had taken a toll on Robert and Nine Toes, both men still recovering from their injuries.

"We'll make camp here," Jake said.

"Are we close?" Boom asked.

Jake nodded but offered nothing more, and thankfully, Robert kept the location of the vein to himself. No reason to have any of them sneaking off before the others could get there as well.

With darkness soon to be upon them, they made camp, but Jake's whole body prickled with awareness. They were being watched. He pulled his rifle from the scabbard and stepped away from the fire to better scan the tree line beyond. Ivan and Boom joined him, weapons drawn.

Jake nodded at both men then quietly slipped away, blending into the terrain. The camp and animals were a beacon to whoever was out there. No reason to be a sitting duck.

He paused and listened, something he'd learned in Morocco. Quieting the mind, as well as the body, he'd honed the ability to access another sense beyond the five used every day.

When the figure rounded on him, he had the rifle at the ready so fast the man jumped back.

"Don't shoot, Jake." Boom's voice filled the darkness from beyond. "They won't hurt us."

Two Ute Indians stood before them.

Jake slowly lowered his rifle as Boom materialized from the darkness. Both Indians looked young, with longs braids draped down each shoulder.

"I know 'em." Boom acknowledged the Indian standing opposite Jake with a nod. "That one's Coho, and this one is called Antelope."

Ivan caught up to them. "I've seen these boys as well."

"You two are a little far from home, aren't you?" Jake asked. The Southern Ute Reservation was over a hundred miles away.

"We have permission," Antelope said and produced a piece of paper from a leather pouch. Coho did the same.

In the dark, Jake held the passes close to read them. They were written by the agent who ran the reservation.

Antelope's said, "This Indian is all right."

Coho's said, "This is a damned son of a bitch. Look out for him."

Jake considered Coho, who offered a wide grin, then returned the papers to the men.

"We're hunting deer," Antelope said.

"How's it been?" Jake asked.

"Good enough. We're almost ready to return home. We've been smoking the meat on the other side of that rise."

"You boys best come with us," Ivan said. "There's been shenanigans back here, and we'd like to pick your brain."

The Utes stared back, clearly perplexed.

"I've got whiskey," Boom cut in. "Come on back to our campfire and sit for a bit."

Clarity registered on their faces, and they agreed with a smile. They retrieved their horses and trailed Jake and the others.

When Nine Toes saw them approach from where he sat by the fire, he sputtered, "What the hell?"

Robert glanced up from his reclined position where he rested his leg.

"Why are they here?" Nine Toes demanded.

Antelope and Coho stopped abruptly, disgust registering on their faces.

"What did you do, Nine Toes?" Ivan asked.

"I don't get along with these two." The injured prospector set his jaw in a rigid line. "They set about haunting me."

Jake glanced back at the two Utes, both sporting youthful faces. "Yep, they sure are scary lookin'."

"That one," Antelope narrowed his gaze upon Nine Toes, "is a dishonorable man."

Jake didn't doubt it.

"He stole meat from us," Antelope continued, "and sold it to other prospectors."

Boom loomed over Nine Toes. "What's wrong with you?"

"Nobody can prove I did that," Nine Toes said in defense.

"So it's true?" Jake asked.

"I'm not sharing a fire with them," the old prospector groused.

"Then you best scoot away into the dark," Jake replied. "They'll be staying for now."

Nine Toes looked away, nursing a pout, and hugged himself as if the gesture made him smaller.

"I'll put your ponies with the others," Jake offered and took the reins from the Ute men, who still appeared annoyed by Nine Toes' presence.

Jake led the animals to a patch of grass where the other horses were hobbled. As Jake picketed the ponies, he noticed markings on one of the saddles, etched just below the horn. He squinted in the dark and leaned closer to read the word on the well-used and worn leather—BLUEBIRD.

As he returned to the group now sharing Boom's bottle of whiskey, he asked, "Why is 'bluebird' written on one of the saddles?"

Ivan and Boom became quiet while Nine Toes stopped mid-swig with the bottle of liquor in his hand. All of them, along with Robert, stared at Jake.

Coho and Antelope, sitting side-by-side, glanced at the group crowding the campfire. The flames crackled, illuminating the dark sheen of their hair and smooth facial features.

"There is a legend among our people," Coho replied, his demeanor subdued.

Although Jake had heard bits and pieces from others, he'd never heard it from a Ute. "Will you tell us?"

Jake sat opposite the two Indians, settling between Robert and Nine Toes. He took the whiskey from the prospector, wiped the mouth of the bottle on his shirt then took a swallow. Damn, it was strong. Jake looked at Boom as he suppressed the urge to cough. Since when did the burly Russian get the good stuff and share it to boot?

Coho nodded. "Back when we freely roamed the mountains, a band camped in a valley surrounded by high granite walls. They sought protection from a group of Apache. To their surprise, they found a small encampment already present, but they did not believe it was their enemy the Apache. There were supplies and a horse and a mule but no sign of the man or men it belonged to.

"For three days, the warriors in the band kept watch for these others, but they never came. Then a man tumbled from a high ledge above, and it was he who owned the horse and the mule. He had been frightened of the Ute men and afraid they would kill him, so he had stayed hidden. But then he fell, and they discovered him. The man offered all of his supplies in exchange for his life. The Ute warriors were ready to kill him, but they decided not to.

"They let him keep the mule, but the rest they took, and they sent him away. That saddle was his. They called him Bluebird because of it. He said that it was the name of his horse."

"Do you know where this was?" Robert asked.

"There is one who still lives on the reservation who remembers. He is the one who gave me the saddle. There are not many valleys with high walls on every side, so it should not be hard to find."

They happened to be camped right beside one. Jake's pulse kicked up a notch. This tale only further confirmed that he'd found the mythical Bluebird lode. But one thing nagged him. "Were there women and children in the Ute band?"

"Yes, I believe so," Coho answered.

"If the valley was so inaccessible, how did they gain entry?"

"There was a hidden path, or so the elder told me."

Interesting. Such a pathway could prove useful in extracting the ore. Jake handed the whiskey to Robert, and from the speculation in his friend's eyes, knew he was thinking the same thing.

"Have you come across anyone transporting a dead body?" Jake asked.

Antelope nodded. "Yesterday. They said he died suddenly, and they were taking him back to town."

"Did you know the dead man?"

Coho shook his head. "He was covered. We could not see him."

"Can you describe the men transporting him?"

"Yes, we knew one. He is called Winston."

---

MOLLY HAD JUST SAT down at a table in Cora's restaurant when Bridget entered, surprising her. Once the business at the Claims Office had been handled, Bridget had departed to speak with her father and check on her brother. Molly hadn't expected to see her so soon, especially this evening, although Molly had mentioned that she planned to come to Cora's after freshening up at Zang's Hotel.

"Did your father let you out of the house easily?" Molly asked as Bridget settled her shawl upon the back of a chair and sat.

"He wasn't there. Archie said he'd gone into the hills to settle a problem."

Molly worked to hide her alarm. "What's that supposed to mean?"

"I don't know," Bridget said, her features strained with concern. "I fear it can't be good."

Cora appeared, a wide grin on her elderly face. "Miss Lannigan, it's a pleasure. And Miss Simms, it's wonderful to see you again. I was hoping you might return."

"Thank you." Molly smiled warmly. "I'm glad to be here."

"Did you ever find your brother?"

"I did."

Molly ordered steak and mashed potatoes, and Bridget requested venison and baked apples.

"And coffee please," Molly added.

"Right away," Cora chirped as she left.

Mabel—the woman at Bertha's Saloon who had told Molly that Robert was dead—entered the restaurant, scanned the room, and then headed straight for Molly and Bridget.

Mabel's gaze darted between each woman then settled on Molly. "I need to speak with you, miss." With her hair swept from her face in a polished and well-kept bun, she appeared quite respectable, except for one thing—the plunging neckline of her simple cotton dress. Molly tried not to stare.

"Yes, of course." Molly gestured to an empty chair. "Please join us."

Bridget's face reddened, and anger flashed in her eyes. She clearly didn't want Mabel at their table, but it was too late now. Molly had already invited the woman.

"I'm not sure we have anything to discuss." Bridget's voice held a hint of contempt.

"Perhaps we should let her speak before we decide that," Molly gently chided.

A ghost of a smile tugged at the corner of Mabel's mouth, her back rigid as she settled at the table. "I promise this won't take long, Miss Lannigan. Your reputation shouldn't be covered in mud from it."

Bridget's response was stoic silence.

"What can we do for you, Mabel?" Molly asked.

Cora interrupted and poured coffee for Molly and Bridget, then stepped back and stared at Mabel, arching her brow in displeasure. "Is this woman bothering you?"

"No," Molly reassured. "Please, pour her a cup of coffee as well."

Cora paused then completed the task and left before Mabel could order a meal. Molly let it go since she doubted the fancy woman would stay that long, especially if the climate at the table got any chillier. Bridget must know that Robert had sometimes frequented Bertha's.

Hopefully, Robert's fiancée wouldn't fly across the table like a wild mountain cat and attack.

"In my line of work, I hear things," Mabel said. "That day I saw you, you were with Jake McKenna."

Molly nodded. Did Jake have a woman like Mabel stashed somewhere? The idea chafed. Try as she might, though, Molly couldn't dislike the woman. Mabel seemed far more comfortable in her own skin than the rigidity that Bridget often displayed. But Bridget had certainly let Robert take liberties the other night while they were at Ivan and Pearl's house.

Is that how a woman held a man when he could easily find company like Mabel?

She'd tried such tactics on Jake, and he'd basically said no.

Now that they were engaged, perhaps she should try harder. She had no intention of sharing Jake with any woman.

"I've heard that you two are...smitten?" Mabel smiled. "Don't worry. He's never been to Bertha's, except for that day with you, but it's true that any of the ladies would be happy to catch him, if only for a night." She glanced at Bridget. "I think you were after him for a while, weren't you?"

Stunned, Molly flicked her eyes to Bridget as a deep shade of crimson overtook the woman's face.

"It wasn't like that, Molly," Bridget said quietly.

A sick feeling began to form in the pit of Molly's stomach. "How was it, then?"

"I'd rather explain in private."

"Of course," Mabel interjected. "I'll just get to it so you two can discuss matters of the heart. Lord knows women like me don't have one."

Molly dragged her attention from Bridget. "I'm certain that's not true, Mabel."

Mabel looked at Bridget. "You're lucky to have Robert. He's a good one."

While there was a tone of deep sentiment in the woman's voice, Molly was certain she also sensed a sliver of resentment.

Mabel turned her attention to Molly, a false flash of joy permeating her face. "All the ladies at Bertha's were impressed that you marched right inside to speak with me. It was no surprise to me that you're Robert's sister."

"But what you told me about my brother was wrong," Molly said, remnants of that piercing pain still present in her heart.

"I'm sorry about that, but I'm glad it wasn't true." Mabel glanced around then lowered her voice. "What I'm about to say could get me in trouble, but I'm sayin' it anyway. James Winston is a regular, but several nights ago, I wasn't available. He roughed up the girl who took my place, which ain't right, in my book. So I plied him with whiskey and got him to talk. He told me he's out to steal a big contract from under Shep Lannigan. He's also got his eyes set on marrying you." She glared at Bridget.

Bridget leveled a cool stare at Mabel. "Yes, I know."

"Although I suspect it will drive you straight into Robert's arms, I'm gonna tell you not to do it. Winston is cruel, and I don't wish that on anyone." Mabel pressed her lips together. "Even you. Winston told me there's a prospector by the name of Charlie Cohen who's been more than just grubstaked by Shep—this Charlie being carefully watched while searching for the elusive Bluebird."

Mention of the Bluebird caught Molly's attention. "What's so special about this man?"

Mabel paused, glancing around to insure their conversation was still private. "Charlie Cohen is no man. Her name is Charlotte. She came to town many months ago and got herself involved with Shep."

"Do all men visit prostitutes?" Bridget asked sharply.

"Not all," Mabel replied coolly. "Besides, their attachment is not a romantic sort. Charlotte knows details of the Bluebird that Shep thinks will help him find it."

Molly met Bridget's gaze. Bridget knew that the Bluebird was likely already staked because Molly had told her of Jake's claims. Had that been a huge error on her part? And had she compounded it when she'd filed the claims?

"James Winston plans to get there before Shep," Mabel added. "He was trailing a man named Pedro. He thought that Pedro knew the real location, but Pedro was also feeding bad ore samples to Charlotte so that she could give those to Shep."

"Pedro's dead," Molly said.

"I know," Mabel replied. "Charlotte and Pedro were in love, and now she's out to get the man who murdered him."

"Winston?" Molly asked.

Mabel shook her head. "I don't know if he did it or not. But right now, that doesn't matter, because Charlotte *thinks* it was Jake."

"It wasn't Jake." Molly's voice was low but firm.

Mabel leaned forward. "Well, whoever did it isn't really the issue. This Charlotte may take matters into her own hands. Where are Jake and Robert right now?"

Molly sat mute, clutching the napkin resting on her lap. The truth as she knew it kept shifting. Things were happening way too fast. It nagged her that Mabel was being so helpful. What if she was working with Winston, not against him?

"They're in the hills," Bridget answered.

"Do you know where exactly?" Mabel pressed.

Molly frowned and snagged Bridget's gaze. "No. They could be anywhere."

Cora appeared with two plates of food.

Mabel took a sip of coffee and waited to speak until Cora left again. "Are they with anyone else?"

"Ivan Krupin, Boris Orlov, and Nine Toes Bishop," Bridget replied.

Mabel gave a slight nod. "Do you think they're all trustworthy?"

"Someone shot Robert," Bridget replied, her voice filled with anger, "and it wasn't them. Did Winston do it?"

Mabel shrugged. "Or maybe Charlotte." She cleared her throat and stood. "Well, I should leave you both to your meal. If I hear anything else, I'll be sure to let you know."

"Thank you," Molly said.

Mabel stepped around the tables, her lemon-colored skirt swaying back and forth, and quit the restaurant.

Bridget vigorously cut her meat, her eyes downcast.

"I know you don't like her," Molly said, "and I'm beginning to think you're right."

Looking up, Bridget froze.

"But first, I think you owe me an explanation about Jake."

"Nothing happened."

"But he chased you?" Even as she said it, it made no sense to Molly. Jake had been nothing but indifferent to Bridget during every interaction they'd had.

Bridget set her fork and knife aside and dabbed her napkin on the sides of her mouth. "No. It was more like I pursued him."

"Is that why you were always warning me away from him?"

Bridget's expression relaxed and appeared filled with regret. "I warned you off because I honestly didn't think he was as truthful and as loyal as you'd like him to be." She took up her fork again and pushed at the food on her plate. "For what it's worth, he never had any interest in me...at all. I won't lie—it rather irked me at the time."

"But you're with my brother. Do you still have feelings for Jake?"

Bridget shook her head. "I don't. And that's the honest truth."

Molly glanced out the window, watching men and wagons and mules heavy with sacks of ore pass by. In all her childhood, trust had never been an issue, even after she fell in that well. Now, everyone she'd become acquainted with in this town was a challenge to her faith in people. "Does Robert know?"

"Yes. It was why we fought a few days ago. Look, I'm not proud of it, but my father encouraged me to draw men into the fold."

"Men like Jake and Robert?"

Bridget nodded. "I'm head-over-heels in love with Robert, but it caught me quite by surprise. I'm trying to do the right thing. You can trust me, Molly."

Doubt hung heavy in Molly's heart, and not just for her brother and the woman who may or may not love him. Was Bridget right about Jake? Was his loyalty a hard-won battle, one that was likely never to be conquered?

"I hope so." But at this point, she didn't have a choice. "We need to go back into the mountains and find Robert and Jake," Molly said as they finished their meal. "I'm worried that Winston—or your father—may find them first."

"I can get horses," Bridget said, her expression earnest.

"And I'll get supplies."

# CHAPTER 21

Climbing in the dark proved more difficult than Jake had imagined. A moonless sky made the shadows impenetrable, and he had more gear than before, but he'd wanted to make sure he had what he needed. Despite the cool night air, sweat trickled down his back as he strained to be as silent as possible so not to disturb the other men in camp.

It had been his only option—going in alone. There was no way in hell he was going to guide Nine Toes to the Bluebird. They'd follow soon enough, but at least he'd have a few hours to himself with the lode.

He tied a rope at the base of a tree, tugging hard to make certain it would hold. This was his safety net in case he fell from higher up. He shed his coat and rested it on a low-hanging branch, then balanced the knapsack on his shoulder, the pick and shovel awkward, just one Colt nestled in the holster at his hips.

Methodically, he moved upward, one hand-hold and foot-hold at a time. He marveled that he'd come this way with Molly a few days ago. At the time, he hadn't felt trepidation, but a twinge of guilt confronted him when he remembered how she'd looked white as a ghost when she'd reached the top of this steep climb. He'd need to be more aware of her feelings from now on.

With the heavens a sheen of muted sparkles, he at last crested the ridgeline, scrambling over a patch of scree, sending shards of rock crashing below.

Damn.

The others might likely have heard that.

He paused to catch his breath and drink from his canteen, then he moved swiftly into the valley to the location of the claims he'd staked as well as Robert's Chigger Lode. He didn't hear the report of the rifle until it was too late.

"You can hold it right there, McKenna."

Shep had finally caught up to him.

---

MOLLY RODE as hard as she dared in the darkness, Bridget trailing behind her. She didn't stop until they'd reached the Krupins' cabin and the golden light shining through its window.

Molly dismounted and led her horse to the corral, where she knew water and oats awaited. She hoped the animals Bridget had acquired could eat and drink quickly.

Bridget followed suit, but they didn't remove the saddles since Molly intended to keep riding through the night.

"Don't move."

Molly jumped at the sound of a strange woman's voice. A female stood in the shadows, pointing a gun.

"Who are you?" Bridget asked in a rush.

Molly took a step back, but the woman gave a slight shake of her head.

"No, no. Come on with me." The woman waved the tip of the pistol. "Let's all go into the cabin now."

Molly raised her hands, as did Bridget, and carefully walked around the building and onto the porch, then entered the cabin, the lady with the gun behind them. At the table sat Pearl, bound to a chair and gagged.

"Pearl?" Alarmed, Molly moved to her friend. "Are you all right?"

The woman closed the door and herded Bridget toward them.

"What's going on?" Molly demanded. "Who are you?"

Light brown hair peppered with gray hung in a loose braid and framed a surprisingly youthful-looking and pretty face. Still, the woman had to be in her forties.

"I'm doin' the talkin'."

Then it dawned on Molly. "Are you Charlotte Cohen?"

"How would you know that?"

"I've heard talk of you. Why are you holding Pearl hostage?"

Charlotte raised the pistol. "Tell me what I wanna know, and I'll leave you all be."

"And what's that?" Bridget asked.

"Where is the man called The Jackal?"

Bridget edged against the table. "We don't know. Why are you looking for him?"

"He hurt someone I cared about."

"Are you sure about that?" Molly asked.

Charlotte's face blanched white. "As sure as I can be."

The woman's voice held the barest whisper of doubt, and Molly latched on to it. "I can tell you with utmost certainty The Jackal didn't murder Pedro Elizondo."

Charlotte's eyes snapped to Molly's face. "How do you know that?"

"Because I was with him when Pedro was killed. I know people are saying it was Jake McKenna, but it's more likely a man named James Winston who did it."

"Winston?" Confusion played across Charlotte's face.

Molly advanced a tiny step. "You know him, don't you?"

Charlotte narrowed her gaze.

"Please lower the gun and sit down." Molly moved a bit closer. "We can talk about this."

Charlotte hesitated, but to Molly's surprise and relief, she let the weapon drop to her side. Molly stepped carefully forward and took the gun from the woman's hand, and then set it on the floor in a far corner behind where Pearl sat. Molly grabbed a knife from the kitchen and sawed at the rope binding Pearl's hands while Bridget pushed the bandanna from Pearl's mouth. Once free, Pearl rubbed her wrists and took a deep breath.

Molly went to Charlotte and guided her to a chair. She and Bridget then took a seat while Pearl disentangled her legs from the rope at her ankles.

"I'm Molly Rose Simms and this is Bridget Lannigan. We'd like to help, if you'll let us."

Charlotte's eyes snapped to Bridget. "Lannigan, you say? Are you related to Shep Lannigan?"

"Yes," Bridget replied. "He's my father. May I ask if you're working for him?"

Molly wondered if she really heard hurt in Bridget's voice, or if she had simply imagined it, hoping that Lannigan's daughter had truly taken a turn for the better.

Charlotte pursed her lips together and squinted as if she was taking their worth. "He's never mentioned me?"

Bridget shook her head.

"I guess it's no secret. When I came to town, I had no money. But now I realize that Shep took advantage."

"In what way?" Molly prodded, but Charlotte didn't reply.

Bridget leaned forward. "He believes that you know the location of the Bluebird, doesn't he?"

At the mention of the mythical claim, Charlotte stilled. Had Bridget just pushed the woman into silence?

Bridget softened her demeanor. "What kind of split do you have?"

Charlotte crossed her arms tightly over her chest and exhaled, clearly frustrated. "I thought it was a good deal at the time, but I soon realized that I'd signed away too much. He put bodyguards on me night and day to make sure I didn't get out of line."

"Men like James Winston?" Molly asked.

"Yup."

"Did you sign a contract?" Bridget articulated her words into the taut atmosphere of the cabin. Molly had a new appreciation for her brother's fiancée as she carefully attempted to extract information from the woman.

Charlotte sighed, her shoulders sagging. "Yup."

"I expect you have it on you. Can I see it?"

Wariness clouded Charlotte's eyes. "I don't know why I should show it to you."

"I've a feeling something's wrong with it. I might be able to help you, Miss Cohen."

The woman considered the request, then reached into a haversack draped across her body and rummaged around until she found the document. She handed it across the table.

Bridget scanned the paper.

"I'll admit I regret the ninety-ten split," Charlotte said. "I didn't have much negotiating power at the time. When I met Pedro, and he told me what the Bluebird could really be worth, I realized the mistake I'd made."

"Is that why Pedro was trying to hide anything of worth that you found?" Molly asked. "Was he going to file the claim himself when you located it?"

Charlotte nervously licked her lips. "Somethin' like that."

Bridget raised her gaze and took a deep breath. "The terms of this contract are terrible—the worst I've ever seen, but you'll be happy to know that it's not valid."

"It's not?" Charlotte asked, surprised.

"I've drawn up such agreements for my pa and have been present at the signings. Such transactions usually occur at First National Bank and are witnessed by Charles Henderson, the president. He and my pa are good friends. But there are no witnesses on this contract. If you show this to a judge, you could make a very strong argument against its validity. I believe that you could win."

Shock froze Charlotte's face. "You think I could?"

Bridget gave a curt nod. "I just can't figure why my pa did this. He has to know this wouldn't hold up if any subsequent claim ever went into a dispute."

"He'd have to make certain the claim was in his name then," Pearl said.

Molly looked at Charlotte. "He must've planned to have you find the Bluebird, but then he would file the claim himself. With a bad contract, you'd have no recourse."

"Molly's right," Bridget said. "He never intended to give you a cut."

Charlotte's eyes flashed with anger, reminding Molly that the woman might still carry a vendetta against Jake. It would help if they could gain her confidence.

"Why does Shep Lannigan think you can find the Bluebird?" Molly asked.

Charlotte ruminated for a long moment. "It's a good story," she nodded and laughed, the cackle ripping into the silence, "and now you tell me that Shep can't take it from me. Alright, I'll tell you.

"I'd never been close to my pa when I was a girl. I grew up in Ohio with an aunt because my mama died young, and my pa went west to find his fortune. One day, when I was grown, he reappeared, and we had a few years before he up and died. He would tell me the most outrageous tales of his experiences in the mountains searching for silver and gold. But there was one story in particular. It went like this.

"He got himself trapped high up on a ledge 'cause Indians came. They made camp and all he could do was wait and hope they didn't find him even though his gear and animals was down below in the valley. So while he was trapped, he made an incredible find—a thick vein of what he was certain was gold."

A sly smile tugged at her mouth. "Who around here doesn't speak of the Bluebird in hushed tones? Who around here doesn't dream of finding it?"

"You know the exact location?" Bridget asked.

"I have information my papa gave me, but he was never able to return, and it's clear now his memory may have been faulty. But Pedro was helping me. I know I'm close."

"How about we go with you into the mountains," Molly said, keeping the knowledge of Jake's claims to herself. There was no guarantee one of them was the Bluebird anyway. And if one was, Molly was uncertain how Charlotte might react to the news. It was probably best to keep an eye on the woman.

"Why?" Charlotte asked.

"I have some idea where this ledge of your pa's might be."

Charlotte eyed her with suspicion. "What're you sayin'?"

Too late, Molly tried to cover her tracks. "Time is of the essence right now, Charlie. If you want to have your hand in the pie, we need to ride now."

"*I aim* to have the *whole* pie." Charlotte angrily bit out each word.

"I'd say the time for that has passed," Pearl said, "but let's get moving so we can get you better than ten percent."

Molly hoped that what she'd done at the claims office had been the right thing.

# CHAPTER 22

Shep pointed a rifle at Jake. "Drop your holster."

He didn't think Shep would really shoot him...but then again, maybe he would. The lure of riches did funny things to a man's mind. Jake unbuckled his gun belt and dropped it to the ground.

"Did you really think I wouldn't find out about this?" Shep asked.

"It hasn't been for lack of trying," Jake said. No sense in attempting to sugarcoat it. "There's been a lot going on behind your back."

"No doubt." Shep flicked a nod in Jake's direction. "Step back."

Slowly, Jake moved five paces from his gun. "How'd you find me?"

"Archie told me."

*How in the hell did Archie know?* Had it been Molly? And if it was, had she spoken deliberately or under duress?

Jake had managed to hide his surprise, but he gave the warning in his voice free rein. "You'd better leave the girls out of it."

"And which girls are those?"

Jake frowned. Was Lannigan being purposely obtuse or just playing plain dumb?

"Well, your own daughter for one," Jake uttered.

"Bridget's loyal. Did you think you could sway her with your charms?"

"There seemed to be a time when you thought she could do that to *me*. But what's done is done. She's got her sights set on Robert, and for some goddamned reason, he's willing to put up with her."

"Any man would be lucky to have Bridget, but I'm not about to hand her over. Make no mistake, any interest you might've had in her would never have led to anything permanent."

"I guess Robert didn't get that memo."

"Robert served a purpose, but he's not behaving as he should."

"Careful, Shep," Jake said. "You're starting to sound like the monster everyone thinks you are."

"I'm just a good businessman, that's all."

Jake couldn't contain his laugh of derision. "That's utter bullshit. You're a liar and a cheat. You take what doesn't belong to you."

"You're still sore about the Shanghai, but that doesn't entitle you to the Bluebird."

"It sure as hell doesn't entitle *you*." Jake sobered. "So tell me how you do it? Who doctors the paperwork in the claims office?"

"That's a bold accusation to be making, son, even for one called The Jackal. You best be careful, lest the evidence find its way back to you."

*Shit.* A tendril of fear shot through Jake's gut. Lannigan's threat was real.

"You better show me what you've found," Shep added.

Reluctantly, Jake grabbed his knapsack and moved away from his weapon, heading into the valley.

MOLLY LED the way on horseback, Charlie riding double with her, since she had no mount. Pearl followed on her mule, and Bridget brought up the rear. They rode in the dark, Molly struggling to stay on course.

She halted her horse and waited for Bridget and Pearl to catch up. "I'm just not certain this is the right way. It's so dark, it's difficult to recognize the path."

"Are you headed to the Glen Valley?" Pearl asked.

"I don't know the name of the place where Robert staked the Chigger."

"Based on what you've said, I believe it's one and the same. Ivan and I have poked around. We never did find anything of value, but—"

"Then why are we headed there?" Charlie demanded.

"It doesn't mean there isn't anything to discover," Pearl continued. "Do you have any idea how hard it is to locate decent lodes in these hills?" Pearl shook her head, clearly fed up with the woman. "How long have you been searching for the Bluebird? A month or two? There are men in these parts who've been looking for years, and they have some idea of what they're doing." Pearl paused and let out an irritated huff. "I know an easier way into that valley."

Molly nearly wept with relief. "There's a different path?" She didn't want to climb that treacherous, steep wall of granite again. "Can you find it in the dark?"

"I think so," Pearl replied. "Let me take the lead."

Molly gratefully let her horse fall in line behind Pearl's mule.

———

THE ALTERNATE ENTRANCE to the valley proved tricky to locate. After three false leads, Pearl finally found it. Ducking under a low overhang of rock, they were able to lead their horses on foot. When they cleared the narrow pathway and emerged into the valley, Molly knew that Jake's claims could be worked far easier with this passageway.

The snap of a twig had the horses dancing and tugging at the reins. As Molly sought to soothe her animal, Charlie raised her gun from where she stood off to the right.

"I'll shoot!" she yelled.

"Pearl, is that you?" a man's voice called from the shadows.

Pearl pushed past Charlie. "Ivan?"

He stepped out, weapon at the ready, along with Robert limping by his side.

"You hold it right there," Charlie demanded.

"This is my husband. Put your gun down!"

"What're you doin' here?" Ivan asked.

"Looking for the Bluebird, what else?" Pearl wrapped her arms around him.

When Charlie noticed Robert, she raised her gun again. "You were in that tunnel."

Robert tensed but didn't move. "You're the one who shot me?"

"There were samples in there and they was mine."

Bridget rushed from behind Molly, but Robert barreled into his fiancée, pushing them both to the ground as Charlie discharged her weapon.

Pearl screamed.

In a red rage, Molly punched Charlie square in the jaw, howling as pain shot through her hand and down her arm. As the woman went down, she swung her pistol, catching Molly on the cheek with the barrel and sending her stumbling backwards, reeling from the blow.

As Molly sought to get her bearings, Robert scrambled along the ground and wrested the gun from Charlie's hands. Both Ivan and Pearl grabbed the woman and held her in place.

Robert stepped back, glancing at both Molly and Bridget. "Who the hell is this?"

"Her name is Charlotte Cohen," Bridget said. "My pa hired her to find the Bluebird."

"Is there anyone your pa hasn't hired?" Robert asked, his anger hanging around him like a cloak. He shifted to his injured leg and winced.

"I'm not sorry I shot you," Charlotte spat out, still struggling against Pearl and Ivan. "You need to stay away from what's mine."

Robert pulled Molly to her feet and nailed her with a look that said, "This woman is unhinged." Maybe he was right. Charlotte had tried to hurt her brother twice now. There was no telling what might happen when they found Jake.

"You've left us no choice, Charlotte," Molly said, trying to calm her nerves. "We need to tie you up."

She retrieved a coil of rope from her horse. It took all of them to hold the writhing, cursing she-cat down while Robert bound both her hands and feet.

Molly stepped back to catch her breath. "Where's Jake?"

"He left camp alone sometime during the night," Robert said. "Ivan remembered this pathway, and we only just got here before you all came along."

The pain in Molly's hand was suddenly gone, eclipsed by icy fear coursing through her veins. "Have you seen James Winston?"

"No. Why?"

"I've a feeling he's looking for you. We should get to the Chigger."

Ivan looked at Charlotte squirming on the ground. "What're we going to do with her?"

"I guess we take her with us," Robert replied, but his voice conveyed his reluctance. "Ivan, help me lift her atop the mule."

The two men hefted Charlie across the animal, face down, her stomach hugging the saddle.

"You no-good, rotten bastards," she screamed. "I *will* have the Bluebird, goddammit. You've no right to it."

Robert stepped away from the volatile woman. "What the devil is wrong with her?"

"It seems her father was the mythical prospector who found the lode years ago after being trapped on a ledge by Indians," Molly said. "She didn't seem this crazed earlier. I thought we'd gotten through to her."

"Does she have a contract with Lannigan?" Robert asked.

"She does, but it's worthless," Bridget replied. "My pa saw to that."

"I can hear you!" Charlie spit.

"Then why don't you calm down?" Molly demanded. "I was of a mind to let you have an adjacent claim, but now you're just acting like a lunatic."

Molly grabbed a bandanna from her saddlebag and roughly tied it off around Charlie's head, muffling the worst of the woman's noise. "I'm sorry for this, truly I am, but you could've killed my brother or Bridget, for God's sake."

Charlie screamed and tried to fling herself from the mule. Robert got more rope and secured her to the animal.

Bridget took Charlie's weapon for herself, and Molly pulled the Colt Lightning from her gear.

"Let's go," Robert said.

In a single line, they entered the hidden valley as dawn began turning the sky to gray.

---

JAKE PAUSED to catch a breath as a ray of sunlight crested the ridge and blinded him.

"Don't stop." Lannigan nudged him from behind.

They stood on the steep, east-facing cliffside, where Robert had staked the Chigger. And if all had gone well in town for Molly, then Jake should now be the proud owner of two claims in the same locale. The big question was just how far was Lannigan willing to go to take what he thought belonged to him.

Jake made a mental note to find a damn good lawyer when he got back to town—one preferably not from Creede, so as to avoid Lannigan's influence—and shore up his claims as quickly as possible to avoid what had occurred with the Shanghai.

"Show me the vein, goddammit," Shep demanded.

Jake bit back a retort and glanced upward. His eye caught a flash of movement on the upper slope. Not wanting to alert Lannigan, Jake moved forward slowly. Was it friend or foe?

An explosion blasted the rock above. Jake instinctively ducked then took off running. A second splintering crack knocked his feet out from him, and he rolled and slipped more than ten feet before regaining his balance.

Rocks and boulders rained down on him. Shep was nowhere to be seen, but Jake didn't wait around to find him.

A third thundering rumble made everything go dark.

---

THREE DYNAMITE BLASTS shook the mountain. Stunned, Molly and the others watched the ensuing avalanche of rocks and debris as it careened down the mountainside.

Jake!

Molly bolted, leaving the others, and frantically ran upward. Carrying the gun proved awkward, but she didn't want to abandon it. She hiked her skirt up and climbed, her legs muscles straining, sweat trailing down her back.

Periodically she stopped to gain her bearings and catch her breath, and saw that Robert and Bridget weren't far behind, Robert somehow making good headway despite his injured leg. Farther back were Pearl and Ivan and, surprisingly, Charlie. They must've untied her.

Molly kept going, not wanting any of them to pass her.

They'd have to deal with Charlotte Cohen later.

As Molly came to the worst of the debris field, she slipped repeatedly on the unsteady surface. Her knees ached with bruises, and she winced from her ankles twisting.

"Jake!" She searched for signs of anyone. "Jake!"

She continued scrambling over the scree, the sun now beating down on her.

*Maybe he isn't here.*

She hoped it was true, but she had to keep looking. What if he was buried? She began scanning the rubble for any sign of a body or clothing. She was pretty certain she was near the place where she and Jake had found the Chigger, where he had probably discovered the gold nugget.

She took a horizontal path, thinking that a body would've been pushed downward, moving quickly but at the same time frantically examining the rocky remains.

The hump of a man, slumped over, materialized at the same time a gunshot ricocheted nearby. Screaming, she crouched and crawled toward the body. When she encountered a dip in the ground, the gunman stopped shooting, having likely lost her. She scrambled desperately to the man and tugged at his shoulders to flip him over.

*Shep Lannigan.*

Blood covered his face and stained his shirt, but his chest moved. He was alive.

Molly peeked upward, wondering where the shooter was. The compulsion to keep moving and find Jake was nearly overwhelming, but she didn't want to get shot. Looking behind her, she couldn't see Robert or Bridget.

Molly shook the man lying unconscious beside her. "Mister Lannigan, wake up." She hesitated for a moment, then slapped his cheek. "Wake up, sir. I can't leave you here, and I certainly can't carry you."

Another shake produced a moan from the man.

"Are you hurt, Mister Lannigan?"

His eyes opened. "What the hell..." He focused on her. "What are you doing here?"

Molly ignored the question. "Can you sit up?" She grabbed his arm and pulled him to a sitting position.

His hand came to his head. Molly backed away from him, searching for the shooter.

"Give me your gun," Lannigan demanded. His disorientation was gone, and he watched her with clear eyes, his hand outstretched for her weapon.

"No." She scooted back farther and pointed the Colt at him.

"You don't need to fear me."

She didn't believe him. "Where's Jake?"

She saw the slightest flicker of hesitation in Lannigan's eyes.

"I don't know," he answered.

She suspected he *did* know. "What have you done? Is that dynamite your doing?"

"No, it was mine."

James Winston stood above them.

---

WHEN JAKE CAME TO, a cornflower blue sky greeted him. Sprawled on his back, he thought he was in Morocco, greeted by yet another day in the unforgiving Sahara, stalked by stealthy jackals, fearing they might turn on him at any time. As he moved his arms and legs, a groan escaped his mouth, and awareness flooded him.

*Creede. Shep Lannigan. The Bluebird.*

And most importantly, *Molly Rose Simms.*

He rolled to his side and wiped his mouth, his hand coming

away smeared in blood. Someone had blown chunks out of the mountain. He pushed to his feet and, despite the pain, decided nothing was broken.

He scanned the area littered with rocky detritus and dusted off his shirt, stained with more blood. After locating his hat several feet away, he began an upward climb, staying low and keeping an eye out for whomever planted the dynamite. He wondered if Nine Toes had somehow found his way into the valley.

Hefting himself onto a ledge, he crouched on his knees. When he saw what the blasting had exposed, he stopped cold in his tracks.

Large and thick, the vein sparkled like a seductively draped woman, gorgeous beyond all measure. Jake stared, utterly stunned.

"God Almighty," Nine Toes said.

Jake hadn't noticed his approach. The prospector fell to his knees, prostrating himself before the altar of riches. Jake gaped at the most extraordinary lode he'd ever seen, unable to speak.

He hadn't expected this. He doubted any of them had, not even the prospector those Utes had kept trapped so long ago. The man must've known he'd found a viable vein, but had he suspected this was here, he would've likely killed all those Indians single-handedly instead of walking away from it.

It was a wholly unimaginable find.

Unfathomable...unbelievable...inexplicable...

Robert and Bridget appeared, followed closely by Ivan and Pearl.

What they saw halted them en masse and caused the women to gasp.

"What the hell?" Robert couldn't hide the veneration in his voice.

"It does exist," Ivan said quietly, then with more excitement, "Praise be, there is a God!"

Nine Toes pierced the solemnity of the moment by weeping loudly.

Boom joined them, out of breath. "You're all staring at something like it's Jesus Christ himself." He stopped when his eyes caught sight of the lode. "Well, I'll be a son-of-a-gun. It's gold. And a helluva lot of it."

"It's mine, you sonsabitches!"

Jake tore his gaze from the spectacle to face a wild-eyed woman he didn't recognize headed straight for them. She shoved past Jake and threw herself in front of the vein.

"It was my pa that found it," she yelled. "I've got the rightful claim."

"No you don't," Shep Lannigan said from several yards away, answering the question of whether he'd survived the blasts—he had.

Molly trailed behind Shep, putting all of Jake's senses on alert. He stood, realizing only then how mesmerized he'd been by the power of gold—how they all had been—but now he needed to be smart. Bewildered by how quickly a crowd had formed in such a remote place, the precariousness of the situation became apparent as James Winston brought up the rear holding a gun to Molly's back.

"Our contract is worthless," the woman said to Lannigan, then pointed at Bridget. "*She* told me so."

Shep cast a cool eye on his daughter. When he reached the crowd and saw the gold-bearing lode, his stoic façade turned to shock.

Molly squeezed between Shep and Robert, then mumbled, "Oh my God."

"Too many goddamn people here," Winston said, waving his gun. "Everyone get back."

Jake had to give Winston credit—he was the only one not to drool like an idiot over the find. Winston skirted the crowd and positioned himself in front of the vein.

"It's not yours, Winston," the woman spat, looking up at him from where she was sprawled across the vein.

"I beg to differ," he answered.

"It's not either of yours," Jake said. "I've already staked this claim. Right where you're standing, to be exact, and it's already been filed with the claims recorder." He knew his coordinates were in this vicinity. It would be close enough.

"Bullshit," Winston replied.

"I've got two more claims just down the slope." Jake indicated the direction with a nod of his head.

"Actually, Jake, you only have one," Molly said.

Confused, he slid his gaze to her, a bad feeling taking root in his stomach.

"You and I own the Chigger, which is down the slope as you said. The one beside it—the Molly Rose—and this one—the Bluebird—are owned by two people."

He'd always prided himself on being smart when it came to women and had been so certain she wouldn't betray him. But it was obvious his luck had just run out, and he would've laughed if didn't cut through him like a knife.

"And who would that be?" he asked.

"Me and Bridget."

---

PANIC GRIPPED MOLLY. She hadn't expected the look of hurt that crossed Jake's face when she said who owned the other two claims. *His* claims.

She'd tried to help, and now she may have irreversibly botched everything that Jake—and Robert—had worked for. She needed to explain.

Standing off to the left, Bridget stared at her. "What?"

"Perfect," Winston said, his gaze locked on Bridget. "We can be married in a few days."

Robert took a step forward. "There's no way in hell that's happening, you dirty, egg-sucking dog."

Molly grabbed her brother's arm, not wanting Winston to shoot him.

"Cut the crap, James," Shep said. "Miss Simms did the right thing."

"I intend to marry Robert," Bridget said.

"And I intend to marry Jake." Molly searched Jake's eyes, his face bruised and streaked with blood, hoping for a hint of... something. But all that reflected back at her was a blank slate, with no hint of affection. Gone was the man she loved; all that remained was The Jackal.

"I'm sorry," she pleaded. "I did it to protect you, to protect the claim."

He looked away from her, the dismissal striking her like a hard slap on the cheek.

Winston pointed the gun at Lannigan. "You'll fix it."

"I don't know what you're talking about," Shep answered.

"You'll *fix* the claim."

"Is it true, Papa?" Bridget demanded. "Have you changed claims?"

"It's all just hearsay," Shep said. "Doing such a thing is illegal."

Jake shook his head, clearly disgusted.

"That's why I did it," Molly cut in, her focus still on Jake.

The Jackal—the keeper of her heart—flicked his gaze to her, guarded and cold.

"I knew if I put your name on it, then Lannigan would steal it from you," she continued in a rush. "You'll have my half."

"And you just handed the other half over to *him*." Jake flicked a hand at Shep.

"No! I gave it to Bridget because, if she really loves Robert, she won't let her father take it from her." Molly looked at Bridget.

Shock and indecision played across Bridget's pale cheeks and wide eyes.

A wave of tears threatened Molly. Maybe she'd been wrong.

She'd gambled it all, and now it was clear that she'd sorely miscalculated.

"You can have my half, Jake," she whispered, but she knew from the vacant look in his eyes that he believed it was all lost. She grasped onto another truth. "This claim might not be all of the vein. It might not even be the apex."

All eyes landed on her. She could feel the attention on her skin as if everyone's hands had just grabbed her.

Charlie shot to her feet, a flash of savage awareness in her eyes.

"Jesus, Mary and Joseph," Nine Toes exclaimed, throwing himself onto the ground to the south of the Bluebird as if he were staking a claim with his body.

Charlie landed atop him, and the two began to fight for ownership.

"You're one jackass of a woman," he yelled, pulling her hair.

"You're a blowhard, and I'm gonna kill you because of Pedro!" She slapped him hard across the cheek.

Molly jumped back to avoid being pushed off the cliff as the two of them struggled like two wild animals fighting over a fresh kill.

Jake bolted to the north side of the Bluebird and hastily started stacking rock cairns. Within seconds everyone had scattered except for Molly and Bridget. Even Winston had abandoned holding everyone at gunpoint, in an effort to gain higher access farther north of Jake's suddenly new claim.

Molly watched in horror as Robert climbed straight up with nothing to stop his fall should he lose his grip. He crossed horizontally in an effort to guess where the vein might be farther up.

Pearl and Ivan and Boom went lower, hastily blocking out rectangular plats with rocks. Shep scrambled past Jake, then Winston, eyeing Robert's progress as the two of them honed in on the same spot. Robert slipped and barely stopped himself from falling off the mountain.

"Robert!" Bridget's hand flew to her mouth.

Molly stopped breathing.

"This is madness," Bridget said, her voice laced with panic.

With Robert momentarily safe again, Molly let her own panic loose on the other woman. "Do you love my brother? Because I'm sure not seeing it."

"You know I do." Bridget's lips pinched in a defensive gesture.

"Then stand up to your father!"

Bridget hesitated, blinking rapidly, her cheeks now flushed red. She took a steadying breath. "I will."

*Thank God.*

For a moment, a weight lifted from Molly.

If the Bluebird claim played out, she and Bridget would own one of the most lucrative mining lodes in the Creede area. She just hoped that Jake and Robert didn't fall to their deaths before she and Bridget could marry the gold-crazed buffoons.

Having gained the upper hand with Charlie, Nine Toes now straddled her, his hands gripping her throat and choking her. "I didn't kill Pedro. It was two other prospectors that done did it." He struggled to keep her still. "Now, I don't wanna kill you, so let's settle this. We'll share the claim, goddammit."

Molly stepped closer. "Take the deal, Charlie."

The woman finally stopped fighting against Nine Toe's restraint. "Fine," she said through gritted teeth.

When Nine Toes released her, she spit in his face.

"No doubt the worst deal I ever did make," he muttered, standing. "Now get up off your ass, woman, and help me stake this claim."

# CHAPTER 23

I t was mid-afternoon as Molly stood beside Robert on the porch of Henry and Esme Patterson's home. She smoothed her hands down her freshly-laundered wool skirt, then patted her hair to make certain it was contained in the bun she'd worked at for over an hour. Impatient frustration was her friend these days.

Robert had told her that Henry would be the best resource in addressing issues involved with the Bluebird, and he'd arranged to bring her for a meeting. Bridget hadn't accompanied them, which she suspected was in deference to Molly's *Jake* problem. Namely, that he wouldn't see her or respond to repeated visits to his cabin, or even to notes sent to him. It had been two days since the craziness in what was now called the Bluebird Valley. She prayed that Henry could help her smooth out the mess she now found herself in.

Robert knocked, and in short order, Esme Patterson opened the front door.

"Molly, my dear." Esme brought her into a hug, which Molly gladly sank into. "It'll be fine. You'll see. My Henry will help."

Leaning back, Molly forced a smile on her face and suppressed an urge to cry.

Esme turned to Robert, and he stooped to let her kiss him on the cheek. "It's good to see you, Robert."

"And you, Esme."

"Come inside. I've got refreshments in the parlor. Let me just drag Henry from his study."

Robert guided Molly into the sitting room. A piano hugged one wall beside a stuffed rocking chair. Molly took a seat on the blue velvet couch, the coffee table opposite displaying a tray with a silver coffee set, ceramic cups adorned with roses, and a plate of cookies and cakes. A portrait of the Pattersons hung on the wall—a young Esme on a horse and a very handsome Henry standing at her side. Molly couldn't help but smile at the obvious love and adventure displayed in the picture.

At the same time, the abrupt loss of Jake—of her own love and adventure—pierced her.

What if there was no working this out?

Henry entered—his hair mussed and his shirt rumpled, the sleeves rolled to his elbows. "It's good to see you both."

"I apologize for his appearance," Esme said, following him. "He's been working hard since news of the Bluebird broke."

"Thank you for seeing me," Molly said.

Henry and Esme sat on chairs across from them. "You've got yourself quite a find, young lady," Henry said, admiration in his voice.

Molly nodded, uncomfortable with how much to say about the details of the claim. Instead, she jumped right to her problem. "I want to give my share to Jake. Will you help me?"

Henry regarded her with shrewd scrutiny while Esme poured coffee and passed each of them a cup although he waved his off.

Molly began to fidget as if she'd misbehaved somehow.

Henry glanced at Robert then focused on her. "I know a bit of what happened out there, and I understand why you would want to set things right by giving Jake half ownership of the Bluebird claim, but I'm going to advise against it."

Molly frowned. "Why?" She balanced the saucer and cup on her knees. Did everyone in this town dislike Jake?

Henry sat back against his chair and crossed his arms. "You and Bridget Lannigan are in a very unique situation at the moment. I've no doubt you have many opposing interests tugging at you, and it will surely get worse as the days go by. But if the Bluebird plays out like most folks think it will, then the necessity for a cool head is of utmost importance.

"Shep Lannigan and Jake McKenna don't get along. If those two are allowed to make critical decisions on the development of that lode, the only result I see is the inability to extract any ore."

"Why would you say that?"

Henry sighed. "I've seen it happen before, and with claims far less lucrative than yours. The lawyers get involved, and the litigation drags on for months, sometimes years. And during that time, any progress is prohibited. Everyone suffers. It's simply a losing proposition."

Henry leaned forward, bracing his elbows on his knees. "You're a bright girl, Molly. Robert has said as such." He gave a nod toward her brother. "Keep the claim. If Bridget is amenable, the two of you can open up that area to the benefit of everyone involved."

Molly considered the gravity of the situation. She'd never dreamed she would ever be in a position such as this, and Henry tugged at her conscience, her sense of responsibility to the larger picture. The Bluebird was the biggest lode ever found in Creede, and it was owned by two women. The town had been in an uproar since the news had broken.

Molly would be lying if she didn't find it all a tad bit exciting.

However, she knew that withholding the claim from Jake was only going to further ruin her relationship with him. Was it worth the risk?

But if Jake got involved and mucked it all up, wasn't that far worse? Wasn't that why she'd placed the claim in hers and Bridget's names in the first place? She'd wanted to protect his interests. She could still do that, even if he was too stubborn to ever forgive her.

She took a sip of her coffee then nodded. "I'll do it."

Henry smiled. "Thatta girl. First, I know you filed the claim in Hinsdale County, but you ought to file it in Rio Grande and Saguache as well. This will strengthen your stance legally. I can help you with that. Second, we need to get the surveyor out there for an official report, and discovery shafts need to be dug. We need samples assayed as soon as possible. I've got two investors back east who are very interested, and I can help you negotiate with them. And third, you and Bridget need to form a company."

It all sounded overwhelming. Molly set her coffee onto the table and clasped her hands together.

Robert reached over and squeezed her arm. "You can do this, Molly." He smiled. "I'm very proud of you."

"You are? But my behavior appears to be that of a woman who romanced the town jackal in order to steal from him."

"That's not who you are."

"Actually, Molly," Esme said, "most of the talk is filled with admiration. Men dominate the mines in this town. That two young women snatched the coveted Bluebird out from just about every prospector, vagabond, and scoundrel within fifty miles of here is a feat well worth celebrating."

"But it was Jake who found it, based on Robert's previous find of the Chigger. There's nothing admirable in me taking it from either of them."

"Then make it right moving forward," Henry said. "I've got faith in you."

Esme smiled. "We all do."

MOLLY STOOD in the assayer's office and waited. The door opened, and as she glanced over her shoulder, her heart galloped in her chest when her eyes met Jake's. He paused, clearly surprised to see her, but removed his hat and entered anyway.

It had been two weeks since her meeting with Henry, and Jake had done nothing but avoid her. It was obvious that he no longer desired to marry her although he hadn't come straight out and said it to her face, and for some crazy reason, this gave her a sliver of hope.

Since she never knew when she might run into him these days, she always made certain she looked her best, and today was no exception. She wore a navy dress that flattered her figure with a hat angled atop her coiled hair.

He tossed his Stetson on a table, sat on a stool, and crossed his arms, watching her. He'd let himself go, his dark hair longer and his days-old face stubble fast turning into a beard and mustache. Shadows hovered beneath his molasses-colored eyes. He wasn't sleeping, of that she was certain.

Shoring up her nerves—something she'd been doing a lot of these past days as the owner of the famous Bluebird claim—she raised her chin. "Are you going to stop pouting like a child and speak to me?"

"You think I'm a child?"

She swallowed against the dryness in her throat. "Hardly."

Of late, during the occasional times they'd been in one another's vicinity, she was witness to the ruffian he was at heart. His aloofness and brooding behavior drove home that he was The Jackal—smuggler, spy, wanderer. Nothing but a scamp.

What had she been thinking?

And yet, it was maddening how even more devastatingly handsome he became each time she saw him.

She repeatedly scoffed at her ability to swoon over him, but it didn't end the desperate longing she felt. Only pride kept her from begging. If they were to be together, she'd find a way to keep her self-respect. After everything that had happened, it was the only way.

And if they weren't together, she'd get over him. She would travel and see the world on her own, and then she would return to Tucson and marry.

So why was she still here?

The Bluebird, of course. She'd wired her folks and told them she planned to extend her visit, keeping the details of the claim to her herself for now. Once it was all put in order, she'd share her news.

"Checking on your samples?" he asked.

She gave a curt nod. Exploratory shafts had been sunk on all the claims that now dotted the entire mountainside in the Bluebird Valley, the previous, less-well-known name of Glen Valley having quickly fallen by the wayside. The value of samples of ore extracted was slowly trickling in. If rumors were to be believed, everyone in town was eagerly waiting for the results from Molly and Bridget's claim, and not just the Bluebird, but the Molly Rose as well. If the appraisal came in high, it would bolster the value of all the neighboring claims.

Investors hovered with bated breath. Molly had already fended off more than she could count. A few had relentlessly hounded her and Bridget to sell now, at ridiculously low prices, pressuring them that they knew nothing because they were women. Thank goodness for Henry Patterson and his help in managing it all.

Many lawyers had become involved in the Bluebird Valley, as everyone had taken pains to protect their claims from any shenanigans from Shep Lannigan, or anyone else for that matter. Thankfully, the Sheriff had stepped in, and several employees at the Claims Office that Shep frequented had been replaced. In the end, however, there wasn't enough evidence to pin anything on Lannigan. Molly suspected this was a bur under Jake's skin. Just one of many, it would seem, although based on his behavior, she surmised she had the honor of top bur these days.

The door opened again, and Robert and Bridget entered. Everyone silently acknowledged one another.

"Is the assay finished?" Bridget asked into the awkward silence.

"Mister Mathers said he'd be out shortly," Molly replied.

The office door opened again, and Ivan and Pearl crowded in along with Boom and his lady love, a short rosy-cheeked, flaxen-haired woman with wide hips. Molly shuffled toward the wall to allow more room, disappointed that the action took her further from Jake.

Molly didn't think another body could fit in the foyer of the assay office, but she was proven wrong when Shep Lannigan, James Winston, Nine Toes Bishop, and Charlotte Cohen insisted on gaining entry.

She flashed a look at Jake, who continued to keep an eye on her, but she honestly couldn't tell if it was desire she saw in his gaze or irritation.

Pearl jostled her way over. "Has he come around?" she asked quietly.

Molly gave a slight shake of her head.

Pearl gave a knowing smile. "Have you tried seducing him?"

Molly leaned closer, concerned someone would overhear. "Of course not. You were the one who warned me of the pitfalls of such a thing."

"That was then," Pearl whispered. "If you want him, you have to go after him, and the surest way is with physical relations. You'll have him in the palm of your hand."

Molly frowned with indecision. While she appreciated the truth that Pearl no doubt spoke, uncertainty outweighed the advice. She was far from confident in her ability to hold Jake's attention with her womanly abilities, and he would no doubt be skeptical of her advances now that she owned the claim.

Her skin flushed with perspiration. She wiped a hand along the back of her neck. Being in the crowded room was beginning to remind of her of the panic she'd felt in the well, and Pedro's tunnel, and Pearl's abandoned mine.

The desire to flee welled up as her heart pounded in her head, her chest aching, her breathing shallow.

"What's wrong?" Pearl asked. "You don't look well."

"My stomach is a little queasy." She began to push her way to the door. "I need a bit of air."

"Molly?" Bridget asked, but Molly ignored her.

Keeping her head down, she made no eye contact with Lannigan or Winston where they stood at the entrance as she pried the door open just enough to slip outside. Once free, she took several deep breaths, steadying herself with a hand on her chest. The mountains cast a shadow in the late afternoon sun, making the air much cooler than earlier in the day. She immediately began to feel better.

"Are you ill?"

At Jake's question, Molly didn't turn around. "No," she answered over her shoulder. "I just needed a break from the crowded room."

"It appears we're all a herd that moves together."

"How did everyone know the samples would be ready today? Bridget and I have been careful who we tell."

Jake moved to face her. "You and Bridget are the stars of town. You're mentioned in the paper on an almost daily basis."

Molly had heard this although she hadn't bothered to check. "Is that why you're so angry with me?"

"Because you're famous and I'm not?"

She nodded.

He gave a humorless laugh. "No, of course not."

"Then what is it, Jake? Please tell me." So much for her pride. She was slowly dying without him. Looking into his eyes, shadowed with pain and confusion that mirrored her own, she knew she couldn't live without him. In a matter of minutes, she'd commence the begging.

He didn't respond right away, but Molly waited, her stomach in knots, needing to know but at the same time fearing he would tell her he didn't love her—had never loved her—and now that he'd realized it, wanted to go his own way.

"I won't lie—I was stunned that you stole my claim right out from under me."

"That's not true," she said in a rush.

"But it is." His eyes narrowed, contemplative. "I've always been an opportunist. I've never had the tables turned on me, at least not by someone I cared about."

"Jake—"

"For the first time in my life, I realized the one thing I'd been missing...the one thing that was important to me. And that's loyalty."

"I told you why I did it. You said you wanted to marry me. When...," she faltered, "*if* we marry, it will be yours. Bridget hasn't handed over her share to her father. She and Robert will keep it. They still plan to wed."

"Well, be that as it may, I'm not convinced everything will be tied into a neat little bow."

He was slipping through her fingers. "Haven't you ever trusted anyone?"

"I wanted to trust *you*. And I suppose that was my mistake, not yours. Honestly, I'm impressed that you pulled it off."

Words clogged Molly's throat with rebuttals to his implication that she'd been planning this all along. Nothing could be further from the truth.

Bridget exited the assayer's office, a huge grin on her face. She handed a certificate to Molly.

Having spent several meetings with the Pattersons, as well as picking Robert's brain, Molly had learned much about the history of mining in Creede and, more importantly, what would make the

Bluebird special. As she scanned the results of the assay, she knew the outcome was beyond expectation.

Excitement thrummed through her, and she couldn't suppress the smile that spread across her face and matched Bridget's. Not wanting to hide it from Jake, she read the findings out loud.

"The samples contained a fine-grained amethyst quartz carrying a considerable amount of gold, nearly eight percent lead, and zinc as well." She took a deep breath. "Some of the samples tested at three thousand ounces of silver per ton."

"Sonofabitch," Jake muttered under his breath, his stunned tone filled with disbelief.

Molly glanced up, wanting to share her joy with him, but he turned away and shut her out. As he reentered the assayer's office, the last bit of news she'd wanted to share with him died on her lips.

"I've never seen him like this before," Robert said. "Did you tell him what the surveyor said?"

"No." And just like that, her momentary happiness faded away.

# CHAPTER 24

Jake downed another glass of whiskey as he played faro at the Orleans Club. He'd found himself here more often than not in the past two weeks. Sitting alone in his small house—not far from Zang's Hotel, where he knew Molly rested her pretty self—gnawed at him like a rabid animal, so every night he'd sought distraction with liquor and gambling.

Robert materialized from the crowd and took the seat beside Jake, offering him a cigar. Jake took it.

"I never really pegged you as a prideful ass," Robert said.

Jake waved the waitress over. "And I never pegged you as a Nancy-boy." The buxom, black-haired woman winked at him, bending close to get his order. "Another whiskey for me and a sarsaparilla for this whipped dog."

"Right away, sugar." She made sure he got an eyeful of cleavage before she left.

Disdain filled Robert's gaze. "I was too nice. You're just a piece of horseshit." He struck a lucifer on the edge of the table and lit his cigar. He produced a second match and handed it to Jake.

Puffs of smoke settled in the air, hanging suspended, much like the tension between them.

"So, you're gonna bury your face in a woman like that?" Robert asked, waving a hand at the departed fancy girl.

Jake knocked his hat back. "I know it's hard to believe, but I don't carouse. Not like you with Mabel."

"That's ancient history, and I'm engaged now."

"Yeah, to the Devil's own daughter."

"What exactly are you so angry about?"

Jake paused while the flirty saloon girl deposited his drink and the bottle of soda at the edge of the faro table, and then sauntered away. There was only one female who haunted his thoughts, and this afternoon she'd looked unbearably enticing in a dark dress that hugged every last curve she possessed. Well, that wasn't entirely true, but his mind did a fine job filling in the blanks.

Jake took a swallow of the firewater, then said, "What's happening in the Bluebird Valley is a farce, and you know it."

"How exactly is that?"

"Lannigan will get his hands on it, and he only has to get fifty percent of it. Bridget will cave any day now."

"No, she won't."

"I'm not an idiot, Robert. I know about the survey. I know the Bluebird claim is the apex. We all staked claims around it—Lannigan, Winston, you, me, the Krupin's, that crazy Cohen woman—but it won't matter. The Bluebird will own that mountain. It may take months—hell, even years—to figure it all out in court, but that claim will prevail."

"So what're you gonna do?" Robert demanded. "Leave?"

"I'm thinkin' about it." Jake slumped in his chair.

"Why don't you honor the promise you made to my sister and marry her? We can both help Molly and Bridget manage this. What the hell is wrong with you?"

What the hell *was* wrong with him?

He'd spoken to Molly of loyalty, and he couldn't deny that her actions had sliced him open, shocking him with the intensity of the hurt. Nights of drinking and denial had worn down that pretense, however; beneath it lay a truth that had ripped him open clear to his core.

He wanted Molly's love.

After his parent's deaths, after the isolation of the orphanage and the sheer terror of living on his own from a young age, he'd never acknowledged that love was important.

He'd wanted Molly, from the first second he'd laid eyes on her, and that lust had been enough justification for marriage in his eyes. But his heart wanted something else, something he hadn't been totally aware of until that moment on the mountain when she'd betrayed him. He wanted her soul—bare and open and only for him. He wanted it so much it stole his breath, nearly knocking him to his knees.

And he was terrified that Molly didn't feel the same for him. That she might never feel the same.

"It's just easier this way," he muttered into his glass, the alcohol the only tonic able to erase the misery in his gut.

"You're a coward," Robert bit out. He stood and plowed into the crowd of men and bar maids, quickly disappearing.

Jake resumed his game, determined not to think about the Simms family anymore.

And he knew it would be impossible.

---

"Son, you need to come with me."

Jake glanced up from the faro table.

Henry Patterson watched him with concern in his elderly eyes. "You're so deep in your cups these days, you're not thinking straight. C'mon." Henry waved him to stand up, his voice stern. "Let's go."

Jake obeyed and followed the old man to a less crowded side room. He tried to stay focused with the liquor dulling his senses, which had been his goal all along. But damn it all to hell, no matter how hard he tried, not even the liquid gold could erase Molly Rose from his thoughts.

"Sit down." Henry directed Jake to a stuffed chair. Normally, men would congregate here to drink and smoke, but Henry's stern demeanor implied this wasn't a social meeting.

Jake sank into the furniture. "It's much too late for you to be out, Henry. Esme will have your head."

Henry narrowed his eyes. "It's Esme who sent me. There's not much that woman doesn't know in this town. She loves you, you know. Like a son."

Jake softened, feeling chastised. "I know."

Boom appeared and shut the door behind him. Jake nodded at the burly Russian. Since Boom now fancied a girl at the Orleans Club, he likely frequented the establishment more than usual these days.

"Glad you could make it, Boris," Henry said.

Boom sat beside Henry on a couch that had seen better days, the ivory material discolored from smoke and spilled drinks. Orlov looked at Jake, disappointment marring his features. "I've never seen you like this. The Jackal never loses his way."

Feeling suddenly cornered by the two men, annoyance pricked Jake, and he suppressed an urge to tell them both to jump off a cliff.

"She loves you," Henry said.

Jake laughed. "And who would that be?"

"She filed that claim to protect you."

"Did she tell you that? She could've signed it over to me at any point these past few weeks."

Henry sighed. "She wanted to, but I advised against it."

Jake went still.

This was news.

"I know your history with Shep," Henry continued. "It showed remarkable insight that Molly Rose filed the Bluebird claim the way she did. But you'll be happy to know that she wasn't so diabolical about it—she was simply trying to do what she thought was right at the time." Henry drew a deep breath. "It's important to handle the Bluebird carefully because this claim could be one of the most important discoveries to ever be found in the Creede district. To be honest, Jake, you're not the right person to make these decisions."

"Bullshit," he muttered, but clamped down on reacting further. Despite everything, Henry was the last person he wanted to get in a pissing match with.

Henry twisted his mouth then laughed. "She's a smart girl, and she holds some sway with Bridget Lannigan. I doubt you'd handle the situation with as much finesse."

Jake gritted his teeth. "Why am I here, Henry? To tell me I should be happy I got bilked out of a fortune?"

"No. You're a part of this, whether you like it or not," Henry said, his displeasure clear. "And I can't tell you who to give your heart to, but if I could, I'd instruct you not to botch this up and let that girl go. But actually, we've got another problem." Henry glanced at Boom. "Shep's about to box that valley in, and we can't let that happen."

# CHAPTER 25

J ake dismounted his horse in front of the Patterson's house. A young boy took the reins and led the animal away. Tonight the Pattersons were hosting a party in honor of the Bluebird mine, or at least the future of the mine, and several lads had been employed to aid the guests as they arrived. During the past ten days, Henry had been less than forthcoming about the details concerning investments and buy-outs and the formation of companies, and since Jake wasn't on speaking terms with Molly or Robert, asking them was out of question. Maybe he was just a coward as Robert had accused.

But Jake had done Henry's bidding and solved a potential setback for the Bluebird Valley. It didn't hurt that it would sink a thorn deep into Shep Lannigan's side. The thought brought a smile to Jake's lips.

Strengthening his resolve, Jake had decided he needed to speak to Molly, and about more than just the Bluebird. He'd ceased his nightly drinking binges, and what remained was an ache the size of the Grand Canyon for her. If she'd still have him, he'd take whatever he could get from her, even if, in the end, it was only affection and not love.

He could live with that.

The alternative was a life without her, and agonizing visions of that outcome had awakened him more and more in recent nights, leaving him drenched in sweat and despair.

Jake tugged at his best jacket, a slight breeze ruffling hair that was free of a hat. He'd shaved the mess of facial scruff that he hadn't cared about maintaining, determined to make this evening count. With her.

As Jake stepped into a throng of other townsfolk and moved to the porch, he came face to face with James Winston.

"Nice of you to tear yourself away from the Orleans Club, McKenna."

Jake coolly assessed the man. "I didn't have the chance to say this before, so let me be clear on one thing. If you *ever* point a gun at Miss Simms again, I'll do more than just rough you up." Jake stepped closer and added in a low voice, "And no one will ever find your body."

For a brief second, something close to fear flashed in Winston's eyes. Jake was still certain Winston had had something to do with Pedro Elizondo's death and the subsequent disappearance of the corpse, but as with most circumstances surrounding Winston and Lannigan, no evidence could be brought to light. Pedro's remains had never surfaced although rumors around town whispered that the Mexican had skipped town. Jake didn't doubt the gossip had been started by Winston himself, but it had been readily accepted by many, including Charlotte Cohen, who had purportedly been in love with Pedro.

Jake stepped away from Winston and entered the house. Esme greeted him in the parlor. He leaned down as she hugged him and planted a kiss on his cheek.

She beamed. "It's good to see you, Jake.".

"Thank you for the invite, Esme."

"You're always welcome in our home. Don't ever doubt that."

She glanced past him with a twinkle in her eye and gave a nod. "Molly Rose is looking especially fetching this evening."

Jake turned and stared. The woman of his heart stood beside Robert and Bridget in the parlor, wearing a deep-forest-green gown with little adornment. It suited her well. She smiled as she chatted with her brother and, for a moment, Jake was mesmerized.

"I think she'll surprise you." Esme moved beside him and latched her hand around Jake's arm, much as she'd done that evening at Lannigan's party.

"She already has," he replied.

Esme chuckled and guided him into the bustle of guests crowding the room. Shep Lannigan stood in the corner and watched the proceedings with an impassive glower on his face.

Jake stopped abruptly when Charlotte Cohen moved from the crowd and blocked his and Esme's passage. She looked very presentable with her hair combed and pinned away from her face and wearing a simple yellow gown, but Jake still watched her with a wary eye.

"I never had the chance to thank you," Charlotte said. "I understand it was you who found the Bluebird."

Jake gave a curt nod. He didn't know of any prospector grateful for another staking the claim they'd been after. He'd lost the Shanghai to Shep, and then he'd lost the Bluebird to Molly. Gratitude had been the farthest sentiment on his mind both times. It suddenly galled him that he'd grouped Molly in with the likes of Lannigan. Deep in his bones, he knew it was unfair.

"I never could find it," Charlotte continued. "If not for you and Robert Simms, none of us would be here."

Jake balked. "You're wrong. We're here because of Molly Rose."

"Yup. She's gonna make it all right in the end."

Charlotte stepped away, sidling up to a man that Jake didn't recognize, but upon closer inspection, he did a double-take. It was Nine Toes Bishop, all cleaned up and looking like a gentleman.

Esme excused herself, and Jake continued forward, still headed toward Molly. She finally glanced in his direction and saw him, but the welcoming smile he'd hoped for didn't materialize. Her unsettled gaze looked more like storm clouds brewing. He really couldn't blame her, yet he'd hoped that her feelings for him had softened during their estrangement. The sentiment was illogical, but Jake was learning that love followed no reasonable rules.

Ivan and Pearl cut him off.

"I'm glad you're here," Ivan said, his good eye watching him intently.

Jake swallowed his frustration at another interruption and shifted his attention to the couple. "How are you both?" he asked.

"We're worried about you," Pearl said.

"There's no need. I'm fine." Not really, but Jake didn't need to whine about it.

"Striking it big does funny things to people." Pearl cast a glance at Molly.

"I'm sure you're here to tell me that I've been an ass to her," Jake said, "and you'd be right."

Ivan chuckled. "I sided with you. Pearl, on the other hand, has been oddly proud of your girl, even if she did steal the biggest piece of the pie for herself."

"I told you," Pearl said, her voice hard, "Molly didn't steal it. I've a feeling it all happened this way for a reason, and I suspect we're about to learn that reason this evening."

"I'd like everyone's attention please." Henry's voice rose above the chatter, and the room quieted, the attention shifting to their host. Jake chanced a glance in Molly's direction, but she'd already moved to stand beside Esme, both of them watching Henry as he spoke.

"Esme and I are pleased to have you all here," Henry continued. "We thought it was fitting to celebrate this latest boom in Creede—namely the discovery of the long-sought and infamous Bluebird vein. I know many of you already know the particulars, so I won't bore you with a rehashing of what has led us to this point. Instead, we have exciting news to share. And, for that, I'll invite Miss Molly Rose Simms to say a few words."

Molly smiled warmly, shaking his hand as she changed places with him, and then turned to address the room. "Thank you, Henry."

A slight flush crept up her cheeks, and Jake could tell that she was nervous. He wanted nothing more than to go to her, to offer support in some way, but he remained where he stood and waited along with everyone else.

As Molly started to speak, Bridget began to move through the crowd and distribute a piece of paper to each person.

"Some of you may not know, but the surveyor did confirm that the Bluebird claim—owned by me and Bridget Lannigan—is the apex of the Bluebird vein. In an effort to expedite mining in the area, Miss Lannigan and I have formed the Bluebird Mining Company. It's our hope that everyone with claims in the area will consolidate their holdings and become a partner in the company. This way, all claim holders will benefit from a common infrastructure that will alleviate any potential concerns over claim overlap and the general removal of ore from the area. Bridget is passing around a prospectus to anyone who currently owns a claim in the area. We invite you to consider it and to, hopefully, join BMC."

Jake took the paper from Bridget and scanned the contents.

*What the hell?*

"These percentages are absurd," Shep bellowed from the far end of the room.

Jake read them again: Robert Simms – 20%, Charlotte Cohen – 20% and Jake McKenna – 20%. Investors would take 10% and the remaining 30% was to be distributed evenly among all remaining claim holders on the eastern face of Bluebird Mountain.

"Bridget should have at least fifty percent," Shep demanded.

Having distributed the outlines for the company, Bridget moved to stand beside Molly. "No, Papa. Molly and I agreed that neither of us would have any share of the company. We didn't find the claim. Jake McKenna did." Bridget rested her gaze on Jake. "And he located it because of the early work that Robert did in staking the Chigger."

"While working for me, I might add," Shep all but yelled.

"Well, be that as it may, you did none of the work to find it."

"Then why does Charlotte get such a high percentage?" Shep demanded.

"It was her father who initially found the vein all those years ago," Molly said. "If he were alive, he would be entitled to it, but since he's not, his daughter will receive his shares in his stead."

Conversation broke out in the crowd as everyone tried to make sense of the announcement. Jake wanted to ask why Molly wasn't anywhere in the company—why had she given it all up?—but Shep raised his voice above the din, grabbing everyone's attention.

"I have an announcement of my own to make," he said. "We all know that short of scrambling over a steep pass on the west side, the only way in or out of the Bluebird Valley is a hidden pathway to the southeast. And that's the key to getting the ore out in any type of timely and economical fashion. I now own the forty acres at the mouth of that entrance. I demand a better percentage, or else your company will be building expensive and dangerous tramways to get to that vein."

The room broke into a cacophony of nervous chatter and bickering.

"You're wrong," Jake said, but his words were lost in the noise.

"What did you say?" Molly asked, staring at him.

Jake raised his voice louder. "Shep's wrong."

The room quieted again, and Jake shifted his gaze to Lannigan. "You don't own all the land at the entrance."

"Like hell I don't," Shep replied.

"You missed one sliver just to the east."

Lannigan smirked. "It doesn't matter. You'll never access the valley without my parcel."

Jake settled his attention back on Molly. "It'll work. I purchased the adjacent piece last week. Boom and I checked it out. We can dynamite the area, and there'll be enough room to lay track. Lannigan's got nothing."

Gratitude filled Molly's eyes. If not for the roomful of people, Jake would've swept her up into his arms and kissed her.

More arguing filled the air, and guests began to hash out what it might all mean. Without taking his eyes from Molly, Jake pushed through the crowd until he stood before her.

"Why didn't you tell me this was your plan?" he asked.

"Because you're a stubborn, mule-headed male, and you wouldn't give me the time of day." Her eyes flashed with defiance— and hurt. He deserved it.

"I'm sorry. I was going to apologize to you anyway, even before your big announcement."

She watched him, a cloud of mistrust in her eyes.

"Why did you cut yourself out of the company?" he asked. "It would've given you independence. With the money, you'd be able to travel anywhere you'd like, just as you imagined."

"Yes, but it was never about the money. It was never my intention to steal it from you, Jake. You're rightfully entitled to the shares."

"What will you do now? Leave?"

"Is there any reason for me to stay?"

He hoped he didn't mistake the expectation reflecting back at him. He hoped that she might feel even one-tenth of what he felt for her.

One thing he was certain of—he wasn't about to let her go without a fight.

"Yes," he said and took her hand.

With everyone's attention diverted by the details of the Bluebird

Mining Company, he waded through the throng of people, pulling Molly with him. They exited the house, and Jake instructed one the boys to get his horse, throwing the lad a coin when he brought the animal from the stable.

Jake removed his jacket and placed it on Molly's shoulders to keep her warm, then helped her onto Fernando. He took a seat behind her and wrapped his arms around her as he took hold of the reins.

"Where are we going?" she asked over her shoulder.

"Zang's."

She shook her head. "Take me to your place instead."

She didn't have to tell him twice.

## CHAPTER 26

J ake spurred Fernando to a gallop, only slowing to a trot as they neared his cabin on Main Street. He brought the horse to the rear of the dwelling, swung down and reached for Molly, catching her as she slid off the saddle with a surprised whoop.

Once she was in his arms, he kissed her. She didn't retreat and instead met him full on.

Tasting her only inflamed his desire. He'd never anticipated something as much as he had this.

He knew where this would go, and there'd be no holding back this time. Tomorrow he'd drag her to the courthouse and make it legal.

She held him close, running her hands from his hair to his neck to his shoulders, as he showed her what she meant to him, branding her with his mouth, tasting her lips and cheeks and the soft skin of her neck.

"Please don't stop this time," she whispered.

He brought his face to hers. "Not a chance."

Silently promising to tend to Fernando shortly, he clasped her hand and led her inside.

"I apologize for the place being a mess." He hadn't been

concerned with housekeeping of late. Had there been an inkling that Molly would be with him tonight, he would've cleaned up.

"I don't care." She threw off his jacket, grabbed him by the back of the neck, and kissed him hard.

Jake gave his hunger free rein and was rewarded by Molly's sighs and groans, her fingers fumbling with the tie at his neck. He helped her remove it, pulled his shirt over his head and tossed it to the floor, then attempted to push the gown from her shoulders, but it wouldn't budge. Nuzzling her neck, he moved his hands to the back of the dress and endeavored to unbutton the garment.

He struggled with first one button then another, but the damn things fought his efforts.

She laughed, her breath heavy against his chest. "You could just raise my skirts and take me that way."

"No," he growled. "You deserve better. Besides, if I don't see all of you, I'm fairly certain I'll go mad."

She stepped back and placed her hands on his forearms. His eyes flicked to hers, and he attempted to quiet his frustration. Despite the darkness cloaking them, her face was visible in every lovely contour. No sultry, flirty gaze beckoned him, and neither was there fear or trepidation. Instead, her expression shone with...joy. He had no other word for it. Humbled by her response, he knew he was damn lucky to have her.

A smile tugged at her mouth and lit her eyes. She turned, giving him full access to the troublesome buttons. He went to work, but the minutes stretched as he tried to get the dress to open up to him.

"I thought maybe you had more experience with such things," she said quietly over her shoulder.

He laughed, pausing to kiss the back of her neck. "Nothing that ever mattered. I promise to get better at this."

The gown gave way, and Jake gently pushed it down her arms, over her hips and finally into a pile of deep-green material at her feet. Still facing away from him, Molly wriggled to remove the petticoats. All that remained was a chemise.

Facing him, she chewed on her lower lip then surprised him by lifting the thin coverlet over her head. He drank in the sight of her bared breasts—perfect in every way. He placed his hands on her hips, his chest brushing against hers, and followed the curves of her buttocks, thighs, knees and calves as he removed her bloomers.

Drinking in the sight of her completely naked form, he basked in the scent of her and pressed his lips to her abdomen. She inhaled sharply then buried her hands in his hair. His mouth climbed upward, never leaving her skin, and when he covered a breast, her fingers tightened on his scalp, painfully tugging at his hair, but he paid it no mind. He suckled until her back arched and her breathing became labored, then he shifted to the other breast and repeated the same sweet torture.

Slowly he stood and took her in a long, deep kiss, plundering her mouth, pressing her against him with one hand and cupping a breast with the other. He lightly bit her neck and felt her legs falter. Guiding her toward the bed, he released her when they reached the edge.

Her chest heaving with rapid breaths, Molly's hand came to his trousers. He complied and removed his boots then his pants, gazing often at her delectable curves.

When her eyes flicked downward, he was reminded that she'd never been with a man. She might find his arousal a bit daunting. Leaning forward, he slipped his hands against her cheeks and kissed her gently.

"You can tell me to stop at any time," he murmured against her mouth.

"There is one thing."

He paused.

"I'm still wearing my shoes."

He glanced down. In addition to her shoes, her bloomers were now tangled around her ankles. He guided her to sit on the edge of the bed then kneeled down and removed the offending items. Still on his knees, he raised his head and her mouth found his.

Jake wanted to go slow, but the anticipation nearly overwhelmed him. He pressed her onto the bed and came atop her, careful not to crush her, suppressing the urge to join in one swift thrust.

He explored her with his lips—nipping at her mouth, then her neck, then the niche above her collar bone. His arousal brushed against her, and he wondered how much longer he could hold on. Moving lower, he lavished attention on her breasts, then carefully brought a hand between her legs.

She gasped, startled, and he increased the pressure. He brought his face to hers and kissed her, feeling the build-up inside her. She gripped his shoulders, trembling, and Jake couldn't keep himself from her any longer.

He pushed her left leg wider and barely joined with her, trying to give her a moment to adjust to him. Her breathing came in rapid bursts, and her mouth devoured his as her hips moved upward.

He slid into her fully, the coupling tight.

So much for restraint.

Reaching back, he guided her leg to hook behind his thigh, then he withdrew and thrust once, then twice. That's all it took. As he went over the edge, he held her tight, and she succumbed alongside him.

She was his soul. She was his everything. If he could be with her, like this, for eternity, then he would require nothing more. He drank her in with a kiss.

The musky smell of sex and the sweet aroma of her skin, her hair, her breath surrounded him, his release leaving him content.

It had never been like this with a woman. Ever.

He braced himself above her with a forearm and looked down into her face.

She opened her eyes and smiled, serene and satisfied.

"I love you, Molly Rose. I'm not looking to ever lose you again."

"You never did lose me." She touched his cheek with her fingertips. "And we weren't careful about this. We didn't avoid a baby the way Pearl had said we should."

"I don't care." He kissed her. "Let's get married tomorrow."

She laughed. "You're crazy."

"Maybe. Probably. I can't live without you."

"People will think I married you to get my hands on your claim." She shifted her fingers to play with the hair on his chest.

Jake pressed forward to remain inside her.

"Anything I have is yours, Molly. I'm sorry I doubted you."

She squeezed her legs around him. "I'm glad you don't anymore. And yes, I'll marry you although how I'll explain this to my folks, I have no idea."

"I'll help you." He stole another kiss.

"I love you too, Jake."

He stilled and looked at her again. "You don't have to say it if you don't mean it."

She released a frustrated sigh and pushed against him. "You're such an impossible man."

He held her in place. "I have no intention of letting you leave this bed."

She lifted her face to his and began covering his cheeks and nose and chin with kisses. "Then tell me you love me again."

"I'll do better." His body responded. "I'll show you."

They didn't speak again for some time.

---

MOLLY LAY in Jake's arms, her naked body draped against his. He'd only left the bed once to remove Fernando's saddle and settle the horse for the night.

Three times he'd loved her, and Molly wondered if he might again before daybreak. Feeling sleepy and happy, she snuggled closer. His fingers splayed across her scalp and tangled in her hair, which flowed down her bare back.

Jake tugged at the blanket to further cover her.

Molly didn't know what the future held, but a huge weight had left her this night. As long as she had Jake, nothing else mattered. They would work through whatever obstacles came their way.

"How did you know about Shep and the land?" she asked.

"Henry and Boom clued me in. Esme had heard what Shep was trying to do, so I tracked down the owner of the nearby parcel and made him an offer."

"Why on earth would he sell? He must've known about the Bluebird and the potential value of that valley."

"I offered him twenty thousand, and he took it."

Molly raised her head. "Where did you get that kind of money?"

"I had a bit stashed away."

"Is there any left?"

Jake ran his thumb along her lower lip. "Nope."

"Why would you do that when you were so angry at me?"

"Because it's my job to protect you. In my anger, I lost sight of that. I promise never to do it again."

Molly climbed atop him, giving him a flash of her breasts. His eyes flicked downward, and judging by his focused gaze, she had his full attention. His open satisfaction with her body emboldened her to explore how *she* might arouse *him*.

And so began round four.

# CHAPTER 27

The following morning Jake entered Cora's Restaurant, scanned the room, and then approached the table where Robert sat. As he neared, he gave a nod to his old friend and took the chair opposite him.

"Thanks for meeting me," Jake said.

Cora appeared and poured steaming black coffee into two cups. "It's sure nice to see you two breaking bread." She grinned. "The usual?"

Jake nodded. "Thank you, Cora."

She winked and departed.

Robert leaned back in his seat. "My sister disappeared last night from the festivities at the Patterson's house. I'm guessing you had something to do with that."

Jake sipped the bitter brew. "I was wrong about her, and for that I'm sorry."

"Did she forgive you?"

The night of holding her in his arms, of loving her with every last ounce of strength he had, still thrummed in his veins. In the early morning hours, he'd accompanied her back to Zang's. He'd done nothing but miss her since. "I'm grateful that she did," he said, his voice thick with emotion.

Cora came to the table and deposited two plates piled high with fried eggs, potatoes, steak, and biscuits. "Bon appétit."

Jake dug in. It was the first decent meal he'd had in the past few weeks, and now that things were finally right between Molly and him, his hunger was back in full force and for more than just food. He'd go to Molly as soon as he and Robert were done.

"We'll need to finalize the paperwork on the Bluebird Mining Company this week." Robert bent forward over his plate and swallowed a forkful of egg dripping with yolk.

"How do you think this partnership will go with Charlotte Cohen?"

Robert raised an eyebrow. "I think we'll need to let Molly handle her. Charlie seems to feel indebted to her. I'm not sure why. But she's more wary of Bridget, probably because of Shep and all that he put her through. She had a contract with him, but I've shown it to a lawyer. It can easily be invalidated."

Jake cut his steak. "And what about Shep? Is he gonna play nice?"

"Bridget's working on that."

"And you trust her?"

Robert pinned him with a glare. "Yeah, I do. We've *all* stumbled, but together we can work through this."

Jake paused, and a smile formed on his lips. "Then let's run ourselves a mining company. We're going to need capital, though."

"Henry has two sources he's been negotiating with out of New York City."

Having disposed of the food on his plate, Jake wiped his mouth with a cloth napkin. "Can you believe this? That we're sitting here, majority owners in the Bluebird mine, and we're actually going to have a chance at this."

Robert smiled, mischief in his eyes, reminding Jake of their early days prospecting together, when they combed the mountains using grit and gumption, luck high on their wish list.

"It's going to be a hell of a ride," Robert said.

"I have a favor to ask."

Robert tossed his napkin on the table. "What's that?"

"Stand beside me when the judge comes to town tomorrow."

Robert snorted. "You have no goddamn patience."

"When it comes to your sister? No."

"And what about my folks?"

"As soon as we get things going with the mine, I'll take her to Tucson and smooth things over with your father."

Robert laughed. "They won't like it, but then they know Molly, so I doubt they'll be surprised. Although I'm sure I'll get a tongue-lashing from my mama for letting you near my sister in the first place."

"You know I love her, right?"

"And that's the *only* reason I'll let you marry her tomorrow."

———

MOLLY STARED at the gold band on her left hand as she sat on the bed, light flickering with a soft glow from the oil lamp on the nightstand. Jake reclined opposite her, his head propped on pillows against the wrought-iron headboard, and watched her. She liked him this way—naked as the day he was born although a sheet covered him from the waist down, his muscled torso still sweaty from their lovemaking.

They'd chosen to spend their wedding night in her room at Zang's since the bed was bigger.

Jake wrapped his hand around her calf and began caressing the skin, causing an instant reaction in her abdomen and other sensitive places. In fact, all Jake had to do was look at her, and she could all but feel him touching her.

Molly couldn't suppress the sigh of contentment that washed through her.

"Happy?" he asked.

"Yes." She shifted the gauzy material of the wrap that Pearl had gifted to her for her wedding. It was quite provocative, if Jake's brooding gaze on her body was any indication. Pearl had instructed her to wear it only with nothing underneath. "Are you?"

"More than you'll ever know."

She resisted throwing herself at him. But if he kept talking to her like she was a rare jewel, she'd give him all the loving he could muster.

"I've been thinking," he said.

She slipped the wrap from her shoulders. "About what?"

He hissed as she bared herself. "Let me get my thought out before you distract me."

She threw the material on the floor. "I'll give you ten seconds."

"When things settle here, I want to take you somewhere." His hand began to slide from her calf to her knee.

"Where?"

"Some place far away."

His fingers found his goal and she gasped. He sat up, clasped his other hand behind her head, and kissed her, his mouth hungry and demanding.

He broke the kiss. "You want to see the world, and I want to be the one to show it to you."

A wide smile spread across her lips, and a giddy laugh escaped her. "All right, Jackal, show me."

# EPILOGUE

*Constantinople*
*One year later*

M olly threaded her way through the busy Turkish bazaar, surrounded by men in turbans and loose-fitting pants and women in silky garments. Molly wore similar attire, including covering her face with a veil. During her travels with Jake, she'd garnered a healthy respect for local customs and did her best to blend in whenever possible.

Constantinople—Istanbul, or Stamboul as foreigners sometimes called it—was fairly progressive in how women were treated. Since the British had a strong presence, western females were tolerated better here than other places in the Middle East.

She ducked past a donkey loaded with rugs and entered Demir's Bakery.

"*Merhaba, Bayan* McKenna," Demir said, grinning behind his counter. "What can I do for you today?" He prided himself on his English usage.

"*Merhaba,*" Molly replied. "I need your best Baklava, Demir."

"It is my pleasure." Demir gathered several portions of the flaky pastry into a box.

Molly paid and took her treasure, thanking her Turkish friend. It was her treat for Jake for the evening, since today—June 2—was their one-year anniversary.

She left the bazaar and walked along a narrow passageway to the tiny apartment she and Jake shared in a crowded neighborhood of latticed Turkish houses.

They'd left Creede six months ago and had spent several weeks in Tucson with her folks and Evie, then they'd stopped in Texas to visit with her Aunt Molly and Uncle Matt and her cousins and other uncles and aunts. After that, they'd traveled to New York City, then London. Jake had taken her to Paris, where she had practiced her French, then eventually they rode the Orient Express to Constantinople, visiting Munich, Vienna, and Budapest along the way.

Once in Turkey, Jake had wanted to remain for an extended time, and Molly hadn't objected. The cosmopolitan city of Istanbul was exotic and foreign in a way that mesmerized her. She was fascinated how it straddled two continents—Asia and Europe, the Bosporus Strait separating it. She'd been wooed by the Muslim culture and fascinated by the flat dome of Saint Sophia, a miracle of construction from the early days of the city, when it was known as Byzantium.

She loved watching the sun set on the Sea of Marmara and eating strange and delicious Turkish foods in local restaurants, her favorite being stuffed dolmas—grape leaves wrapped around a vegetable filling. She further indulged her curious mind with visits to the opera—her favorite so far had been Mozart's *The Abduction from the Seraglio* about lovers separated after a pirate's abduction—and reading about the explorations of David Livingstone in Africa.

Jake promised a visit to that continent would be their next adventure.

But Molly was aware that the news she had to share with him might likely change their plans, and not entirely in a bad way.

She hoped he would be as pleased as she was.

She let herself into their apartment and waited for him to return from his business meeting.

Muffled thumping preceded Jake's entrance. Dragging a large, rolled rug through the door, he smiled as Molly set her book aside and rose from the sofa to help him.

"I take it the meeting went well?" she asked.

"We're going to be rug dealers, Chigger."

She shut the door as he dropped his goods on the floor. "Did you bring me a sample?"

"It is our anniversary, and I know you've been wanting one." He pushed the kitchen table and chairs back then unrolled the rug.

As he unfurled the exquisite and intricate red-hued design, Molly couldn't contain her excitement. "Oh Jake, I love it." She helped him adjust the rectangular piece then stood back to admire the gift.

Standing behind her, he wrapped an arm around her and kissed her neck. *"This is how I would die into the love I have for you: as pieces of cloud dissolve in sunlight."*

Molly sighed. She easily succumbed when Jake quoted Rumi, and he knew it.

"Red is a symbol of the mystery," he murmured, his breath tickling her ear. "Red is present in a rose, a ruby, in the blood that courses through our veins. It's the fire inside a cook stove and in the brilliance of a sunset. It's at the root of all that is. Love is painted in all shades of crimson and scarlet."

She peeked over her shoulder at him. "Wait a minute. I thought blue was your favorite color."

He raised her left hand to his mouth and lightly bit the inside of her wrist. "Quit ruining my seduction."

"My apologies, but I have news first." She stepped from his arms and faced him. "I'm pregnant, Jake."

His eyes lit with joy, relieving a burden of worry. "Are you certain?"

She nodded.

He folded her into his arms and kissed her, his touch gentle, almost reverent. He moved his gaze to her abdomen and placed his large hand upon it. "I love you, Molly. Nothing is more important than you and this child. If you want to leave Constantinople, just say the word. Should we return to Arizona?"

Molly knew he worried over taking her so far from home, and it was true she experienced sharp twinges of homesickness that she'd never expected, but being with her husband was more important to her than anything.

"No." She laid her hand over his. "My place is with you. We'll have this child here. Mama and Papa have said they'll visit—this will be the perfect excuse for them. They've even said they would leave Evie with us for a time. She'd be a great help with the baby, and we can introduce her to the marvelous riches of Europe and Asia."

He kissed her, lingering.

"You're not missing the excitement of Creede, are you?" she asked.

"No. I sold my shares to Robert at the right time although I am sorry the price of silver has plummeted so drastically."

"I know, but he and Bridget were smart and invested in horses and cattle. They'll survive."

Jake knelt down so he was face to face with his future offspring. "And I suspect the exchange rate of silver will eventually recover. Robert is far more patient than I am."

Molly knew that was true if their hasty marriage had been any indication, but nothing in her life had been more genuine or more right.

"Before I thank you for the rug," she ran her hand through his hair, "you should know that I have Baklava."

He groaned. "You make impossible ultimatums."

"What if I said I'd serve the pastry to you in bed?" She arched her eyebrow. "Without a shred of clothing?"

He stood, then cupped her backside with his hands and kissed her deeply. "Then I shall quote Rumi to you all night long."

*"I want to sing like the bird sings, not worrying about who hears or what they think."*

Jake watched her with amusement. "Since when did you start reading Rumi?"

"I'm a quick study, Jackal."

His laughter filled her with love, while the intensity in his dark eyes made her want to meet him in a place filled with need and longing and soul-deep hunger.

He led her to the bedroom. "Believe me, I know."

---

THANK you so much for reading *The Bluebird*. I truly hope you enjoyed the story. If you would consider posting a review, I would be forever grateful as it helps tremendously in the discoverability of a book. ~ Kristy

---

SIGN up for Kristy's newsletter at kmccaffrey.com/subscribe/ to stay updated on her latest news and releases.

# AUTHOR'S NOTE

L ocated in the San Juan Mountains, the Creede mining district sits in the southern part of Colorado. The San Juans are sometimes called the "Alps" of America, with high rugged peaks separated by deep valleys. The landscape is filled with forests of spruce, pine, fir, and aspen, open meadows filled with wildflowers, rushing mountain streams, and sparkling lakes. The area is also rich with valuable metals—gold, silver, copper, lead, and zinc.

Early prospecting in the 1870's revealed silver-bearing ore, leading to a major discovery in 1889 by Nicholas C. Creede. In August 1889, Creede and his partners—E.R. Naylor and G.L. Smith—were prospecting on Campbell Mountain when they located the Holy Moses claim. The Creede mining boom began in the fall of 1890 when word spread that the Holy Moses had been sold for $70,000 to Denver investors. Hundreds of prospectors descended on Campbell Mountain as well as nearby Bachelor Mountain, where the Amethyst Vein was discovered, becoming Creede District's most productive lode.

During Creede's early years, the area was often referred to as 'No Man's Land' because parts of the camp were located in

Saguache, Hinsdale, and Rio Grande counties. Due to this confusion, it was necessary to file mining, homestead, and lot claims in all three counties. And although each county fought to gain control of the potential riches of Creede, none would assume jurisdiction or provide police protection. The issue was resolved by an act of the Colorado legislature in March 1893 when the County of Mineral was formed from parts of each of the three counties, and a provisional city government was organized.

As prospectors staked out their claims in the early 1890's, there were many cases of claim jumping, overlapping boundary lines, and moving of boundary stakes. The result was litigation that often led to the suspension of activities until the cases could be resolved in the courts. The case between the Last Chance Mining and Milling Company and the Del Monte Mining Company went all the way to the United States Supreme Court, delaying production from these mines for several years.

From 1891 to 1899, mines on the Amethyst Vein had the greatest economic impact on the Creede District, with most of the production coming from high-grade oxidized ores in the southern portion. (Oxidized ores are preferable since they can be shipped directly to smelters without further processing.) The majority of the value was silver. In 1892, the total estimated output of mines in the Creede District was $4,215,800, for which the Amethyst Mine accounted for over half.

In 1893, a silver panic dealt a devastating blow to the Creede economy. U.S. President Grover Cleveland sought to solve an economic crisis by repealing the Sherman Silver Purchase Act, which had been passed in 1890 in response to a large overproduction of silver by western mines. It required the U.S. Treasury to purchase silver using notes backed by either silver or gold. This legislation was critical for Creede and other silver mining towns because it had stabilized silver prices.

While the panic of 1893 didn't completely shut down silver mining in Creede, it did seriously decrease production. The dollar value of silver produced in 1894 was only 31 percent of the 1893 number, but by 1898-1899 it had rebounded to approximately 60 percent of the 1893 figure.

# ACKNOWLEDGMENTS

For this book, I have many people to thank. Author Ann Charles contacted me after reading several of my books and not only became a fan but a friend and mentor. She graciously beta-read this novel while in manuscript form, offering unwavering support and enthusiasm. A big thank you to my proofreaders: Marcia Montoya, Tanya Brown, Janet Lessley, Judy Tucker, and Sandra Brown (who actually read the book twice), and a special shout-out to reader Deborah Dunham who went above and beyond, offering an in-depth line-edit that brought to my attention many improvements to my grammar. One thing is certain—a writer is always learning.

My editor, Melissa Maygrove, has once again done a tremendous job in clarifying my thoughts and pointing out story discrepancies. I've had several editors throughout the course of this series but it's been Melissa who has taught me the most.

This book proved to be my wake-up call when it came to technology. I lost an early, and nearly complete, version of this story when my external hard drive failed. To my heartbreak and chagrin, I had no backup. It was my 22-year-old and IT-savvy son, Sam, who helped me through it, trying in vain to recover the data (in the end he couldn't) and advising me on how to manage my files better. After re-writing the entire manuscript again, I lost the story a second time but thankfully had a backup. Needless to say, I'm happy this book is finally complete and published before another computer gremlin strikes again.

I must, of course, include a big thank you to my husband. His endless support makes it possible for me to pursue a writing career, and his brainstorming abilities have aided me through many a plot-conundrum; his viewpoint has frequently helped me see a different perspective that's hiding within a scene. He also makes me laugh every day.

And finally, a huge thank you to the readers. While writing is done inside a bubble, it's what happens later when a reader engages with the story that the work transforms into something more. In the end, it's the joy we share in this life that makes all the difference. I hope my work brings a small amount of delight to your days.

**Don't miss The Wren**
**Wings of the West Book 1**

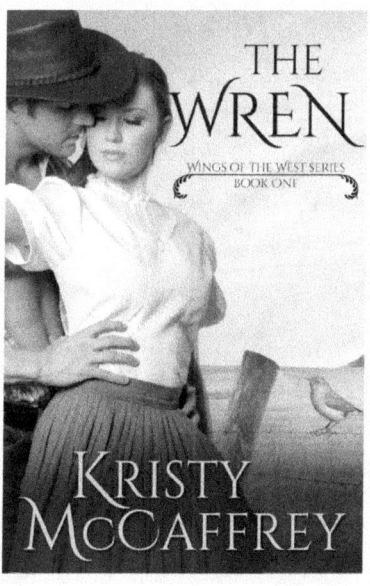

Ten years have passed since her ranch was attacked, her folks murdered, and Molly Hart was abducted. Now, at nineteen, she's finally returning home to north Texas after spending the remainder of her childhood with a tribe of Kwahadi Comanche. What she finds is a deserted home coated with dust and the passage of time, the chilling discovery of her own gravesite, and the presence of a man she thought never to see again.

Matt Ryan is pushed by a restless wind to the broken-down remains of the Hart ranch. Recently recovered from an imprisonment that nearly ended his life, the drive for truth and fairness has all but abandoned him. For ten years he faithfully served the U.S. Army and the Texas Rangers, seeking justice for the brutal murder of a little girl, only to find closure and healing beyond his grasp. Returning to the place where it all began, he's surprised to stumble across a woman with the same blue eyes as the child he can't put out of his mind.

kmccaffrey.com/the-wren/

### The Dove
### *Wings of the West Book 2*

Disappointment hits ex-deputy Logan Ryan hard when he finds Claire Waters in the midst of a bustling Santa Fe Trail town. The woman he remembers is gone—in her place is a working girl with enticing curves and a load of trouble. As a web of deceit entangles them with men both desperate and dangerous, Logan tries to protect Claire, unaware his own past poses the greatest threat.

Plagued by shame all her life, Claire is stunned when Logan catches her on the doorstep of The White Dove Saloon dressed as a prostitute. She lets him believe the worst, but with her mama missing and the fancy girls deserting the place, she's hard-pressed to refuse his offer of help. As she embarks on a journey that will unravel the fabric of her life, one thing becomes clear—opening her heart may be the most dangerous proposition of all.

kmccaffrey.com/the-dove/

## The Sparrow
## *Wings of the West Book 3*

In 1877, Emma Hart comes to Grand Canyon—a wild, rugged, and, until recently, undiscovered area. Plagued by visions and gifted with a second sight, she searches for answers about the tragedy of her past, the betrayal of her present, and an elusive future that echoes through her very soul. Joined by her power animal Sparrow, she ventures into the depths of Hopi folklore, forced to confront an evil that has lived through the ages.

Texas Ranger Nathan Blackmore tracks Emma Hart to the Colorado River, stunned by her determination to ride a wooden dory along its course. But in a place where the ripples of time run deep, he'll be faced with a choice. He must accept the unseen realm, *the world beside this world,* that he turned away from years ago, or risk losing the woman he has come to love more than life itself.

kmccaffrey.com/the-sparrow/

### The Blackbird
### Wings of the West Book 4

Bounty hunter Cale Walker arrives in Tucson to search for J. Howard "Hank" Carlisle at the request of his daughter, Tess. Hank mentored Cale before a falling out divided them, and a mountain lion attack left Cale nearly dead. Rescued by a band of Nednai Apache, his wounds were considered a powerful omen and he was taught the ways of a *di-yin*, or a medicine man. To locate Hank, Cale must enter the Dragoon Mountains, straddling two worlds that no longer fit. But he has an even bigger problem—finding a way into the heart of a young woman determined to live life as a bystander.

For two years, Tess Carlisle has tried to heal the mental and physical wounds of a deadly assault by one of her *papá's* men. Continuing the traditions of her Mexican heritage, she has honed her skills as a *cuentista*, a storyteller and a Keeper of the Old Ways. But with no contact from her father since the attack, she fears the worst. Tess knows that to reenter Hank Carlisle's world is a dangerous endeavor, and her only hope is Cale Walker, a man unlike any she has ever known. Determined to make a journey that could lead straight into the path of her attacker, she hardens her resolve along with her heart. But Cale makes her yearn for something she vowed she never would—love.

kmccaffrey.com/the-blackbird/

***Into The Land Of Shadows***
***A Stand-Alone Novel***

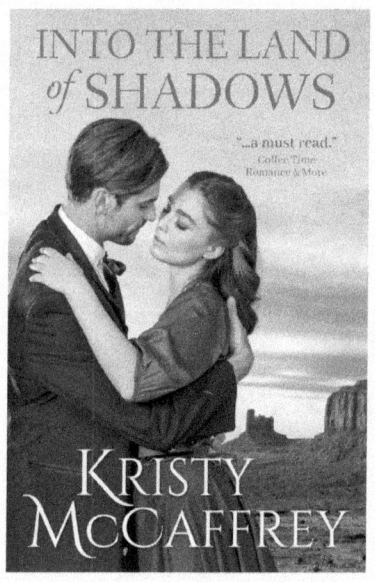

This book was previously published in 2013 under the same title. While the text and cover have been updated, the story remains the same.

It's been five years since a woman came between Ethan Barstow and his brother, Charley, and it's high time they buried the hatchet. When Ethan travels to Arizona Territory to make amends, he learns that Charley has abruptly disappeared after breaking more than one heart in town. And an indignant fiancée is hot on his trail.

When Charley Barstow abandons a local girl after getting her pregnant, Kate Kinsella pursues him without a second thought. She's determined he set things right, and even more determined to end her own engagement to him, a sham from the beginning. But an ill-timed encounter with a group of ruffians lands her in the company of Charley's brother, Ethan, who suggests they search together.

As Ethan and Kate move deeper INTO THE LAND OF SHADOWS, family tensions and past tragedies threaten to destroy a love neither of them expected.

kmccaffrey.com/into-the-land-of-shadows/

# ABOUT THE AUTHOR

Kristy McCaffrey has been writing since she was very young, but it wasn't until she was a stay-at-home mom that she considered becoming published. A fascination with science led her to earn two mechanical engineering degrees—she did her undergraduate work at Arizona State University and her graduate studies at the University of Pittsburgh—but storytelling has always been her passion. She writes both contemporary tales and award-winning historical western romances.

An Arizona native, Kristy and her husband reside in the desert where they frequently remove (rescue) rattlesnakes from their property, go for runs among the cactus, and plan trips to far-off places like the Orkney Islands or Machu Picchu. But mostly, she works 12-hour days and enjoys at-home date nights with her sweetheart, which usually include Will Ferrell movies and sci-fi flicks. Her four children have all flown the nest, so she lavishes her maternal instincts on Jeb, an American Bulldog her family rescued in 2021. He has his own Instagram account at @jeb_therescue.

Connect with Kristy
    Website: kmccaffrey.com
    Newsletter: kmccaffrey.com/subscribe/
    Facebook: facebook.com/AuthorKristyMcCaffrey
    Instagram: instagram.com/kristymccaffreybooks/
    BookBub: bookbub.com/authors/kristy-mccaffrey
    TikTok: tiktok.com/@kristymccaffrey